fortune

fortune

megan cole

HarperCollins*Publishers*

First published in paperback in Great Britain by HarperCollins 2010

HarperCollins*Publishers* Ltd
77–85 Fulham Palace Road, Hammersmith, London W6 8JB

Visit us on the web at www.harpercollins.co.uk

Text copyright © HarperCollins*Publishers* 2010

ISBN 978-0-00-736470-1

HarperCollins*Publishers* reserves the right to be
identified as the author of the work.

Typeset in Meridien by Palimpsest Book Production Ltd,
Falkirk, Stirlingshire

Printed and bound in England by Clays Ltd, St Ives plc

*To every girl who wants
to be somebody.*

*With thanks to Hannah,
for the inspiration.*

chapter one

New York City
July

'Why the hell shouldn't I have Botox? It's my face.'

Nineteen-year-old Madison Vanderbilt, ice-blonde hair cascading down her back, eyed her mother belligerently over the fifteen-foot breakfast bar.

Candy Vanderbilt, a stretched-face forty-something with diamonds dripping from her ears and neck, showed the first bit of common sense she'd had in her life. 'Honey, don't you think you're a little bit young?'

'Heidi Montag had, like, everything done.' Madison

offered up a smooth, blemish-free face, courtesy of regular facials at the most expensive beauty salon on Fifth Avenue. 'I'm covered in wrinkles, look!'

Candy frowned, or rather tried to. Her own forehead was so frozen that she had difficulty registering any expression at all. 'Why don't you leave it for a few years? Twenty-one is as good a time to start as any.'

'That's if I don't look 112 by then,' huffed Madison. God, her life sucked! Come July, she'd normally be joining the rest of her friends in the Hamptons for a summer of sunbathing and scoping out hot guys. This year, however, she and her mom were stuck at home in their five-million-dollar apartment in New York. Madison stomped over to the floor-to-ceiling window to look down at the sticky, traffic-clogged streets below. New York in July was so not the place to be. Her best friends, Tiffani and Chelsea, would be heading down to the beach now, while she, Madison, was cooped up in this stupid condo.

It wasn't fair.

'What am I supposed to do now?' she said, turning back to her mother.

Candy looked up from her stool, where she was readjusting the diamond collar on her lapdog, Dolce. 'Honey, you live in the greatest city in the world! There's so much to do.'

'Like what?'

'Shopping! And Fabrizo has opened up that new nail bar around the corner. His French manicures are to die for.'

Madison carelessly examined a perfect pink nail. 'Whatever.' She was so over manicures, so over her mother, so over this dumb city. It was like being a prisoner in a cage with no end in sight. Madison couldn't believe the injustice of it all. 'Oh my God, of all the times to get sick, Hank has to do it now. Doesn't he know he's ruining my life?'

Candy's baby-blue eyes widened. 'Madison, that's a dreadful thing to say!'

Madison sighed. 'You know what I mean.'

Exasperated, she turned and walked over to one of the many full-length mirrors adorning the luxury apartment. Her stepfather Hank, her mom's third husband and a self-made millionaire, had recently been diagnosed with colon cancer and was now in one of the most prestigious hospitals in New York. The good news was that Hank was responding well to treatment... the bad news was that he was going to be in hospital all summer, *ruining* their annual family holiday.

Madison scrutinised herself in the mirror. Five foot eight and an American size six, she was perfectly proportioned, with a pert chest, flat stomach and shapely legs. Madison turned round, admiring her high, peachy butt, courtesy of three-hundred-dollar-an-hour Pilates sessions with the same woman who trained Sarah Jessica Parker. She was looking hot, even for her. Her brow furrowed crossly as she thought of it all going to waste. She could *kill* Hank!

The intercom sounded, making her mother's little lapdog jump.

'Go and get that will you, honey?' asked Candy.

Sighing again, Madison made her way to the front door and looked through the peephole. Juan, the young Puerto Rican bellboy, was standing outside, smoothing down his hair. Madison pulled the door open and leant on the door frame, giving him the full benefit of her white denim hot pants. The young man's eyes widened. He had a monster crush on Madison. She looked down at the shiny black envelope in his hand.

'That for me?'

'Yes, it just came by courier. I thought I would bring it up personally. I was going to—'

But Madison had already snatched the envelope out of his hand and shut the door in his face. Then she returned to the kitchen to show it to her mother.

'It's heavy, it must be a super dooper invite,' said Candy approvingly, handing the envelope back to her daughter.

Madison opened the envelope quickly and threw it on the floor. Dolce jumped down and started ripping the paper apart, but both women were so engrossed in the contents they didn't notice. Madison had only got three lines down before she started squealing.

'Oh my God! Brad Masters! He's invited me to his fiftieth birthday party!' Her eyes widened. 'In *Capri*! Oh my God, *Brad Masters*!' She clutched the invitation to her chest. 'I bet I get flown over in his private jet.'

Madison couldn't believe it.

Brad Masters?

In the worldwide fame league, you had the Pope at number one, followed by Madonna, then Brad Masters in a close third place. A British-born billionaire, he spent his life jetting round the world making millions in property, running record companies and throwing lavish, high-profile parties. Despite his fame and good looks, though, Brad was still something of an enigma – a confirmed bachelor who never talked about his private life. The mystery only added to his allure.

'The party's at his beachfront house,' Madison breathed excitedly, her eyes darting back and forth across the invitation. 'Oh my God! Courtney Richard's sister Cara went to one of his parties at Nobu last year! Cara is, like, this *top* model and she says Brad's people only handpick the best guests.' She gasped. 'O.M.G! What if he can get me a part on *The Hills*?'

Her mother's expression was less-than-pleased.

'Why would Brad Masters invite you to his birthday party?' Candy said. 'If anyone should go, it should be *me*.'

Madison shot her a look. Her mother really had to

get over herself – Candy's partying days had ended with, like, the dinosaurs. 'Mother, you are way too ancient. Brad's obviously seen me on the scene, hanging with the beautifuls,' she said, re-reading the invitation.

'Madison, it's entirely inappropriate. You're not going!'

Madison looked at her mom in disbelief. Candy never said no to her! 'Excuse me, yes, I am.'

'No, you're not!'

'I'm nineteen. I can do what I like.'

Candy fixed pleading eyes on her daughter. 'What if your father takes a turn for the worse?'

'*Step*father,' corrected Madison. 'And if you hadn't married him, I wouldn't be stuck in this sucky city in the first place.'

'Madison!' Looking pained, Candy stood up. 'I've got another one of my headaches coming. I need to go lie down.' She scooped up Dolce and shot her daughter a look. 'You're not going and that's it!'

'You just don't want me to go off and have fun,' Madison shouted after her. 'Hank's your husband – *you* stay with him.'

Candy's bedroom door slammed. Madison rolled her eyes; her mom was such a drama queen! She turned back to the invitation, turning it over in her hands. This was her ticket out of Dullsville – wait until Tiff and Chelsea heard about it!

It was going to be the best summer *ever*!

chapter two

London

The doorbell of the dusty little shop tinkled. Sapphire Stevens looked up from behind the counter, where she had been gently strumming on one of the guitars. The lyrics had come to her easily, but she just couldn't get the melody.

'How's it going?'

It was Jerry, back from his lunch-break. He was the friendly-faced owner of the Camden music shop where Sapphire worked part-time. Unlike other places she'd worked, Jerry didn't mind if she practised when the shop wasn't busy. Even though he was quite old – at least in his forties – he was really encouraging about her music and always took time out to help her or listen. Sapphire's dad had died when she was little and she thought of Jerry as the father figure she'd never had.

Sapphire gave a rueful smile. 'Oh, you know.'

Jerry grinned. 'Don't tell me, the melody again.'

'I just can't get it right,' she sighed. 'I don't know why the words come so easily, but the tune won't.'

'It'll come, don't worry,' he assured her. 'Even the most successful artists struggle with one or the other. Elton John has worked with loads of lyricists, for example.'

Sapphire laughed. 'He's ancient!'

'Ancient, but very rich,' Jerry pointed out. He eyed her over the counter. 'Why don't you knock off? It's really quiet today.'

'If you're sure? I really don't mind staying.'

'Nah, it's cool.' Her boss's eyes twinkled. 'Go home and start practising. Those melodies won't sing themselves.'

* * *

Five minutes later, Sapphire was taking her usual route home through the twisty streets of North London. It was a fifteen-minute walk home, or a five-minute bus ride, but Sapphire preferred the fresh air. Her life was so hectic, what with college and work, it felt like the only time she could think. As she pounded the pavement, Sapphire noticed a hole beginning to appear in one of her Converse trainers. It was last thing she needed. All her wages from her job went on supporting herself through her art degree at the prestigious Central Saint Martins college. Her mum helped where she could, but money was tight at home. There was just about enough for the two of them to live and eat comfortably, with the odd takeaway or cinema trip thrown in.

A white van drove past and the driver honked his horn.

'All right, sexy!'

Sapphire blushed beetroot and pulled her jacket round her. At five foot six, with soulful brown eyes and a petite figure, there was no doubt she was a natural beauty. Not that Sapphire ever thought that. Her long, brown hair seemed to have a mind of its own and her double-D breasts were a source of constant embarrassment to her. Instead of flaunting them in tight tops, Sapphire covered up her assets in baggy T-shirts and oversized checked shirts.

She put her head down and hurried home, away from beeping drivers and sleazy comments. Five minutes later she reached an old Victorian mansion that had been converted into flats. It was a rather dilapidated building, with crumbling brickwork and ivy climbing up the walls, but Sapphire liked it. It had character. She and her mother, Leonie, lived in a cramped little flat on the ground floor.

As Sapphire opened the front door the smell of herbs and spices greeted her. 'Hi, Mum!' she called out, as she took her jacket off and hung it on one of the hooks in the narrow corridor. A fluffy black and white dog wearing a red neckerchief appeared at the end of the corridor, ears cocked.

'Hello, Beatle, come here, boy!' The ancient collie ambled up to Sapphire and stuck his wet nose in her hand. Beatle was named after her mother's favourite band – The Beatles – and was nearly as old as

Sapphire. He was like the third member of their family.

'In here, darling!'

Sapphire walked into the cluttered, cosy kitchen. An older woman, with the same tumbling hair as her but tinged with grey, stood stirring a big pot on the Aga.

'That smells good,' Sapphire said, as she came over to kiss her mum on the cheek. She caught a whiff of patchouli oil, her mother's signature sent.

'Lentil curry. I thought I'd make up a big batch and we could freeze the rest.' Leonie Stevens watched her daughter as she went to the fridge and opened it. 'You're home early.'

Sapphire came out from the fridge holding Beatle's lead. 'Mum, what's this doing in here?'

'That's where it was!' Leonie laughed. 'I must have put it in there by mistake when I came back from our walk. I remember walking in and...'

Sapphire shook her head fondly. 'What are you like?'

Leonie's absent-mindedness was a bit of a family joke. She had been the ultimate rock chick when she was younger, and her party-loving lifestyle had left its mark on her memory. Sometimes Sapphire felt more like the mum in their household, but she wouldn't swap Leonie for the world.

'Jerry let me off early, the shop was quiet.'

'There's a letter here for you,' her mum said, turning back to stir the pot. 'It looks very posh.'

Sapphire picked up the shiny black envelope from the kitchen counter. It had an address badge on the front, with her name printed in swirling black letters. It was probably a promotion for a product Sapphire could never afford. Carefully, she opened the envelope and pulled out a stiff piece of black card, covered in gold writing.

'You are cordially invited to a party celebrating the fiftieth birthday of Brad Masters,' she read out.

There was a loud 'plop' as her mum dropped the wooden spoon in the curry.

'Brad Masters?' Sapphire repeated, confused. 'He's that big music industry guy, isn't he?'

Leonie kept quiet. In disbelief, Sapphire carried on reading. 'It's being held at his beachfront villa in Capri.' She looked up. 'This has to be some kind of mistake! He's obviously got the wrong person.'

Her mum hesitated. 'Well, maybe not. I used to know Brad Masters, back in the day.'

Sapphire's eyes widened. 'You're joking!'

Leonie nodded. 'We were close for a while. Well, lovers actually.'

'You… *what*?' spluttered Sapphire.

'Sex is natural, darling!'

Sapphire stared at her mum in horror. 'Ewww!' She couldn't believe her mum had dated Brad Masters!

Leone smiled. 'Maybe he's decided to look me up again; he always was wonderfully generous.'

Sapphire frowned. 'The invite should be addressed to you then. Brad Masters doesn't even know me!'

'Well…' Her mum started stirring the pot again. 'He and I have stayed in touch a bit over the years. I may… have mentioned you.'

'You and *Brad Masters*?' Sapphire repeated. 'He's, like, a gazillionaire.' She just couldn't get her head round it.

Her mum shrugged, as if being on first-name terms with one of the most famous people on the planet was entirely normal. 'Brad's a very nice man. I've told him about you and what a talented musician you are. Brad's always on the lookout for fresh new talent and he said he'd like to meet you. I didn't want to push anything when you were younger, because I know how the music industry works. But now that you're eighteen...' She left the statement hanging in the air. 'Well, you're old enough to make up your own mind.'

Sapphire shook her head. She was having a hard time taking all this in. Then something else fell out of the envelope and she bent down and picked it up.

'What's this, a plane ticket?' She gave a gasp. 'It's got my name on it! British Airways, First Class.'

'Oh my goodness!' said Leonie. She came over to have a look. 'I did say he was very generous.'

Sapphire shook her head. 'I don't get it, Mum. Why he's done this? Did *you* know about it?'

Leonie's heart gave a sudden jump. *What do I say?* she thought wildly. 'I didn't know he was going to do *this*,' she said eventually. At least *that* was the truth.

Sapphire bit her lip. 'What if he's a bit, well, you know... pervy?'

'Darling, I wouldn't let you go if he was. Look, I

know it's a big surprise, but why don't you think of it as a nice holiday, and the chance to meet the best-connected man in the music business? It could really open doors for you.'

The first flush of excitement crept across Sapphire's face. 'You don't mind?'

Leonie smiled at her daughter's expression. 'Of course I don't! I think it sounds fantastic. Just as long as I have the house phone number and you call me regularly.'

Sapphire blew out a big breath. 'Brad Masters. Wow! I'll need a bit of time to think about it though.'

Instinctively, she looked at the old photo on the dresser, of a smiling man with a little girl on his shoulders.

'What would Dad think?' she asked quietly. Her dad, Bill, had been a talented musician himself, until he'd been tragically killed in a motorbike accident when she was younger. Even though Sapphire couldn't remember much about her dad, she treasured this photo.

Leonie felt herself welling up. 'I'm sure he'd be very proud, darling.'

Sapphire shook her head in wonder. 'This could be my big break!' She narrowed her eyes at her mum, humorously. 'Just before I go, Mum, have you got any more surprises for me? Like you're best mates with Mariah Carey or something?'

Leonie laughed. 'I'm afraid knowing Brad is the extent of it!'

Sapphire grinned and bounded out the kitchen.

As soon as her daughter was gone and she was alone again, the smile dropped from Leonie's face. *'Oh God,'* she muttered. She had worked hard to move on from what happened twenty years ago, and now she was starting it all up again. Had she just made the biggest mistake of her life?

chapter three

Rome

Simonetta Mastrangelo breathed in deeply, filling her lungs. She didn't smell the pollution-filled traffic fumes of Italy's capital city; she smelled adventure, glamour and success.

Tucking her portfolio under her arm, she sashayed down the street, well aware of the admiring glances she was getting from passing pedestrians. She got a few dirty looks too, but Simonetta was used to bitchiness from other, less pretty girls. They were just jealous. As she passed a shop window, she caught sight of her perfect reflection and congratulated herself – not for the first time – on leaving behind her boring village in the countryside and moving to Rome to make it as a model.

Standing nearly six feet tall, Simonetta had the posture and long, lithe limbs of a natural. Or so Models Italia, the agency that had just signed her up, told her. With the smoky brown eyes and jet-black hair of Vanessa Hudgens, and the slim physique of Whitney Port, she had the beauty and natural grace to go very, very far. Simonetta had already done a few major catwalk shows, but she wanted more. Naomi, Claudia, Cindy, Giselle – she saw her name up there with all the greats.

It was taking a *little* more time than she'd anticipated, but Simonetta knew she'd get there eventually. She was destined for the cover of Italian *Vogue*. She just *knew* it.

Her mobile went off, rousing her from a daydream about red carpets and Hollywood parties. It was her mother. Simonetta rolled her eyes in irritation. Extremely over-protective and religious, her mother rang her at least four times a day. Anyone would think that Simonetta was a *bambina* of nine, not a beautiful, self-assured woman of nineteen.

'How are you, Simonetta?'

'Same as I was two hours ago, *Mamma*.'

'Are you eating properly? Papa and I are worried about you.'

'*Mamma*, stop fussing.'

'You were skin and bone last time I saw you! That is not what men find attractive, Simonetta. How will we ever find you a husband?' Her mother sighed dramatically. 'You're putting me in an early grave, Simonetta, all this gallivanting about Rome. I will pray extra hard for you at church tonight...'

Simonetta's eyes glazed over as her mother droned on. She'd heard it all before: how she'd abandoned her family for a shallow, superficial life. How she had shamed her local congregation. *Just because I want to make something of myself, Mamma, and not be stuck in a little hick town all my life! Just because I want to be someone!*

Ten minutes later, her mother took her first pause for breath and Simonetta took the chance for escape.

'I'm home now, *Mamma*! I'll call you later.' Before her mother could say anything, Simonetta ended the call. She gazed up at the modern apartment block she lived in now and swelled with pride. Renting in the trendiest part of the city may have left her in tons of debt, but it was *essential* to have the right address. Besides, she could pay all her debts ten times over when she started earning serious money.

As she let herself into the lobby and checked her mailbox, Simonetta noticed one envelope standing out from all the credit card statements and overdue bills. Black and shiny, it looked like an invitation to a hot new nightclub or bar. Simonetta smiled, pleased that her networking was starting to pay off.

She pressed the button for the lift and the doors slid open. Simonetta stepped inside. Trying to open the envelope with a portfolio under one arm and a Chloe handbag under the other wasn't the easiest thing to do, and Simonetta had to wait until she got into her apartment. Kicking the door shut, she dumped her bag and portfolio and ripped open the envelope.

It was an invitation all right, but not the one she was expecting.

You are cordially invited to a party celebrating the fiftieth birthday of Brad Masters.
Location: Casa Eleganza, Capri.
Dress: Elegant.

'Oh, *mio Dio*!' exclaimed Simonetta. She knew who Brad Masters was! He'd obviously noticed her at a catwalk show and decided he had to meet her. Simonetta's lips curled into a smile; she'd known it was only a matter of time before someone influential approached her. Even though Simonetta always went for older men, thirty *years* older was pushing it. Nonetheless, Brad was still very attractive for his age and it would be great to play him along and kick-start the luxury lifestyle she'd always dreamed about. Having Brad Masters on her speed dial would open doors for her, *serious* doors. Simonetta knew how it all worked.

Her phone rang and she snatched it up. It was Lexi, her agent from Models Italia.

'Simonetta?'

'Lexi, you'll never believe whose party I've just been invited to!' Simonetta's normal aloofness had been taken over by excitement.

Her agent laughed. 'Brad Masters?'

Simonetta frowned. 'How did you know?'

'Because his office called the agency, wanting to invite you to one of his parties.' Lexi sounded almost as excited as she was. 'Simonetta, Brad only asks the big-name models to his parties. This could be your break – it could put Models Italia on the map!'

Simonetta rolled her eyes. Typical Lexi, only thinking of herself and the stupid agency. After Brad Masters' party, Select, Models One and all the other top agencies would be begging to sign her up. A beep indicated another call. 'Lexi, I'll call you later,' Simonetta cut her off and switched over to her mother. Normally Simonetta would have ignored the call but she had to share the good news.

'*Mamma*, you'll never guess who has just invited me to his birthday party!'

'I do not know, Simonetta.'

'Brad Masters! You know, the really rich and famous music guy.'

She knew her mother wouldn't approve, but even so, Simonetta was shocked by her reaction. There was a long silence, then her mother let out a high-pitched shriek.

'Simonetta! This is an outrage. Why are telling me this?'

'Because it's exciting, *Mamma*, I thought you'd be pleased for me.'

'*Pleased*?' Her mother could barely get the word out. 'I knew moving to Rome would be the undoing of you. You're on a slippery slope. Mixing with those, those... *people*. Sex, drugs and loose morals, Simonetta – that's all they care about.'

'*Mamma*, it's only a party!'

Her mother let out a stifled sob. 'No, it is not! Simonetta, you do not know what you are doing. I forbid you to go.'

Simonetta had had enough. 'And I forbid you to ring me again. I'm sick of you always telling me what to do.'

'Simonetta, I only have your best interests at heart!'

'Goodbye, *Mamma*,' she said coldly and put the phone down.

chapter four

London

Jerry let out a low whistle.

'Brad Masters, eh?'

Sapphire played with a piece of her hair, as she always did when she had something on her mind. 'What do you think?'

Jerry was silent for a moment, considering. 'I think as long as your mum's OK with it, you should go. Sapphire, Brad Masters wants to meet you and talk about music!'

'But I'm crap at melodies!' she half wailed. 'What if he asks me to sing something?'

Jerry laughed at her anguished expression. 'Then Brad Masters is the man to talk to about it! He knows the best people in the business. They'll help you get it right.'

'You really don't mind if I take time off work? It'll only be a few days.'

Jerry clutched his hand to his chest. 'It'll be hard, but I'll try to survive.'

His silly face made Sapphire laugh, showing off her cute little dimples. 'You're the best, Jerry, thank you!'

'Go get 'em, kid,' he said fondly.

Capri, two weeks later

Simonetta stepped out of the private jet and looked round triumphantly. *This* was what it was all about! She'd told her modelling agency that she was burned out and needed a last-minute holiday, and begrudgingly, they'd agreed. Lexi, her agent, wouldn't have been so snotty if she knew Simonetta was going to stay with Brad Masters! Even though Simonetta had remained her aloof, disdainful self, inside she was bubbling with excitement. This was going to be the start of the rest of her life – the life she, Simonetta Mastrangelo, had always known she was destined for.

An immaculately suited chauffeur was waiting for her at the bottom of the stairs. Simonetta paused and looked over her sunglasses at him, adding to the effect of her tight black dress and towering heels.

'*Buongiorno, signorina,*' he murmured. 'If you would be so kind, your transport awaits.'

He gestured with a white-gloved hand to a sleek, black Ferrari at the edge of the airfield. A smile crept over Simonetta's face. Oh, yes, this was what it was *all* about. Flinging her hair back, she sashayed off, the admiring chauffeur following in her wake.

Sapphire's journey had been just as mind-blowing. After travelling first class for the first time in her life, she had been greeted at Capri airport by another chauffeur, this time in a gleaming Mercedes. After a short journey which made Sapphire feel like she was gliding along silk, the car had made its way with some difficulty down to a little port where a sleek yacht called *Melodia* had been waiting for her. Sapphire knew enough Italian from her GCSEs to know it was Italian for melody.

But I'm rubbish at melodies – is this a bad omen? she thought, worriedly. Despite the stunning scenery around her, tension had been building in her stomach since she landed. Was it really such a good idea coming here? She had never met Brad Masters in her life and she wouldn't know a soul at the party. Sapphire could only imagine the sort of movers and shakers who would be there; what on earth was she going to say to them?

But the handsome young crew waiting aboard the boat soon took Sapphire's mind off such matters. With their deep tans, white teeth and sinewy bodies, they looked like a chartbusting boy band.

'*Signor* Masters especially wanted you to come to his house this way,' Alberto the skipper told her. 'It's the best way to see Casa Eleganza.'

Sapphire sat at the front of the boat, enjoying the sea air and occasional sea spray against her face. After ten minutes, Alberto pointed ahead and shouted something. As the speedboat zoomed round a rocky outcrop, Sapphire gasped. There, nestling above its own private beach and jetty, was a stunning white building the size of a palace. It was early evening by now and the sun was setting, a golden glow reflecting back at them from the windows.

'Beautiful, eh?' Alberto called.

Speechless, Sapphire could only nod in agreement. It looked like something out of a fairytale.

Up close, Casa Eleganza was even prettier, with jewel-coloured flowers tumbling from window boxes and immaculate green lawns stretching out in front. Despite the scorching heat, the grass was a dark emerald. Sapphire could see several gardeners hard at work. She was so busy taking in every detail she didn't realise for a moment that they'd docked. Sapphire felt a warm hand on her shoulder and looked up to see Alberto smiling down at her. She blushed, wondering if all Brad Masters' staff were this good-looking.

A plump, friendly-faced old woman with grey hair tied back in a bun was standing expectantly on the end of the jetty. 'You be careful now, Alberto!' she called. Sapphire noticed she had a strong Irish accent. As Alberto helped Sapphire off the boat, the old lady stepped forward and clasped both of Sapphire's hands warmly.

Sapphire started to feel more relaxed. The woman had a kind, motherly air about her that just made you know she'd look after you. Yet somehow she also fitted in with the opulent, luxurious backdrop of Casa Eleganza, as if she was part and parcel of the place.

'I'm Maggie O'Sullivan, housekeeper,' said the woman. 'And you must be Sapphire.'

'Hi, Maggie,' said Sapphire, suddenly feeling rather shy again. Maggie noticed and put a comforting arm around one shoulder. 'You must be awful tired after your journey, so why don't you come along and see your bedroom. I've had it made up extra-nice for you.'

'What about my rucksack?' Sapphire asked, but Maggie was already guiding her towards the house.

'Ach, that'll be brought up to your room shortly. Come along now.'

If Sapphire had thought the chauffeur-driven car

and the yacht were mind-blowing, her bedroom was something else. In fact, the word 'bedroom' didn't do it justice, as Sapphire found when she walked through her own private living-room on to a sweeping balcony overlooking the sea.

'Maggie, this is amazing!' she gasped.

The housekeeper smiled proudly. 'Mr Masters does like to keep a nice house.'

'It's more than nice,' said Sapphire, flopping on to a huge L-shaped sofa. Vases of exotic lilies stood everywhere, while the walls were cramped with modern art and expensive-looking paintings.

'I'll leave you to it,' Maggie said. 'You probably want a nice, long shower or something.'

Sapphire suddenly felt a bit awkward. 'Er, when is the party? I mean, do I need to change now or anything?'

'The party isn't tonight, pet, don't worry. Mr Masters is flying in tomorrow from a business trip. He sends his apologies and says he looks forward to meeting with you.'

'Oh,' Sapphire said, feeling somewhat at a loss. What was she supposed to do until then?

Maggie seemed to read her mind. 'Why don't you unpack and get yourself straight and then I'll introduce you to the other guests.'

Sapphire felt a jolt of nervous excitement in her stomach. *The other guests,* she thought. *I hope they're nice.*

chapter five

It was 6:55pm and Sapphire was due in the drawing-room in five minutes. Unfortunately, she didn't even know what the drawing-room looked like, let alone how to find it.

She gave herself one final look in the mirror. The vintage flowery tea-dress she'd bought from a second-hand shop in Covent Garden now looked a bit old and frumpy. Still, she didn't have much else to choose from. As usual, Sapphire had left her packing to the last minute and had ended up throwing a mish-mash of random clothes in her rucksack. At least her dress for the party was OK – an All Saints puffball number her mother had bought her for Christmas last year. Sapphire had hung it up as soon as she'd unpacked, but like the rest of stuff she'd pulled out, it looked like it needed a good iron.

She looked at the photo of her dad that she'd brought, on the bedside table. Its presence comforted her. She still thought of her dad often, and loved to tell his photo what she'd been up to.

'Wish me luck, Dad!'

Pulling open the heavy door to her bedroom, Sapphire slipped out on to a wide, marble-floored corridor. She paused to listen. Considering that there was supposed to be such a huge party tomorrow, she was surprised not to hear the sound of any other guests. Then again, the place was so big Sapphire doubted she'd hear them anyway.

The grandfather clock in the hall was chiming seven as Sapphire made her way down the sweeping staircase. The vast rooms yawning off the main hall were motionless and empty. Except for one. Sapphire strained her ears; a low murmur of voices was coming from somewhere. Following the voices, she set off down a corridor which seemed to lead into the heart of the house, pausing to admire the huge, blown-up photographs on the walls – most of them of the famous artists signed to Brad Masters' record label, BMM. Oddly enough, there were no pictures of the man himself.

Finally, she stopped at a dark, wooden studded door. She held her breath for a moment before going in. From behind the door, she could hear what sounded like a young female voice. At least there were going to be people there her own age. Encouraged, she pushed open the door.

Inside, the drawing-room was just as opulent as every other in the house. The lights were turned down low, evening shadows starting to dance in every corner. Sitting in huge sofas opposite each other were two stunning girls – one dark-skinned and smouldering; the other blonde and icy-looking. While they were both slim, the dark-haired one had an angular look that made Sapphire think she might be a model. She was gazing round with a bored expression while the blonde talked in an affected American drawl. Both were wearing tight body-con dresses that definitely weren't off the rack at Topshop.

'So I said to Lauren Conrad, like get *over* yourself bitch, and *she* said—'

The blonde American girl stopped, suddenly aware of Sapphire's presence. 'Oh. Who are you?' She gave Sapphire a snotty once-over and raised an eyebrow. 'I didn't realise tramp chic was in.'

The blonde looked to the brunette for a laugh, but the other girl yawned and went back to staring out the window. Feeling rather stupid, Sapphire introduced herself. The blonde looked disdainfully at her hair, which was still wet from the shower and curling round her shoulders. She sniffed.

'I'm Madison Vanderbilt, and this is Simonetta... er... Mongolla, or something.'

'I've told you, it's *Mastrangelo*,' Simonetta said, shooting Madison a death stare. Sapphire had already decided that she *really* didn't want to get on the wrong side of these girls. Neither looked like they were about to get up, until Madison spoke.

'You can come and say hello if you want to.' She stuck out a hand as if she were royalty. Sapphire walked across and took it, before Madison snatched it back as if she'd just touched something unpleasant. She waved Sapphire away, and without thinking, Sapphire backed away respectfully. As she sat down on a hard little stool, Sapphire laughed at herself in disbelief – she couldn't believe she'd just done that!

Simonetta looked at Sapphire, a secret smile playing on the edge of her lips. 'So, you got the black invitation too, little creature? We were just talking about it.'

'Er, yes I did. It was sent to my home.'

'You're English?' said Madison.

'Yes, I'm from London.'

'Have you met the queen?' Madison asked, her blue eyes showing interest for the first time.

'Funnily enough, no,' Sapphire replied, thinking Madison was winding her up.

Apparently, she wasn't. Madison just sighed, as if Sapphire was just one big disappointment. 'When's everyone else getting here? I need some proper people to talk to,' said the blonde, staring up at the ceiling. So far she hadn't once made eye contact with Sapphire.

'I think Brad is back tomorrow so maybe they're coming then,' Sapphire ventured.

Simonetta turned sharply towards her, incredulous. 'How do you know that? About Mr Brad?' she said.

'Er… the housekeeper told me. Maggie.'

'Ah,' said Madison. 'Already friends with the domestics. Tragic.' She turned a hand over and studied her nails.

After an excruciating five minutes in which Madison talked about herself, Simonetta closed her eyes as if asleep and Sapphire perched awkwardly on the stool wondering what on earth they were all doing there, the door opened and Maggie came in. Sapphire smiled with relief.

'There you are, girls,' Maggie exclaimed cheerfully. 'Madison, Simonetta, I haven't had the pleasure yet, but welcome to Casa Eleganza. I'm Maggie. If you need anything, just let me know.'

'I'll be sure to do that,' said Madison, coolly.

Maggie smiled blandly, as if Madison had said something nice. *She's got the patience of a saint,* thought Sapphire. The housekeeper clasped her hands together. 'I'm thrilled to see you all getting to know each other,' she said. 'Now, dinner will be served in a few minutes. Can I get you anything to drink in the meanwhile?'

'A cosmopolitan,' said Madison. 'Pomegranate. I literally won't drink anything else right now.'

Maggie gave her a steely look. 'Isn't the legal drinking age twenty-one in America?'

'Yeah, if you're a loser. Besides, we're not *in* America,' said Madison condescendingly.

Maggie ignored her and turned to the other two. 'I'll get you all a fresh pineapple juice.' Giving Sapphire a wink, she exited the room with the light movement of someone half her age.

At dinner, which was served in a long, elegant room with chandeliers twinkling above, Sapphire got a better look at both girls. From their manicured nails to their perfect eyebrows and salon blow-dried hair, they had an expensive gloss to them. Sapphire felt a bit like a poor relation, something Madison wasted no time in pointing out.

'So, why is it you say you're here?' she said, toying with the delicious lobster ravioli she had barely touched.

'My mum knows Brad Masters,' Sapphire said. 'She kind of told him I was doing my own thing musically and apparently he wanted to meet me.' Even to her ears, it sounded hollow. *Why* am *I here?* she wondered for the umpteenth time.

She turned to the sultry girl on her left. 'What's your connection to Brad, Simonetta?' They'd already heard at great length how well-known Madison was on the New York/LA party scene, and how Brad must have spotted her there.

Simonetta shrugged her tanned shoulders nonchalantly. 'I am a model. I am beautiful. People recognise me. Brad contacted my agency and invited me out here.'

'Oh, right,' said Sapphire. She looked at Simonetta to see if she was winding her up with the being beautiful bit, but quickly realised she wasn't.

'*I* haven't seen any of your work, you can't be that successful,' Madison said.

Across the table Simonetta's eyes glittered

dangerously, but she didn't dignify Madison's comment with a response.

'And what is it you do?' said Madison, turning to Sapphire. 'Clearly nothing in the fashion industry.'

Sapphire ignored the jibe. 'Actually, I'm a student. I'm doing an art degree.'

Madison looked as if Sapphire had just made her eat a tablespoon of dog shit.

'And I work too,' Sapphire continued, with a sudden urge to displease Madison even more. 'I've got a part-time job in a record shop. To help put me through art school.'

'A *record shop*?' Madison asked, horrified. 'What, you own it?'

'No,' said Sapphire. 'I work at the till.'

'Till?'

'Cash register,' said Simonetta, in a bored tone.

Madison gasped. 'O.M.G,' she said. 'That's so not hot.' She made a show of examining Sapphire's bitten nails and the Top Shop earrings dangling in her ears. 'Are your family really poor or what?'

Sapphire was taken aback by the rudeness of the question. 'It's just me and Mum so it is hard,' she said defensively. 'Well, there was my dad too, but he died when I was young. Before I went to boarding school.'

'Boarding school,' mused Madison. 'That's private, right?'

'Er... yes,' said Sapphire.

'So how did your mother afford that?'

Sapphire opened and then shut her mouth, realising she had no answer. It had never occurred to her before – how *had* her mum been able to send her to the best girls' school in the area when some months in the winter they'd had the electricity cut off?

The door to the dining-room swung open and through it came Tito, the young man who had served their ravioli.

'Ladies, excuse me to interrupt.' Tito had big eyes and slightly goofy front teeth, which gave him the look of a startled rabbit. '*Signor* Masters has just phoned from Monaco. He says he's sorry he can't be there, but hopes this will please you in his absence. Please, follow me.'

Even Madison and Simonetta let curiosity get the better of them. As Simonetta unfolded herself elegantly and stood up, Sapphire realised how *tall* she was. Even without the black stilettos, the dark-haired girl must be six foot. Sapphire felt like a midget in comparison. Sighing loudly, Madison got up and shoved past her. Sapphire watched as the American girl tottered out the room in stupidly high wedge heels. Sapphire looked down at her own New Look thong sandals. She'd break her ankle if she tried to walk in Madison's shoes. The three followed Tito out on to the veranda, where an inky sky hung over the evening sea. He stood there, gazing intently at the view.

'Like, it's the sea at night-time. Whatever,' complained Madison. 'You can't even see that many stars.'

All of a sudden there was a loud *whoosh!* and the sky was lit up by a huge, screaming rocket. It soared up higher and higher before exploding, a cascade of stars falling on to the waters below. Another went up, and then another, until a circus of light danced before their enraptured faces. On and on it went, the display getting more and more dazzling. It was the most incredible thing Sapphire had ever seen.

Some minutes later, when Sapphire thought her eyes couldn't take any more, there was one final burst of colour. They all stood silent, watching the final sparkles fade away into the horizon.

Tito turned to them and smiled. '*Signor* Masters' way of welcoming you to his home. Pretty good, huh?'

'It was OK, I guess,' said Madison, recovering her normal obnoxious manner.

'It was brilliant, Tito!' Sapphire told him.

He grinned. '*Signor* Masters will not be returning until tomorrow night. Until then, he has said you must use Casa Eleganza as if it is your own home.'

They stared over the balcony at the tennis courts, swimming pool and manicured gardens. A helipad stood some way off in the distance, its location marked by a big 'X'.

'I suppose it will have to do,' sniffed Madison.

chapter six

Sapphire woke up a start. Where was she? The soft
silk sheets certainly didn't feel like the ones on her
narrow single bed at home. She opened one eye and
realisation hit. She was at Brad Masters' house in
Capri! Instantly awake, she sat up. She picked up her
mobile; it read 8:10am. Bright sunlight streamed in
through muslin curtains that fluttered in the breeze.
Sapphire threw the silk covers aside and got out of
bed, bare feet padding on the marble floor. She

walked over to the balcony, pulled the curtains aside and stepped out.

It was a stunning day, the sun already high in the cloudless sky. Below her, the grounds of Casa Eleganza stretched out like a kingdom. Sprinklers on the lawns whirred round and round, drenching the lush green grass. Sapphire saw a maid scurry from an outbuilding, her arms full of washing. To her right, the infinity pool glittered enticingly, overlooking the sea. Sapphire had only ever seen such things in the magazines her mum sometimes got.

A surge of excitement coursed through her – she had to get up and explore this beautiful place! Throwing on a vest, shorts and her old Havaiana flip-flops, she brushed her teeth and slipped out.

Downstairs the house was coming alive. Sapphire could hear women's laughter and the clatter of plates from the kitchen. Turning left, she walked towards the huge front door and, with some difficulty, pulled it open. The view stretched before her like a painting. With a little hop and a skip, Saffron ran down the steps into her own private paradise.

* * *

From his bedroom window, the half-naked young man watched the brown-haired girl run off towards the swimming pool. His stomach churned with a mixture of rage and shock, just as it had when he had first laid eyes on the spoiled British girl yesterday. As far as he was concerned, inviting their new house guest was the worst mistake Brad had ever made. Not that *he* would ever tell Brad that. With a dismissive shake, the boy turned away and started to get dressed.

By mid-morning, Sapphire had pretty much covered every square foot of Casa Eleganza's grounds. The more she explored, the more amazing it seemed to get, from the olive groves to the vineyard to the huge garages at the back of the house, which housed a fleet of Ferraris, Aston Martins and Lamborghinis. Brad Masters obviously liked his cars. Sapphire started to make her way back towards the house. She was feeling hungry now and wondered what would be for breakfast.

As she walked up the winding path, Sapphire noticed a building that sat back in a shady corner of its own, surrounded by trees. She frowned. Would it be rude to go and have a look inside? Brad Masters had said to treat the house as their own, after all.

Quietly, Sapphire pulled open the door. Inside it was cool and dark. 'Hello?' she called out. Hearing nothing, she ventured inside. She was standing in what seemed to be the corridor of a little flat. In front of her was a small living-room, practically empty apart from a sofa and a guitar leaning against one wall. Embarrassed that she had walked into someone's home Sapphire turned to walk out, but bumped into a young guy standing behind her.

'Sorry!' she exclaimed, embarrassed. 'I—'

All she could take in was a mop of black hair and luminous green eyes before the boy rounded on her furiously. 'What the hell are you doing?' he shouted, his English strongly accented. 'You have no right to be in here!'

He was much taller than her, and Sapphire shrank back as he stared down at her angrily.

'I'm really sorry,' she stammered. 'I didn't realise—'

He didn't give her time to finish. He gestured at the door. 'Get out.'

Cheeks burning with humiliation, Sapphire started to walk out. Then a wave of anger suddenly swept through her. 'There's no need to be so rude,' she said swinging round. 'I said I was sorry. It was a mistake to come—'

Her words fell away as she realised he was right behind her. They collided and, as she fell against his chest, Sapphire felt the lean, hard muscle underneath and caught the waft of fresh aftershave.

'Oh!'

She stumbled back as the dark-haired boy almost shoved her away from him. He looked at her, his pale face disdainful.

'You kind of girls spend your whole life being rude, what can you expect in return?'

'*What*?' exclaimed Sapphire. 'What are you talking about? You don't even know me!'

His eyes flashed. 'Nor do I wish to.' With that, he shut the door in Sapphire's face.

It was late morning before Sapphire found Madison and Simonetta sunbathing beside the pool. Each was in the smallest of bikinis, showcasing their perfect bodies. Simonetta was wearing huge gold hoop earrings, a selection of gold chains draped round her neck. *The Italians sure go big on accessorising,* Sapphire thought. Simonetta made even lying by the pool into a major fashion shoot. Sapphire dumped her bag and sat on the nearest sunlounger.

'Hi, guys.'

Madison lifted up her Gucci sunglasses and inspected Sapphire as though she was some kind of insect.

'Oh, it's you.'

Simonetta didn't move a muscle, as if she couldn't even be bothered to say hello. Sapphire decided to persevere. After all, she was stuck with these two for the time being.

'What have you two been up to?'

'This,' said Madison, lying back on her lounger. After a few seconds, though, her head lifted back up again. 'Where's your bedroom anyway? Simonetta and I were wondering where they'd put you. The servants quarters, maybe...'

Sapphire gestured at her balcony. 'Actually, I'm up there.'

Madison sat up. '*There*? You've got your own balcony?'

Sapphire nodded. 'Where are you two then?'

Madison looked at Simonetta, who had inclined her head slightly. Her jewellery glowed expensively in the sunlight. 'We're at the back of the house,' she said, sounding annoyed.

'Ah, no balcony?' Sapphire asked, trying to stop herself smiling. She could imagine the dirty look she was getting from behind Madison's mirrored sunglasses.

Madison opened her mouth to say something, but just then Tito appeared with a tray of glasses and iced water. He set it down on a table between Simonetta and Madison's sunbeds.

'I thought you might like some refreshment, *signorinas*.'

'*Grazie*, Tito,' Sapphire replied.

He looked pleased and clapped his hands. 'I see you learn the lingo already. Have you had the chance to have a look round?'

Sapphire nodded. 'It's really lovely.'

'*It's really lovely*,' Madison mimicked in a stupid English accent. She turned on her side with her back to them. Simonetta was completely motionless again, as if she had fallen asleep.

Tito's eyes twinkled at Sapphire.

'And from your observations, Sapphire,' he asked, 'what sort of man do you think *Signor* Masters is?'

Sapphire hesitated. 'Well, he's obviously into his art and music. Mr Masters clearly likes to be surrounded by beautiful things. But…' She stopped, not wanting to seem rude.

'Go on,' Tito said, smiling.

'Oh, I don't know. It really is a beautiful place, but there's just something a bit…' Sapphire wrinkled her forehead, trying to think of the right words. 'Empty about it, do you know what I mean? Like, it's not very homely. I'm not slagging it off,' she added hastily.

Tito laughed. 'I am sure you're not! Casa Eleganza is a little like, how do you say it, a blank canvas?'

'Yeah,' agreed Sapphire. 'Normally you can get a feeling for someone from their house, but I don't feel I know anything about Brad Masters.'

Tito's eyes twinkled again. 'Maybe *Signor* Masters likes it that way.'

Sapphire hesitated, thinking of the boy she'd bumped into earlier – the one who'd been so horrible to her. 'Tito, I ran into this guy earlier. Black hair and green eyes, what's his—'

'Heavens, boy! Are you bothering these girls, Tito?' Maggie walked alongside the pool towards them, wearing what looked like a dark-green version of the navy dress she had been wearing yesterday. 'Haven't you got any jobs to do?' she said to Tito, though her tone wasn't cross. Tito bowed and, giving Sapphire a cheeky smile, waltzed off.

'He's a good lad, Tito, but Lord can he talk the hind legs off a donkey,' Maggie chuckled. She stood over the girls, hands on sturdy hips. 'How are you all doing today?' she asked.

Madison sat up, ignoring the question. 'Are the other guests here yet? When's Brad flying in?'

'Hold your horses, young woman,' Maggie told her. 'I actually came to tell you that Mr Masters will be arriving by helicopter later on today. He'd like you to join him on the terrace at seven o'clock.'

'Seven o'clock?' said Madison. 'You seriously expect me to be ready by then? It's, like, the evening already.'

'It's not even lunchtime yet,' said Sapphire. 'You've got plenty of time.'

'Maybe *you* do,' said Madison, getting up from the sun lounger. 'Some of us *like* to look good.'

Lying on her sunbed, Simonetta's lips twitched into a smile. 'And some of us look good naturally,' she said airily.

Madison stared at her. '*Bitch*,' she said, eventually. 'You do *not* know who you're messing with.'

'I'm sorry, did I offend you?' asked Simonetta. 'I was just making an observation.'

Maggie stepped between the two girls. 'Madison, why don't you go up to your room. I'll help you get ready if you like.' She ushered Madison towards the house. Before she left, she turned to Sapphire and smiled. 'Brad does not know what he's getting himself into,' she said.

No, thought Sapphire. *I'm sure he doesn't.*

But do we?

chapter seven

The tension in the air was palpable. Madison sighed. 'Where *is* he? We've been waiting for *years*.'

Sapphire checked her watch. It was quarter past seven.

'He's probably on the phone or something,' she said. The three of them were on the terrace, waiting for the grand arrival of Brad Masters. They had all heard a helicopter whirring overhead a moment ago and now it sat on the helipad, like a giant insect resting. A man had got out and walked into the house through another door, ignoring them.

Madison sighed. 'I needn't have rushed after all. Do you know I had to do my hair in *two* hours tonight?'

She certainly looked the part in a shocking pink Versace dress and sparkly Dolce and Gabanna stilettos. Simonetta, who was standing in the shadows looking out to sea, was the epitome of Italian sexiness in a backless black dress, her sheet of dark hair cascading down her back. Sapphire, by contrast, had plumped for a smock dress over leggings and flat sandals. She wished she'd bought another pair of heels; she felt like a dwarf next to Simonetta and Madison.

Simonetta turned back towards the other two. 'Something's going on,' she announced dramatically. 'Something weird.'

Madison frowned. 'What do you mean?'

'Think about it,' Simonetta said loftily. 'We are here for a party, but where are the other guests? It has just been us three since we got here.'

'You're right, you know,' Sapphire said. She had been thinking the same thing herself.

Madison's eyes widened. 'But why would he invite just the three of us, all the way out here?' Her eyes flickered over Sapphire. 'After all, I can't imagine what we've got in common.'

A man's deep voice spoke behind them. 'Ah, an inquiring mind. That's what I like to see, young lady.'

They all spun round to see Brad Masters standing on the terrace. Even in the fading light, Sapphire could see he had an aura. He was tall – at least six foot two – with hair that had once been black, but was now greying around the temples. He was dressed in an expensive, lightweight grey suit (Armani, Simonetta noticed) with an open-necked black shirt underneath. He looked tanned, confident and simply oozing with power and money.

Brad Masters stepped forward and took Madison's hand. 'Madison, isn't it? Delighted to meet you.'

'And I'm delighted to meet you, Mr Masters,' she gushed, eyes darting furiously to check him out. The Patek Philippe watch on his wrist must have cost a hundred grand!

He smiled easily. 'Call me Brad.'

Simonetta wasted no time getting in next.

'Simonetta Mastrangelo,' she announced, giving Brad her hand. To her disappointment he didn't kiss it.

'Good evening, Simonetta,' Brad replied. 'I've seen your face before. You're a model, aren't you?'

Simonetta shot a smug look at Madison. Brad turned to Sapphire, who was standing at the back.

'Last but not least, you must be Sapphire. Hello.'

'Hello there,' said Sapphire, blushing. Brad Masters was standing right there, in front of her! He shook her hand formally and his grip was strong and warm. Brad stepped back and surveyed the three of them.

'I trust you're enjoying your stay.'

'Oh, we're having a ball,' Madison breathed, determined to strike up conversation first. 'You have a *really* beautiful home. Of course, I've stayed in places as big as this before, but none quite so amazing. Your décor is really something,' she added.

Brad smiled at her, as if he were slightly amused by something. 'Thank you, Madison. I like it.'

'How was your trip, Brad? Did you make any good deals?' Simonetta asked, casually putting one hand on her hip to show off the outline of her body. She knew that when it came to powerful men, the way to impress them was by talking business.

Brad looked a bit taken aback. 'It was a trip worth making, thank you, Simonetta.'

She smiled, doing that half-closed thing with her eyes she knew made men go wild.

Brad looked at Sapphire instead. 'Have you had the chance to explore?'

'Yes, it's really beautiful, thank you. I'm just wondering, though… why did you invite me here?'

Brad ignored the question. 'Do you play tennis?'

'A bit,' said Sapphire, blushing because he was singling her out. 'I haven't played much since school, though.'

'We must find time to have a game,' he told her. 'Anyway, enough of my small talk, you must be starving. Please, follow me.'

Pushing Sapphire out of the way, Madison went after him, closely followed by Simonetta. All the way down the marble corridor, Brad made easy conversation with the girls, pointing out the famous photographs and paintings adorning his walls.

'I'm particularly pleased with that – it's an original

Andy Warhol,' Brad said as they passed a painting of brightly coloured flower prints.

Madison nodded sagely. 'The name's familiar. Was he on *American Idol*?'

Brad's face stayed neutral, but Sapphire couldn't help raising her eyebrows. She couldn't believe Madison didn't know one of the most famous artists of the last hundred years!

A few yards on, Brad stopped at the door of the dining-room. 'By the way,' he said casually, 'I invited someone else to join us for dinner.'

He pushed the door open. 'Girls, meet Cam Tyler.'

Madison screamed.

chapter eight

Cam Tyler rose from his seat and smiled. Madison realised she was hyperventilating and tried to calm down. She couldn't believe he was standing there in the flesh.

Cam was a twenty-year-old American R&B star who was *the* singing sensation of the moment. His debut single – originally released on his own MySpace page – had shot to the top of the charts on both sides of the Atlantic and he was tipped to be the next Usher, Ne-Yo and Justin Timberlake rolled into one. No wonder the music industry was going crazy for him, and every label was desperate to sign him.

But as usual, it seemed Brad Masters had got in there first.

'Hi,' Madison said breathily. 'I'm Madison Vanderbilt.'

'Cam,' he said easily and stepped forward to take her hand. Madison held it a little longer than necessary before letting go. She stepped back to take a better look at the singer. She knew he was hot, but in the flesh he was even better. Cam Tyler was *ripped*. Six feet of pure muscle, with biceps nestling under his Rocawear T-shirt; Madison just wanted to reach out and *squeeze*. If the body was something, the face was even better – tanned, square-jawed and with chocolate-brown eyes that gave a Labrador puppy a run for its money. Today Cam's short, thick black hair had been styled upwards into a cool quiff.

Madison smiled seductively, running her tongue over her lips. She was satisfied to see Cam smile back.

Brad stepped in to carry on the introductions. 'Cam, this is Simonetta Mastrangelo.'

'*Buongiorno*,' Simonetta drawled. She'd got over her initial surprise of meeting Cam Tyler and was now back to her aloof, studied self. The boy was too young for her; Simonetta normally only dated men in their late twenties or thirties. But there was no denying he was cute. She gave him a casual once-over.

Cam raised his eyebrow interestedly. 'Hey, Simonetta.'

'And this is Sapphire Stevens, our English contingent,' Brad said, gesturing to Sapphire.

Cam looked at her, as if he hadn't really noticed she was there before. 'Hey, Sapphire. Great name.'

'Hi there,' she mumbled, noticing a diamond stud glinting in his ear. Cam Tyler was the best-looking boy she had *ever* laid eyes on. She could feel herself going red under his penetrating gaze. Cam smiled, as if well-aware of the effect he was having on her.

A gong sounded somewhere in the house. Brad smiled.

'Dinner is served.'

Two hours later, the four were still sitting at Brad's dinner table, having seen off a delicious seafood dinner. Despite her claims that she wasn't hungry and 'couldn't eat a thing', Madison had polished off two plates of mussels and a piece of the exquisite dark chocolate tart that had been brought out for dessert. Now they were having coffee while Brad explained why Cam was there.

'Cam's working on his debut album for BMM and we both decided he'd be better off out here, without any distractions.'

'LA's kind of crazy,' Cam said. 'I needed some space to write, so when Brad invited me to stay in his guesthouse, I jumped at the chance.'

Brad looked across at Sapphire. 'You should ask young Sapphire for help if you get stuck. I hear she's quite a talent when it comes to writing lyrics.'

Cam looked at Sapphire. 'Really? That's cool.' He sounded like he was being polite rather than interested.

Sapphire blushed again. 'I've written a few things,' she mumbled.

Madison decided the conversation had gone on

long enough without her. She leaned across the table, giving Cam the full benefit of her cleavage.

'Do you work out, Cam?'

Sapphire and Simonetta exchanged incredulous glances, but Madison was totally serious. 'I bet you go to Benny's Gym in Hollywood. It's where all the hot people hang out, right?'

Cam smiled. 'I've been there a few times, yeah.'

Brad coughed. 'I've got some calls to make. Cam, can I leave you to look after our house guests?'

Cam smiled, showing off perfect white teeth. 'Sure thing, Brad.'

Brad stood up. 'Girls, if you'll excuse me. I've taken the liberty of organising a boat trip tomorrow, so can you meet me on the jetty at nine o'clock sharp?'

Madison and Sapphire looked at each other and nodded excitedly. Brad was getting up to leave when Simonetta spoke. '*Signor* Masters, when is the party?' She smiled seductively. 'I'd like to look my best.'

Sapphire and Madison looked at each other again. In the heat of the moment, they had forgotten about the party.

Brad smiled smoothly. 'My mistake, I should have let you know. It's tomorrow evening, so you'll have lots of time to prepare after the boat trip.'

'Is it being held here?' Simonetta persisted. She had seen no sign of caterers, florists, or any of the usual activity you'd expect to be involved with Brad Masters' fiftieth birthday party.

'Yes, it's being held here. Now, I really must make those calls.' Brad smiled at the table. 'Goodnight, everyone. Sleep well and I'll see you in the morning.'

The door closed behind him and all four looked at each other. A wicked look crossed Cam's face. 'You guys like to swim?'

'I haven't got my costume,' said a slightly panicky Sapphire five minutes later. They were standing by the side of the infinity pool, the starry sky above like a velvet blanket studded with diamonds.

'Don't be so lame, Sapphire. Who needs a bikini?' said Madison. Sapphire watched open-mouthed as the American girl peeled off her dress and stepped out of it, to reveal lacy knickers and a bra. Cam's eyes gleamed in appreciation as they swept over her lithe body.

'Last one in's a total loser,' she said, then dived elegantly into the pool.

Sapphire watched as Cam peeled off his T-shirt and her tummy did a funny little flip. It was like he'd just walked off an Abercrombie and Fitch billboard. His body was a work of art: broad, defined shoulders and a six-pack that tapered into a small waist. Sapphire couldn't help staring at Cam's flat, muscled stomach, where a fine line of hair from his belly button disappeared into the top of his shorts. Cam caught her looking and she blushed bright red. He raised an amused eyebrow.

'Coming in?'

Sapphire shook her head quickly. 'I don't think so.'

'OK.' Cam turned and, with a whoop, launched himself into the pool.

'Cam, you just soaked me!' Madison screamed.

'Well, we are in a swimming pool, Madison,' he pointed out. 'It's kind of inevitable.'

Sapphire came and sat down, dangling her legs in the water. It was wonderfully cool and she wiggled her feet.

'You're making it very easy for me to pull you in,'

Cam told her, a wicked glint in his eyes. Suddenly he looked past Sapphire and his mouth dropped open. Sapphire turned and saw Simonetta shimmying along the side of the pool towards them. Her long limbs moved with the grace of a cat; her black hair gleamed in the moonlight. Sapphire's eyes widened as she saw that, save for a tiny G-string, Simonetta was practically naked. Embarrassed by the sudden amount of flesh on show, Sapphire averted her eyes as she walked past.

'How easy it is to make you blush, little creature,' Simonetta murmured. Pausing to stretch and yawn, showing off her full, firm boobs, Simonetta climbed down the steps into the pool. She ducked her head under the water, coming up like some kind of beautiful sea nymph. Flashing a smile at Cam, she started to do a graceful breaststroke to the other end of the pool. After a moment, he followed.

Madison swam over to Sapphire.

'What a slut!'

Sapphire remained silent, as Simonetta and Cam swam into a corner and started talking.

'Talk about desperate. Guys *hate* girls throwing themselves at them,' Madison sniffed. Suddenly, she pulled her bra down to expose a pair of perky boobs.

Sapphire half-laughed in shock. 'What are you *doing*?'

'Mine are better than hers, aren't they?' Madison demanded.

'Er...' Sapphire said, trying not to look at Madison's dusky pink nipples. To her relief, Madison pulled her bra up again and glanced jealously down the pool. Simonetta and Cam's heads were close together, barely a foot between them. The air had suddenly taken on a charged feeling that made Sapphire feel uncomfortable, out of her depth.

'I think I'll go to bed,' she said.

'Don't leave me,' Madison implored.

'Really, I can't keep my eyes open,' Sapphire lied.

Madison shot another jealous look at Cam and Simonetta. 'Whatever, this is a suck-fest anyway.' Muttering under her breath she climbed out and stalked off.

'So,' Cam said with a lazy smile. 'You go skinny-dipping often?' His eyes strayed again to Simonetta's breasts, just out of reach beneath the water. Simonetta dipped her hair back in the pool again, coming up with it sleek and sexy against her head.

'This is not skinny-dipping, I am still wearing clothes.'

Cam raised an amused eyebrow. 'You Italians have a funny dress sense.'

She smiled seductively. 'And you Americans are far too uptight.'

Cam laughed, but his eyes had taken on a hungry, intense look. 'You're a very beautiful girl, Simonetta.'

'I know.'

'And very confident.'

Simonetta noticed his breathing had got more husky and shallow. She arched her back again and ran her hands through her hair. Cam bit his bottom lip and moved towards her.

'Simonetta…'

Simonetta smiled. He was wriggling on the hook like a fish.

'I have to go,' she suddenly announced.

Cam looked stunned. *What?*

She gave him an amused, haughty look. 'A model needs her beauty sleep.' She pushed off and glided gracefully back across the pool.

Cam stopped her. 'Wait! You're leaving just like that?'

Simonetta turned and saw the lost expression on his face. Men – they were all the same! So easy to manipulate, so easy to tease. And now she'd proved that a world-famous R&B star was no different. It reinforced once again Simonetta's knowledge that she was irresistible to any man.

Now that she knew she could have Cam, she had instantly lost interest. '*Ciao*, darling,' she breathed.

'There's a name for girls like you,' Cam said, but he sounded more disappointed than angry. He knew he'd just been played by Simonetta. He watched her lithe form emerge dripping from the water, this time her hands covering her assets.

Simonetta turned and dropped him a slow, seductive wink. 'There's only one name for me. It's Simonetta.' *One day*, she thought to herself, *you'll see it everywhere.* 'And now, I'm going to bed.' Grabbing her clothes, she slid off into the darkness.

'Jesus!' Cam exclaimed, then dived under the water. He needed a cooling off.

chapter nine

There had been no sign of the other two at breakfast. As Sapphire made her way down to the beach afterwards, she wondered briefly what had gone on last night after she left. An image of Cam's torso, muscled and glistening with water, suddenly popped into her head, making Sapphire's stomach lurch. Had he been with Simonetta last night? Or even both? Sapphire couldn't help feeling a bit gutted; she'd gone to bed last night thinking about his sexy body and dark eyes.

Any thoughts of Cam were temporarily suspended when she saw the huge, gleaming-white yacht moored at the end of the jetty, the name *Spirito Libero* emblazoned across the side. As she approached, Brad was standing on the beach talking on his mobile. Sapphire waited until he was finished and then stepped forward hesitantly.

'Happy birthday.' She gave him the flower she'd plucked from the veranda outside her bedroom.

Brad looked surprised. 'What's this?'

Sapphire blushed. 'It's your birthday, isn't it? I mean, the party's tonight. I'm afraid I didn't get you a card or anything, but I thought you might like the flower instead.' She coughed, embarrassed. 'I mean, even though it's your flower anyway…' She sighed. 'Sorry, it was better in my head.'

Brad smiled back. 'I'm really touched, thank you. My birthday was actually last week,' he added. 'But this was the only available space in my schedule.'

'Oh,' said Sapphire, blushing.

You are such an idiot, she told herself. *Why can't you just keep your mouth shut?*

Behind them, they heard a loud shriek. Madison

had got one ridiculously high heel stuck in the sand and had fallen over. Staff rushed from nowhere to help her. Brad and Sapphire looked at each other and started laughing.

'I've got a feeling this is a birthday celebration I won't forget,' he said.

Simonetta lay still, enjoying the warm sun on her face. They had been on board for a few hours now, and already her dark skin was turning the colour of mahogany. She thought of how she'd left Cam last night and smiled to herself. Not many girls would turn down Cam Tyler – she could already see the cow eyes Madison and Sapphire were making at him. Silly little girls! Simonetta had much more important things on her mind. She wanted a way into Brad Masters' inner circle and there was no way she was going to wreck her chances with a stupid holiday romance.

Her thoughts drifted to her *mamma*. What would she be doing now? Probably preparing yet another meal for her brothers and sisters in the narrow kitchen of their poky little house. Simonetta couldn't understand why none of her siblings, who were all younger than her, had expressed any desire to leave their boring village in search of fame and fortune. Of course, none of them were as blessed as her looks-wise, but still. Her sister Vera had a big sweet habit and even bigger thighs, but you'd have thought she could get a job as a secretary or *something*.

Simonetta thought more about her mother. *Mamma* would have a heart attack if she could see her daughter now, perched atop a luxury yacht in a thong bikini. She had been ignoring her mother's calls since she got to Capri, but she could imagine what the voice-mails would be.

'Why are you such a bad girl, Simonetta? Why do you do this to me?'

Her mother had always been harder on her than her brothers and sisters and Simonetta had never known why. Still, it didn't bother her now. She was free to do whatever she wanted.

'Simonetta.' Sapphire was standing over her, smiling. 'Lunch is ready.'

Simonetta watched the English girl walk away. Such an odd creature! She was quite pretty, but she had clearly never heard of couture. And those eyebrows! If she weren't such a lost cause, Simonetta would sit her down and give her the wisdom of her beauty tips. She was embarrassed to be seen out in public with her.

And yet Sapphire had a secret pass to Brad Masters' world, just like her and that bimbo Madison. Something linked all three of them and Simonetta couldn't for the life of her work out what it was.

'Is this how you spend your time off, Brad?' Sapphire asked, forking a mouthful of *spaghetti alla carbonara*. Although she had initially been intimidated, Brad was surprisingly easy to be around and Sapphire was feeling more relaxed by the minute.

Brad smiled ruefully. 'Days like this are few and far between unfortunately. My work seems to have a habit of taking precedence.'

'Yeah, but you don't *have* to work, do you?' asked Madison. 'I wouldn't if I had all this.'

'I do it because I enjoy it,' he said, smiling. 'Music is my passion. I'd work even if I wasn't getting paid.'

Madison looked puzzled at this revelation. 'Oh.'

'What about you, Sapphire?' Brad said, turning to her. 'You work in a music shop, don't you? It must be pretty interesting.'

'Yeah, Jerry, the guy who owns it, is really nice. He helps me out a lot with my own music.' Sapphire went red as both Simonetta and Madison looked at her contemptuously.

'I'm looking forward to hearing some of your stuff,' said Brad. 'Your mum said it had kind of an Amy Winehouse-vibe.'

Sapphire's heart skipped a beat. 'Er... I'm all right with lyrics, it's just the melodies.'

Brad smiled understandingly. 'That old chestnut, eh? It'll come.'

'Do you really think so?' she asked eagerly.

He shrugged. 'Sure. Anything's possible if you work hard enough. I started out in life with an overnight bag and a couple of quid to my name.' It was well known that Brad had arrived in London from a sleepy town in Devon and worked his way up to the big time.

'Quid?' asked Madison, looking puzzled.

He chuckled. 'Quid, dosh, wonger, however you want to say it.'

'Brad means money,' Sapphire said, smiling at Madison.

Madison returned the smile, happy they were back on familiar ground. 'Money makes the world go round, right?'

Brad studied her. 'Do you really think that?'

'Uh? *Yeah!*'

Brad said nothing as he stared out to sea.

Sapphire smoothed down her dress, checking herself for the umpteenth time in the mirror. The short, strapless number from Miss Selfridge was a bit daring for her, but her mum had encouraged her to buy it on one of their rare shopping trips. 'You've got such a lovely figure, darling!' Leonie had told her. 'You should show it off more.'

Showing it off is what I am doing tonight, Sapphire thought. She had to admit the dress looked pretty good, and even better with the black heels her mother had insisted on buying her as well. Shaking her blow-dried hair over her shoulders, Sapphire applied a coat of lip-gloss, took a deep breath and walked out.

The house was strangely silent for a party and Sapphire had heard no guests arriving. *Maybe they're all being brought in on Brad's yacht,* she thought. As she reached the staircase, she saw Maggie standing at the bottom. On catching sight of Sapphire, the friendly housekeeper let out a happy gasp.

'Don't you look like a princess! Come down here so I can have a proper look at you.'

Careful not to trip up, Sapphire slowly made her way down the stairs.

Maggie's eyes lit up in approval. 'Such a darling dress. Don't you think so, Raphael?'

Sapphire jumped. She hadn't realised the rude boy from yesterday was standing in the hallway. His green eyes seemed to burn into her as he gave her a contemptuous look.

'I will see you later, Maggie.'

'Don't mind him,' Maggie said as Raphael stalked off. 'That's just Raphael's way.'

Well, I don't like his way, Sapphire thought. *It's rude.* 'Why *is* he here, Maggie? He doesn't seem to fit in.'

Maggie chuckled. 'Brad found him on the street

in Rome, busking. He's a music student, a rare talent, Brad says. They got talking and when Brad found out Raphael was busking to pay his way through college, he invited him to be his chauffeur for the summer instead. Brad likes nurturing young protégés.'

'I don't think Raphael likes me very much,' Sapphire ventured.

Maggie smiled. 'Don't take it personally. Raphael's... complicated. He doesn't find it easy to relate to people.'

'Right,' said Sapphire. Like *that* explained anything. Maybe he just didn't like brunettes or something. She asked a question that had been troubling her instead.

'Maggie, where are all the other guests?'

The housekeeper smiled knowingly. 'All good things come to those who wait.'

The three girls were waiting expectantly in the drawing-room. Madison had already surveyed Sapphire's outfit with distaste. Now she looked Simonetta's black silk jumpsuit up and down.

'You say it's Gucci? Looks fake to me.'

Simonetta made a 'pff' sound, giving Madison the once-over back. 'I didn't realise it was prom night.'

Madison looked down at her baby-blue sequinned mini-dress. 'Er, hello? This is Dolce and Gabanna.'

'They must have been having an off day,' Simonetta sniffed.

It was a minute past seven when Brad walked in. 'Girls, you look fabulous. Shall we?' He gestured towards the door. In curious silence they followed him out of the house and down the garden path towards the beach. Hundreds of candles lit their way and at the end of them, Sapphire could see a gazebo ablaze with fairy lights and more candles. In the gathering gloom it looked magical. Brad led them inside, to where an ice bucket containing a bottle of champagne stood in one corner, along with four glasses.

'When's everyone else arriving?' Madison asked, her eyes scanning the sweeping gardens.

Brad smiled. 'Everyone's here.'

'But…' Madison looked in confusion at Brad and then at Sapphire and Simonetta. 'I don't understand.'

There was a long silence before Brad spoke again.

'Girls, I'm going to cut to the chase. I've brought you here under false pretences.'

Sapphire's heart began to quicken. The atmosphere could be cut with a knife as the three girls listened to what he had to say.

'It is my fiftieth birthday party,' Brad said. 'That much is true. But the reason I only invited the three of you is…' He stopped, seemingly stuck for words. 'That is to say… The reason you're here is because I thought it would be a good chance to meet my….'

He looked at them all, face serious.

'A good chance to meet my daughters.'

chapter ten

There was a stunned silence.

'O. M. Fricking *G*!' Madison crowed. 'I always knew that loser Frank was way too un-cool to be my dad!'

Sapphire was barely aware of Madison's shrieks. Her heart was pounding, blood rushing through her ears as she tried to take it in. Brad Masters, her father? He couldn't be! Her father was Bill! She thought of the cherished photo up in her bedroom. Suddenly the image of Bill's face in her mind seemed blurred, as if her whole world was slowly sliding away from her.

'You're not my dad!' she cried, aware of the tears pouring down her cheeks.

Brad took a step towards her, his face pained. 'Sapphire...'

'Don't touch me!' she yelled and turned to run out of the gazebo. She pelted up the garden path, kicking her heels off halfway, stones and grass scratching her feet. As she rounded the corner, she ran into something warm and solid.

'Whoa there!' said Cam. He grabbed hold of both of her arms and then saw her tear-stained face. 'Hey, are you all right?'

Sapphire wriggled out of his strong grip and ran. When she got through the front door, she whirled up the stairs to her bedroom. The photo was sitting there on the bedside table – Sapphire picked it up and clutched it to her chest.

'You're not my dad!' she shouted out towards the open window. Curling up in a ball on the bed, she started sobbing.

A few minutes later she became aware of another

person in the room. Maggie was standing there, her pleasant, wrinkled face full of concern. 'Oh, duckie,' she said. 'Mr Masters asked me to come and see if you were OK.'

The kindly tone of her voice set Sapphire off again. 'He's not my dad, he can't be!' she sobbed. '*Bill* is my dad. He rode a motorbike and he used to tell me bedtime stories. He loved my mother and me very much and he died when I was ten…'

Maggie came and sat down on the bed and put a warm hand on her shoulder. 'No one is going to take Bill away from you,' she said. 'Mr Masters knows he hasn't been a part of your lives, but he would like to start now, if you'll let him. You know, as far as fathers go, you could do worse than him. He's a good man.'

'*This* is my dad,' Sapphire said, showing her the photo of Bill. 'My mum met him at a music festival.'

Maggie smiled sadly. 'Oh darlin'.' She hesitated. 'Maybe you should call your mam and talk to her about it.'

Sapphire nodded. Leonie would tell her it wasn't true.

'I'll bring you a nice hot cup of tea,' Maggie said.

Giving her another pat on the shoulder, she left. Sapphire got her mobile and switched it on. As she scrolled down to 'home' and it started ringing, her hands were shaking so much she almost dropped it.

Leonie answered after ten rings, sounding a bit out of breath. 'Hello?'

'It's me.'

'Hello, darling! I was just putting some things away.' Her tone sounded anxious. 'How are you getting on?'

'Is Brad Masters my dad?' Sapphire asked, voice trembling. Her mother was going to tell her it was all a sick joke, she knew it.

There was a short silence.

'So he's told you then.' Her mum's voice was tight with worry and expectation.

'He's told me, but that doesn't mean it's true, Mum!' she shouted. 'Tell me it's not true. Bill's my dad!'

Leonie's voice wavered. 'Oh, Sapphire, I wish you didn't have to hear it like this, but I thought it was the best way. Please believe me, darling, Brad and I talked about it...'

Shock rippled through Sapphire. 'You've known *all along*?'

'Yes, but Sapphire, we weren't going behind your back or anything. I just thought you could get to know your father a bit first...'

My father? Her mother had actually said the word. Sapphire knew Leonie was telling the truth.

'Leave me alone,' she cried and threw the phone across the room.

In all the fuss with Sapphire, no one noticed that Simonetta had slipped away quietly. When Brad had told them he was their father she had received the news with typical haughtiness, but her mind had been whirling. Brad Masters, her father? But how? Her mother had never left the village in her life! Simonetta knew what she had to do. Walking along the beach until she found a spot with good reception, she dialled her family home. Her sister Vera picked up.

'It's me. Can you get *Mamma*?'

Her sister let out a dramatic shriek. 'So you're alive! *Mamma* has been out of her mind, how could you do this to her?'

'Just go and get her!' Simonetta snapped. She didn't have time for this. She could hear Vera's lumbering footsteps and a few moments later her mother snatched up the phone.

'Simonetta! Why haven't you returned any of my calls?'

Simonetta ignored her. 'Is Brad Masters my father, *Mamma*?' she asked calmly.

A scandalised gasp. 'How can you say such a thing?'

'Just tell me, *Mamma*! I know you're lying.'

Her mother fell silent. 'Let me take the telephone outside,' she said eventually. 'It is more private there.'

Simonetta listened to her mother make her way through the kitchen to the back yard. She could picture the place – the broken kitchen cupboard Papa was too lazy to fix, the never-ending line of washing blowing outside in the breeze.

'Now we can talk more comfortably,' her mother said. Her voice had lost some of its drama and she seemed calmer, almost resigned. 'What is it you want to ask me again?' she said, as if she'd forgotten.

Simonetta cast her eyes upwards. 'For Mary's sake, *Mamma*. Is Brad Masters my father?'

She could hear her mother breathing down the line. Finally she spoke. 'I know what you think of me, Simonetta – that I am a boring old woman who has never lived. But I, too, have a past and secrets.' She paused. 'You must never breathe a word of this to anyone, not even to Papa. The shame would kill him.'

'So that's what I am – an embarrassing secret?' Simonetta demanded.

Her mother sighed. 'That's not what I meant.' She took a long, deep breath. 'When I was young, just after I had become engaged to Papa, I had the offer of a summer job in Rome, as a waitress. Papa and my father were adamant I wasn't to go – it was not the thing for a young girl to do, especially back then. But I was determined. Determined to get out of the little village where I had grown up, where everyone knew my business. Against their wishes I went, but with a strict promise to be back at the end of the summer.'

Simonetta listened, spellbound.

'I was working in this expensive restaurant, where

I met Brad Masters. He was a customer and he used to talk to me. I liked him because he was very handsome and seemed to care about me. One thing led to another and we started dating. Of course, I was torn with guilt over Papa, but there was something about Brad that I found irresistible.'

'What happened next, *Mamma*?'

Her mother sighed. 'At the end of the summer I knew I had to go back. Papa was waiting and Brad was starting to make a big success of himself. So I came back home and a few weeks later I found out I was pregnant. I was able to get away with it because Papa and I were, you know, together.' Her mother gave a short, bitter laugh. 'See what a good Catholic girl I turned out to be!'

Simonetta ignored her. 'How did Brad find out?'

'Because I rang and told him, the day after you were born. I wasn't sure up until then, but the moment I saw you I knew. You looked just like him. Brad was shocked, but insisted he'd pay to help bring you up. I told him no, we had Papa to look after us. I said I wanted to tell him as a matter of principle, but it was probably best if we never spoke again.'

'So how did he find me?'

Her mother made a weary sound. 'I do not know, maybe the surname from when you started modelling. Brad knew I was engaged to a Mastrangelo. Maybe he saw you and realised it was not a coincidence. Brad Masters has ways of finding out things, Simonetta.'

Simonetta sat down heavily on the sand. It was hard to take it all in.

Her mother's voice was softer now. 'So tell me, Simonetta, do you hate me more than ever? I know I've always been tough on you. I just didn't want you to go the same way as me.'

Simonetta smiled in the darkness. 'No, *Mamma*, in a funny way it's made me understand you better.'

She ended the call and stared out to sea. She'd always known that there was something special about her, something that made her different from the rest of her family. And now she knew what it was.

Brad Masters was her father. And that meant a one-way ticket to riches and luxury.

chapter eleven

The three girls stood in the drawing-room, waiting.
Madison tried her phone again for the umpteenth
time.

'Why doesn't my stupid mom turn her phone on?
She's only gone into hospital for chin lipo.'

Sapphire looked at her, not quite believing
Madison was so shallow. Not quite believing she was
Sapphire's half-*sister*. The thought seemed to hit them
all at once.

Madison and Simonetta looked at each other. 'I suppose you and I got our height from him,' Madison said. 'Unlike the runt over there.'

Simonetta took Sapphire's chin in her hand roughly, making her wince. 'Oi!'

'Hmm, I suppose you could say we have the same eyes,' Simonetta said, scrutinising Sapphire's face. 'Not that you can tell under those eyebrows.' She dropped Sapphire's chin abruptly.

Just then the door opened and Brad came in. He looked at them, taking in Sapphire's puffy red eyes. 'I haven't handled this very well. Sapphire, I'm sorry to have upset you.'

She stared at the floor, refusing to meet his gaze.

Brad sighed. 'Girls, I didn't just bring you here to make *that* revelation. There's another reason. A very important reason.'

Despite herself, Sapphire looked up. What could he mean?

Brad walked over to one of the windows and stared out. 'I'm a very rich man, but I've worked hard to get where I am. And working hard meant sacrifices.' He sighed. 'No time to pursue love or have a family.' He swivelled round to face them. 'I've decided that I want more out of life. I want to slow down.' He smiled. 'I want to start having some fun for a change.'

A silence fell over the room. All that could be heard was the distant crash of the waves. Brad walked back, hands on hips, meaning business. 'I've got money. Lots and lots of money. It's more than I could ever spend and is enough to let me lead an extremely comfortable life. But now I have to think about what happens to all that money… once I'm no longer here. I want to pass it down to someone, an heir, to hopefully invest and spend wisely. I want to give it… to one of you.'

Sapphire's mouth fell open.

'Like, how much are we talking about here?' asked Madison, in an awed whisper.

'That remains confidential until I have chosen one of you. Suffice to say it is well into the millions.' Brad paused. '*Hundreds* of millions.'

Madison looked like she was about to faint. 'Hundreds of millions of *dollars*?'

'Wait…' said Sapphire. 'You said one of us. You

want us to compete for it?' She was starting to feel more annoyed by the second. Who did this bloke think he was, coming in here and playing God?

'Not exactly,' said Brad. 'But I do want to make sure it's in safe hands. That's why I invited you all here, to get to know you better. So yes, I'm afraid that I can only choose one heir.'

'What if one of us doesn't want your stupid money?' Sapphire said. 'I'm perfectly happy with my life, thank you.'

'Are you, like, totally *insane*?' Madison asked incredulously.

Brad looked at Sapphire evenly. 'So you'd pass up the chance to have unimaginable wealth and all the opportunities that come with that?'

Somehow Sapphire couldn't find the words to say no.

Brad nodded, satisfied. 'I'm giving one of you the most incredible opportunity, but you have to work for it. I would like you to spend a few weeks with me, so I can decide which of my three daughters deserves the money most.'

'A few *weeks*!' Sapphire cried. 'But I've got a job!'

Brad smiled. 'Ah, yes, Jerry. I believe one of my people has spoken to him and he's more than happy to give you some time off.'

Sapphire's shoulders slumped. Not Jerry as well! It was one huge, great conspiracy against her.

Brad noticed her expression and smiled. 'Come on, Sapphire, a few weeks with all this' – he waved his hand round the luxurious room – 'can't be too bad, can it? And we still haven't had the chance to talk about your music.'

He had her and he knew it. 'OK,' she said stiffly. 'But if I want to go home, I'm going.'

'That's a deal,' Brad said, 'and I'm a man of my word. One more thing, I would like this to remain amongst the four of us until my rightful heir is announced.'

Madison looked pained. She was, like, *dying* to tell her friends she was Brad Masters' daughter!

'Madison?' Brad said sternly.

'Fine, whatever,' she muttered.

'Good!' Brad said, smiling. 'I think we should celebrate – we still have a bottle of champagne waiting for us in the garden.'

Five minutes later they were back in the gazebo, ready to toast each other. Just then, Brad's mobile rang. He took it out of his pocket and pulled a face.

'Excuse me, I won't be a minute.'

The girls looked at each other. To Sapphire, it was more like opponents facing up for a battle than sisters bonding.

'Here's to us, dear sisters. May the best woman win,' Simonetta said jeeringly.

Unwillingly, Sapphire held her glass up to clink with the others.

Madison took a swig, then smiled sweetly at Sapphire and Simonetta. 'This is mine, bitches.'

chapter twelve

Madison retired to bed that evening in a euphoric state. The news that the man she'd thought was her dad wasn't her dad hadn't affected her at all. She hardly saw Frank anyway, he lived in Washington, which was, like, the other side of the world, and he never had much to say to her anyway. And he had nostril hair. And neck spots... Just *ewww*. In one short moment, Madison had dismissed Frank from her life like a last-season Gucci bag.

Although Madison knew she would never win any

prizes for academic ability, she was smart in a different way. Smart enough to know that the biggest prize in her life was up for grabs and she *had* to win it. Apart from sucking up to Brad's billionaire butt, she had to eliminate the competition. With happy thoughts racing through her mind – mostly of pushing Simonetta and Madison over the side of *Spirito Libero* with rocks tied to their feet – Madison drifted off to sleep.

Sapphire, by contrast, slept badly. By dawn she was sitting on the balcony, legs curled up in her chair, watching the sunrise. All around her the world was coming to life – birds chirped a morning chorus and waves crashed in the distance. *It's like paradise*, she thought, and yet she had been plunged into some weird kind of hell.

She wasn't the person she'd thought she was for the last nineteen years. Her whole life had been a lie. *I don't even know who I am any more*, she thought, staring out over the rolling gardens.

She didn't know how long she'd been sitting there when there was a knock at the bedroom door. Throwing a dressing-gown over her pyjamas,

Sapphire went to answer it. Maggie stood there with a tray bearing a pot of tea.

'I thought you might be in need of this,' she smiled.

'Thanks, Maggie,' Sapphire said gratefully. For some reason the gesture made her want to cry.

'How are you feeling?' Maggie asked, her keen eyes roving over Sapphire's face, missing nothing.

Sapphire shrugged helplessly. 'Y' know…'

Maggie nodded wisely. 'Give it time, pet.' She paused. 'I know you feel manipulated. You must be thinking, "who is this guy, to come into my life and tell me he's my father and that I *might* get to inherit a fortune".'

'Er… yeah,' said Sapphire. That was pretty much exactly what she was thinking.

'But you have to trust him,' said Maggie. 'Mr Masters is a good man. I wouldn't have worked for him for so long if he wasn't. Give him the benefit of the doubt.' She started plumping a pillow. 'Oh, and he's organised a little treat for you girls this morning. To make up for the shock of last night.'

'Oh, yeah?' asked Sapphire politely, thinking that the last thing she wanted to do was spend time with anyone, let alone those two. She just wanted to stay locked away in her room.

Maggie beamed. 'He's organised for the best tennis coach in Capri to come and give you lessons. You're to meet him by the court at ten.'

'*Tennis* lessons?' asked Sapphire incredulously. Who wanted to play tennis at a time like this?

'It'll be good for you.' Maggie said firmly. 'You girls need something to do other than laze round the pool all day.'

'But I haven't got anything to play in,' Sapphire protested.

Maggie smiled. 'That's all been taken care of.'

Madison smoothed her little pleated skirt. 'I had *no* idea Ralph Lauren was doing tenniswear this season! This is so hot.'

The three girls were standing by the tennis court, waiting for the coach to turn up. While Sapphire stood in awkward silence, Madison prattled on as usual and Simonetta examined her fingernails, looking bored. What was Simonetta thinking about behind her aloof veneer? Did she care at all?

It's almost as if nothing happened last night, Sapphire thought. It was so weird.

All three of them had been provided with head-to-toe designer outfits, including visors and tennis shoes. The look had been finished off with white Prada sports sunglasses and a solid white-gold Patek Philippe watch with a little half-moon on its face. Sapphire, not quite believing how heavy it was, had taken it off to have a look and discovered her initials had been engraved on the back. Simonetta and Madison had the same.

'Nice touch, Daddy Dearest,' Madison crowed. 'These Moon Face watches are *insane*! Beyoncé's got one, y'know. They're, like, $30,000 or something.'

Thirty *thousand* dollars? Sapphire felt sick. She wouldn't dream of spending that much on a car, let alone a watch. What if she broke it? Her stomach gave another sick lurch.

'*Buongiorno,*' a voice called out. They turned to see a heavily tanned older man in tennis whites carrying a load of rackets walking towards them. He stopped and held out a hand. 'I'm Amadeo. It's very nice to meet you.'

'*Buongiorno*,' they all chorused back.

Amadeo grinned, showing toothpaste-white teeth. 'Shall we start then?' He handed them rackets and they followed him out on to the court.

While Madison was prancing about like a show pony telling Amadeo how good she was, Sapphire's heart was going like the clappers. She was crap at tennis! *Please, someone, take me away from all this*, she thought, willing herself back in her room, in her old clothes, reading a book. As Amadeo lined them up and started to shout instructions, Sapphire caught sight of someone walking past out of the corner of her eye. She turned and saw the lean, mean presence of Raphael. He shot her a look of disgust and stalked off. Sapphire frowned, fears about her crap backhand temporarily forgotten. Why did someone she didn't even know seem to hate her so much?

Amadeo served a ball and Sapphire was so busy looking at Raphael, she didn't notice it bouncing in front of her until it hit her in the boob. She squealed in pain, and dropped her racket.

That was about the best part of the whole day.

chapter thirteen

'I can't *believe* you gave Amadeo a black eye!'

'Nor can I, Madison, so can you please stop going on about it?' Sapphire said.

They were sitting round the pool; Sapphire in the shade, while the other two showcased yet more tiny bikinis. Sapphire cringed again at the memory of hitting Capri's best tennis coach smack-bang in the face with an off-kilter shot. Amadeo's eye had started to swell immediately so they'd called it a day after that.

It was just as well, because once they'd established that Sapphire hadn't blinded Amadeo, Madison had started to kill herself with silent laughter. Even Simonetta had raised a smile as they'd watched the coach limp up to the house to get some ice. Despite letting out a horrified giggle herself, Sapphire had been feeling terrible ever since.

'So you're a loser on *and* off the tennis court!' Madison crowed maliciously from her sunbed.

Sapphire shot her a look. 'Shut *up*, Madison.'

Madison's expression suddenly became sweetness and light. 'Hey, Cam!'

Sapphire looked over and felt a lurch in her stomach. The R&B star was walking round the pool towards them.

'Hey. What are you girls up to?'

'Oh, you know. Just chilling.' Madison stretched out a long leg provocatively and patted her sunlounger. 'Come talk to me.'

Cam grinned. 'Sure. Hey, Simonetta,' he called as he passed her. The model raised a hand briefly before dropping it again. Cam shook his head and gave a wry grin.

Madison didn't miss the exchange. She flashed an extra-bright smile, determined to make sure Cam's attentions were focused on her instead. He looked even more muscular than normal, the white vest he was wearing showing off his broad shoulders to perfection. Madison readjusted her swimming costume to its best advantage.

'So, what have you been doing?' she said, as he sat down next to her. She let her bare leg fall casually against his.

'Writing. I've kinda been stuck on the lyrics, though. Thought I'd come and get some fresh air and clear my head.'

Madison smiled understandingly. 'It must take over your *brain*!' She thought she'd better ask a deep, meaningful question. 'So, like, where do you get your inspiration from?'

'Oh, you know, people. Situations.' Cam's eyes twinkled. 'This place has given me a lot of material.'

'O.M.G, am I in one of your songs?' exclaimed Madison. 'I totally am. I know it!' She looked over at Simonetta. 'Did you hear that – Cam's written a song about me!'

Simonetta didn't stir.

'Hey, I'm not going to name names!' protested Cam. 'But let's just say you ladies have definitely provided some material for me.'

Madison cast a dismissive look at the other two girls. 'I can't imagine you got much from them.'

Cam eyed her curiously. 'What *are* you girls all doing here together? You seem very... different. How did you meet?'

Remembering what Brad had said about keeping their secret, Madison panicked. She scrabbled round for a reason in her head. 'Cupcakes!' she blurted out.

Cam looked confused. 'Cupcakes?'

'Yeah! Uh, there was, like, this charity cake-making competition in New York which Brad was judging and, er, we all met there.'

'You were all making cupcakes?'

'Yeah!'

Cam glanced over at Simonetta. 'I wouldn't have put Simonetta down as a cupcake kinda person.'

'Oh, she's very good!' trilled Madison.

'So who won?'

This time it was Madison's turn to look confused. 'Won?'

'The cupcake competition,' said Cam patiently.

'Oh! Me of course.' To her huge relief she saw Brad walking towards them. 'Hi, Brad!' She jumped up to greet him.

'How was tennis?' he asked.

'Oh, like, totally amazing,' she gushed. Her eyes scanned Brad's outfit. 'That suit is to die for. Gucci, right? You have, like, *really* awesome taste for such an old guy. Er, I mean...'

'Old guy?' Brad smiled.

'Madison was just telling me how you guys all know each other,' Cam said.

'Oh, right,' said Brad suspiciously.

'Yes, I was telling him how we met at the charity cupcake competition in New York,' babbled Madison.

Brad looked perplexed, but didn't say anything. 'Anyway, I just came to tell you girls I've got to fly to Rome for a business meeting. I'll be back in time for dinner.'

From where she was hiding behind her book, Sapphire was disturbed to see Brad walk towards her.

They hadn't spoken since last night and Sapphire felt really awkward around him.

'Hey, Brad, did you hear about Sapphire blinding Amadeo?' Madison yelled after him.

You bitch! Sapphire thought furiously.

'You should have seen it,' continued Madison. 'It was totally LMAO.'

'L... M... what?'

'Duh! Laugh my ass off,' said Madison.

'Right.'

'I'm *so* sorry,' said Sapphire. 'I'm really uncoordinated and I just—'

'Don't worry about it,' said Brad, smiling at Sapphire. 'I spoke to Amadeo and he's fine. Believe me, he's had worse. Ask him about when he coached Vinnie Jones some time.'

'I really am rubbish at tennis,' Sapphire mumbled.

Brad smiled. 'Me too. That's why I've got a coach.'

There was an awkward silence. Brad looked at the book in her hands. 'What are you reading?'

Grudgingly, Sapphire showed him the book. It was a new one that had just been brought out about Michael Jackson.

'I've heard about this, it's meant to be pretty good,' Brad said.

'Yeah, it is,' Sapphire said stiffly. Despite her unease, natural curiously got the better of her. 'Did you ever meet him?' she asked hesitantly. 'Michael Jackson, I mean.'

Brad shrugged lightly. 'Quite a few times.'

Sapphire looked at him in disbelief. 'No way!'

'Way,' he laughed.

Sapphire couldn't help herself. 'That is so cool!' she told him.

They grinned at each other.

'So… are we friends again?' Brad asked eventually.

'I guess so,' she mumbled.

'Have you spoken to your mum yet?' he asked. Sapphire felt herself go red again; she'd been ignoring Leonie's calls and texts ever since their conversation. She'd felt so angry and upset, the last thing she wanted to do was talk to her mum, but suddenly she felt guilty.

'No, but I will do.'

'Make sure you do; your mum's a nice lady.'

There was a short, awkward silence. 'Well, Sapphire, I'll see you later,' he said.

She smiled, happy they'd moved off the tricky subject. 'OK, hope your meeting goes well.' She watched as he walked off.

'You know, I'd really like to hear about Michael Jackson one day,' she called after him. 'You know... since you actually met him.'

Brad stopped and swung round. 'You want to hear all about my celebrity encounters? They're not as glamorous in real life, I'm afraid to say.'

'Not just the celebrities, you know, other stuff.' Sapphire blushed. 'Your life sounds really interesting.' Despite her shock at his revelation, Sapphire had been warming to Brad. He was such a charismatic man.

He gave her a perceptive look. 'And so you will, Sapphire. But for now, my meeting in Rome awaits.'

Sapphire opened her book again as he disappeared.

'Suck-up,' said Madison, before rolling on to her stomach.

chapter fourteen

'I'm sorry, Mum.'

'I'm sorry too, darling. I really am.'

Sapphire bit her lip. 'It was just a shock, y'know. Why didn't you tell me?'

Her mother sighed down the phone. 'Bill and I thought it was the best thing. Brad was off all over the world and I didn't want an unstable routine for you. Bill took one look at you and fell in love with you, Sapphire. He always thought of you as his real daughter.'

'I still want to think of Bill as my real dad. It's just so *weird*. My head's totally spun out.'

'I know, sweetheart.'

'It was a bit of a shock finding out I've got two half-sisters as well. Not to mention that I'll be competing with them to win Brad's inheritance.'

There was a deathly silence at the other end. '*What?*' her mother said eventually.

'Uh, yeah,' Sapphire said confusedly. 'I thought you knew.'

'Well, I didn't!' Her mum's voice was shocked. 'I thought it was just you and Brad getting to know each other. I wouldn't have let you go out there otherwise. And what on earth is this thing with the inheritance? I thought he wanted to help you with your music. If I'd known he was going to pull this money stunt... well, he's going to get a piece of my mind, I can tell you!'

'Mum, *please* don't call and have a go at him,' Sapphire pleaded. She couldn't cope with any more emotional stuff at the moment. 'Maybe he thought he was doing the right thing by not telling you, like you did with me. And the money... well, he knows I don't want it. I hope he does, anyway. But I can use this opportunity to get to know him, even if I don't take any of his cash.'

Her mother sighed. 'Fine. I can't believe it! Sapphire, you have two half-sisters!' She paused. 'What are they like?'

Sapphire gave a hollow laugh. 'Better save that for another time.'

Her mother knew her well enough not to push it. 'OK. If you're sure.'

Sapphire had something else on her mind. 'Mum, did Brad pay for me to go to St Bridies?'

Her mother hesitated. 'I didn't want any money from Brad, but he was insistent he paid for your school fees until you were eighteen. He would have paid for your college fees too, but I wanted you to stand on your own two feet.' She laughed ironically. 'Find out the true value of money.'

'Oh, Mum.' Sapphire's bottom lip wobbled. She knew that in her own misguided way her mum thought she was doing the right thing. She could imagine Leonie standing in the kitchen on the phone, Beatle snoring in his basket in the corner. Suddenly she felt really homesick.

'I love you, Mum.'

'I love you too, Sapphire.'

Madison narrowed her eyes and watched Brad and Sapphire across the dinner table. They'd spent far too much time talking and laughing. The goody two-shoes act might work on Daddy Dearest, but it didn't cut any ice with Madison. From the way Simonetta's eyes kept flicking down the table, it was clear she felt the same.

'Sapphire, you can't have Brad to yourself all night!' Madison interrupted jokingly, but her voice hid a warning.

Back off.

Sapphire flushed. She hadn't meant to monopolise Brad. But his knowledge of music was amazing and Sapphire was surprised to discover they even liked some of the same bands. It was almost like talking to a mate.

Simonetta rested her elbows in the table. 'So, Brad, did you have a good meeting in Roma today? A publishing deal, wasn't it?'

'Yes, it was. And it went well, thank you.' Brad looked at her. Simonetta was a dark horse, but he had no doubt she was very intelligent. *A girl like you could do well with my money*, he thought. Simonetta was definitely one to watch.

After dinner Brad retired to his office, leaving the three girls round the table. Madison's face, which had been the picture of sweetness all evening, suddenly switched to a mask of pure evil.

'Don't think I don't know what you're doing, Sapphire.'

'I'm not doing anything,' Sapphire said in exasperation, 'I was just talking to Brad. I like finding out about people. What's wrong with that?'

'Plenty, when there's hundreds of millions of dollars up for grabs,' she hissed. 'I don't even know why you're here, if money isn't important to you. Why not get lost and narrow down the competition?'

'Perhaps the little English creature has had her head turned more than she will admit,' drawled Simonetta. Sapphire was mortified to feel tears pricking at the back of her eyes. She blinked them away furiously. There was no way she was going to cry in front of these two!

'I don't care what you two think,' she said and, pushing her chair back, left the room. Out in the corridor she took several deep breaths, pushing the tears back down her throat. She couldn't believe she was *related* to Madison and Simonetta!

Wanting to get as far away from them as possible, she headed down to the beach. It was a crystal-clear night and she stared up at the stars, marvelling over how many there were compared to the smoggy skies over London. Sapphire found a spot and sat down, listening to the gentle lapping of the waves breaking on the shore. Somehow the rhythmic sound and movement comforted her.

'Pretty, hey?' The voice came from behind, making her jump. 'Hey, I didn't mean to startle you.' It was Cam, in faded blue rolled-up jeans and a simple white vest. The moonlight fell on his face, highlighting his dark eyes and high cheekbones. *He's beautiful*, Sapphire thought, looking beyond the buff body for the first time. The realisation that it was the first time they'd been alone together hit her. Sapphire was grateful the darkness hid her rapidly reddening cheeks.

'Mind if I sit down?'

Sapphire shook her head dumbly as he crossed his legs and sat down beside her. She'd never been so close to Cam before and the sheer size and strength of his body made her heart beat faster. He smelt of soap and shampoo, as if he'd just got out of the shower.

Say something, she thought desperately. *He's going to think you're some kind of weird mute.* Her heart was beating so hard now it physically hurt.

'W-what are you up to?' she stuttered.

Cam picked up a handful of sand, watching as it ran through his tanned fingers. 'I like coming down here, it helps clear my head when I've been writing.' He turned to look at her, so close she could smell his minty breath on her cheek. 'So what was up with you the other night? You looked pretty upset.'

Sapphire hesitated. 'It's a bit difficult…'

Cam nodded. 'Girl stuff, right?'

It was probably best he thought that. 'Girl stuff,' she agreed.

He smiled at her, his eyes crinkling up sexily. 'Must

be kinda tough hanging out with Simonetta and Madison. They seem pretty high maintenance.'

'I thought you fancied Simonetta,' Sapphire said, immediately embarrassed that she'd brought up the subject.

'Fancied?' Cam was still playing with the sand.

'Er... I thought you were attracted to her.'

Cam laughed. '*Attracted*? I love how you Brits talk,' he said. 'Simonetta's hot. But she likes playing games. I'm not into all that.' He smiled. 'I like an easy life.'

Sapphire was mesmerised by his full mouth, the straight whiteness of his teeth.

Cam changed the subject. 'So what's your thing, musically?'

Sapphire dug her bare feet into the sand, feeling the coolness seep through her toes. 'It's kind of soul meets jazz, with a little bit of blues thrown in,' she told him.

'Like Amy Winehouse?'

'I suppose... but Amy Winehouse is amazing. I'm nowhere near as good as her.' Her mum and Jerry had said her voice was a lot like the London pop star's, before her fall from grace – but Sapphire knew she had a long way to go yet. 'I'm just… ordinary.'

'I don't think you're ordinary at all, Sapphire.' He studied her face. 'You're a very pretty girl, you know that?' He moved his hand up, and touched her cheek lightly. 'And I love your freckles.'

Sapphire's heart nearly burst out of her chest. 'They always come out in the sun,' she mumbled. Suddenly a loud siren went off somewhere close, making her jump. Cam reached into his jeans and brought out his iPhone.

'Shoot, it's my manager. I'm gonna have to take it.' He gave a slow, sexy wink. 'I'll see you around, Sapphire.'

'See you around,' she started to say, but Cam was already striding away down the beach. Sapphire flopped back on the sand, looking up at the stars above. She touched her nose, where she could still feel the tingle of Cam's touch.

Oh my God. Did Cam Tyler and I just have a moment?

chapter fifteen

The long, hot days slid into balmy nights and the three girls quickly established a routine at Casa Eleganza. Sapphire spent her days reading and sightseeing. The other two girls spent their days sunbathing and... sunbathing.

Sapphire persuaded Tito to take her out in his battered Citroën to explore the island of Capri, and was constantly amazed at how beautiful it was. One afternoon they were just returning from a trip to an orange grove when they came across a man walking along the road. As Tito slowed down, Sapphire was surprised to see it was Brad. He looked strange out by himself in a shirt and chinos – no mobile phone, expensive suit or staff running round him.

The Citroën pulled up beside him.

'*Buongiorno, Signor* Masters, can we offer you a lift?' Tito asked.

Brad bent down to peer in the window and looked surprised to see Sapphire in the passenger seat. 'Oh, hello. Where have you two been?'

'Sapphire wanted me to show her the orange groves,' Tito said. 'She is treating me like her own personal tour guide!'

Sapphire laughed. 'I am not! It's just such a beautiful island, I want to see as much of it as I can while I'm here.'

Brad smiled at her. 'Fancy joining me? It's not far back to the house.'

Sapphire looked at Tito uncertainly. 'You can't say no to the boss!' He smiled. She unbuckled her seat belt and got out. They waved goodbye to Tito and the old car zoomed off in a cloud of dust.

'I hope Tito doesn't drive like that when you're in the car,' Brad said. 'I don't want one of my daughters...' He stopped, both of them awkward. 'If it's any consolation, I'm finding it hard to get my head round it as well, Sapphire,' he told her.

She smiled, grateful he had tried to make her feel better.

'So what are you doing out here? Has the limo broken down?' she asked mischievously.

Brad grinned. 'Very funny. Actually, I like to go for long walks when I've got the time. I see Capri very much as my home now.'

'Have you got any other, you know, family?' Sapphire asked, realising as she said it that his answer would affect *her* life as well.

Brad's voice was wistful. 'Unfortunately not. My parents died when I was thirteen and Maggie bought me up from then. She was my nanny. And even though I didn't inherit any money from my parents – there was a problem with the will – she sort of adopted me.'

'Maggie was your *nanny*?' Sapphire asked incredulously.

'Yep, and she's not averse to telling me off even now,' he grinned.

Sapphire laughed at the thought of Brad getting an ear-bashing. 'That must be so funny!'

He gave a mock grimace. 'Not if you're on the receiving end. Maggie's got quite a tongue in her. She's kept me grounded over the years. Maggie's family.'

'I thought she was your housekeeper,' Sapphire said, a little too sarcastically.

Brad sighed. 'Look, I've told her a thousand times to retire! I wanted to set her up in her own villa in the sun. But Maggie said she'll work until the day she dies, so I thought if she was going to insist she might as well come and work here for me.' Brad chuckled. 'She's some lady.'

'She obviously thinks the world of you,' Sapphire said.

Brad smiled by way of answer. 'How's the music going?' he asked, changing the subject. 'I'm sorry I haven't managed to have a chat with you yet; I've been busy with Cam's stuff.'

At the mention of Cam's name, Sapphire's stomach dropped. Last night she'd had a dream in which *she* had been the one in the pool with him, not Simonetta. She'd wrapped her legs round his waist as his soft lips had kissed hers, his hands wandering over her body, from her waist up to her chest...

She jumped, realising that Brad was saying something to her. 'Sorry, what was that?'

'I said, have you met my chauffeur, Raphael? He's one of the other young people here. I wondered if you'd bumped into each other.'

'Um, yeah,' Sapphire said. There was no way she was telling Brad she'd wandered into Raphael's house by mistake.

'He's incredibly talented,' Brad continued. 'That kid's got star quality written all over him. I don't think he'll be a chauffeur much longer. Mind you, he does struggle a bit with his lyrics...'

'Hmm,' said Sapphire. 'He struggles a bit with being civil to people too.'

'Ah,' said Brad. 'I see he's been working his trademark charm again. Give him a chance, Saph. He's got huge potential.' He gave her a meaningful look. 'As do you.'

Sapphire shrugged, though she had a warm feeling

inside from when Brad had called her Saph instead of Sapphire. 'I might be able to write songs, but I can't seem to play them,' she sighed. The truth was she'd struggled to pick up her guitar since she'd been on Capri. She was having a total block.

'Come on, you'll get there. Your mum says you're really good.'

'That's because she's my mum,' said Sapphire, smiling.

'Leonie always had good instincts when it comes to spotting raw talent. You know, she persuaded me to sign up The Hollywoods.'

Sapphire was too shocked to speak for a moment. 'My *mum* did that?' The Hollywoods were a hugely successful band signed to BMM, Brad's record label. Even thought they were in their forties now, kids her age still listened to them. Sapphire had seen them at Wembley last year, along with a whole stadium full of screaming people.

Brad smiled. 'Yes, she did. Which is why when she sent me some of your stuff, I took it very seriously.'

Sapphire went bright red. 'You've read my lyrics?' She could kill her mum!

'And a recording of you singing *Back To Black*. You've really got a great voice, Sapphire, you need to have more confidence in yourself.'

'I didn't realise I had such a pushy mother,' she grumbled, deflecting the compliment. She had never been that good at receiving them. They walked in silence for a few moments, before she spoke again.

'What happened, you know, with you and Mum?'

Brad paused. 'Lots of things happened. It was a case of the wrong timing. Things got... complicated.'

'What, like her being pregnant with me?' said Sapphire, too sharply again. Brad brought out such mixed-up feelings in her.

Brad was silent for a moment. 'No,' he said. 'I would have liked to be in your life. It didn't work out that way, and I regret it every day. I regret it every time I look at you.'

Sapphire flushed. 'Sorry. That was out of order.'

'You have every right to feel angry with me, turning up in your life like this.'

'I know,' she admitted. 'It's just all such a...'

'Whirlwind?' he suggested. Sapphire smiled. 'Yeah, something like that.'

He reached a hand up to her face and then dropped it away again. 'You know, when you smile, you have your mother's dimples.'

Sapphire flushed, but it was a nice, warm feeling. In companionable silence they continued back.

Madison walked confidently up the path to the large guest-house on the edge of Casa Eleganza's grounds. She was pleased to see Cam sitting outside on the terrace, working on a laptop. He had his shirt off, a heavy silver chain round his neck. Discarded dumbbells lay stacked against the wall.

'Hey, Cam!'

He looked up over his sunglasses. 'What's up, Madison? What brings you out here?'

'Oh, I was just passing,' she lied. 'Aren't you going to invite me in?'

He eyed her amusedly. 'Sure, do you want a guided tour?' He jumped up and Madison followed him in. The place was state-of-the-art, with a huge sound system and plasma TV screens in every room.

'Pretty cool, huh?'

Madison fluttered her eyelashes at him. 'Totes. You could have some crazy parties here.' *Or you and I could have one of our own, gorgeous,* she thought, hitching her hot pants a tad higher up her tanned thighs. She moved closer to Cam and ran a manicured finger across his chest. 'How often do you work out?' she asked, sticking her chest out so he couldn't miss her pert 32 Cs.

'Enough.' Cam gave her a wry smile. She was pretty full-on, this one. A real handful – and not just her chest. Cam had met plenty of girls like Madison – hot rich chicks out for the take. He was kinda over it. Even though she *did* have a killer body. He and Madison could have some fun...

He took a deep breath.

'I've gotta get back to work,' he said with a tinge of regret. Man, he'd come out here to avoid distraction and there were hot girls all *over* the joint!

Madison pouted. 'Don't be so boring.'

Cam laughed, 'Hey, dude's gotta earn his living somehow.'

She smiled, showing sharp white teeth. 'OK, I'll come see you again.'

'Sure thing,' Cam said and watched her wriggle out. An idea popped into his head and he went back to the laptop, where he'd been writing his lyrics.

'She looks like an angel, but she's got her eye on your Amex...'

'Thanks, Madison,' he said aloud. He'd been stuck on that line for days.

chapter sixteen

Brad was in his study, a wood-panelled room with a huge mahogany desk that overlooked the sea. He had just finished an important business call when there was a knock on the door and Simonetta walked in, radiant in a long olive-green dress.

'Am I disturbing you?' she asked, with a self-assured tone that suggested that, even if she was, Brad should stop what he was doing. *The girl's got balls,* he thought with an inward smile. *I'll give her that.*

Simonetta sashayed across the room in a way that reminded Brad of when he had first set eyes on her mother Sophia, twenty years previously. He wondered fleetingly what Sophia looked like now, if she had kept her beauty, or softened and become more matronly over the years.

Simonetta lowered herself into the chair opposite him. 'I thought I would come and see how everything is going.'

'With business, you mean?' Brad asked, watching her eyes move round the room, taking in the gold and platinum discs adorning the walls.

'Of course. I know business is a man's world, but I have a strong interest in it too.'

'I don't believe that,' Brad told her.

'You don't believe I'm interested? You—'

He smiled at her, raising a hand to cut her off. *As fiery as her mother too.* 'I meant that I don't believe business is a man's world.'

Simonetta shrugged. 'Of course not. You are... modern, you move with the times. But in my village,' at this her lips curled in disgust, 'men go out to work and women are expected to stay at home, having babies and washing and cleaning.'

'Is that why you left?'

Simonetta nodded. 'I got spotted by a scout in the street when I was in Rome one day, but I would have moved there anyway.'

'And your mother, how is she?' Brad prompted.

Simonetta gave another, dismissive shrug. 'I was glad to get out. She suffocates me.'

Brad leaned back in his chair and studied her. 'What do you want out of life, Simonetta? Are you going to stay in modelling?'

'That and other things. You don't just have to be a model these days. Look at Elle Macpherson – she is a very successful businesswoman. Underwear lines, art, property... that is what I want. I don't think small.'

'Good for you,' Brad said, smiling.

Simonetta nodded regally.

'I think, Brad, that you and I are similar people. We understand money and what can be achieved with it.' She gave him a meaningful look and with a murmured *'Ciao'* got out of her chair and wafted out.

After she had left, Brad put his hands behind his head, thinking. Simonetta *was* a smart cookie, there was no doubting that. If he made her his heir he had no doubt that she would become very successful. But he couldn't underestimate Madison – she might come across as an airhead, but Brad was sure a sharp brain was ticking away under all that fluffiness. She was her mother's daughter, after all, and Brad remembered how resourceful Candy had been when it had come to setting her sights on *him*. His lawyers had drawn up a watertight contract to make sure Madison would be looked after, but he knew Candy would have pushed for more if she could have. Brad sighed. He didn't want that woman getting her hands on any more of his money, but at the same time there was no way he could deny one of his daughters the right to become his heir.

This was going to be very interesting indeed...

'Look at the size of my bush! Does anyone know where I can get a Brazilian around here?'

'You are disgusting,' Simonetta said, as Madison hitched her cutaway swimsuit even higher to examine her bikini line.

'I can't help it! I didn't know we were going to be here for so long.' Madison eyed Simonetta suspiciously. 'Why, what are *you* doing to keep yours under control?'

'I had it all lasered off. Waxing is *so* last year, darling.'

'Slut,' muttered Madison.

Simonetta looked up from her sunlounger. 'What did you say?'

'Nothing,' Madison sighed, throwing herself back on the sunlounger. 'I'm bored of all this lying round. I want to *party.*' She shot a conspiratorial look at Simonetta. 'Brad's away with Cam tonight, we could always raid his bar.'

'Not with that Maggie woman hanging around. She always seems to be watching us,' Simonetta grumbled.

'Oh, I'm sure we can get rid of her,' said Madison. Then she clocked Sapphire walking up the path to the pool. 'Oh, great, it's Little Miss Goody Two-Shoes,' she said under her breath.

'Hi, guys,' Sapphire said moments later. There was a heavy silence. *Busy slagging me off again,* she thought. Luckily, she was beginning to care less with every day that passed.

At that moment, a plan started to formulate in Madison's devious little mind. 'Come and sit down next to me,' she said in an over-friendly voice. Sapphire looked at her strangely, but sat down.

'Simonetta and I were just talking about tonight. Brad said we can help ourselves to drinks from his bar.'

Simonetta shot a look at Madison, but didn't say anything.

'That's cool of him,' Sapphire said. She wasn't much of a drinker, although she did like a cold beer.

'Yeah, but because Simonetta and I have some urgent business to attend to, we wondered if you could get the drinks sorted. We can meet in your bedroom – it's much bigger than ours. And you've got the balcony,' she added.

Sapphire raised a cynical eyebrow. 'What's this "urgent business" you've got?'

'Emergency bikini waxes. I swear, mine is, like, the size of Texas!'

As if Madison knew where that was. Sapphire wished she hadn't asked. She hesitated. 'I suppose it would be nice to hang out. We haven't had any proper girl time yet.'

'Our thoughts *exactly*,' gushed Madison.

'So I'll get a couple of beers, maybe a bottle of wine. That should do us.'

'Oh, no, no, no!' Madison sat up. 'Bring the whole caboodle, sweetie. Champers, spirits, we want it all! We can take all the unused stuff back,' she said, seeing Sapphire's disconcerted expression.

'If you're sure Brad said so—'

'More than sure!' Madison interrupted brightly. 'In fact, Brad said to help ourselves to a particular bottle of champagne. I think it was the Dom Perignon White Gold Jeroboam.'

'The White Gold what?'

'White Gold Jeroboam. Brad insisted we have it.'

Sapphire grinned. 'Cool, see you at mine later?'

Madison winked. 'Not if we see you first!'

As Sapphire walked off, Simonetta turned to Madison. 'Is this the same Dom Perignon Brad told us about – the one Michael Jackson bought him?'

'Yup.'

'The Dom Perignon he was saving for his sixtieth birthday?'

'That's the one.'

Simonetta exhaled. *'Mio Dio!'*

'We're going to have to watch Sapphire tonight,' Madison told her. 'That girl's shady.'

And I'm going to have to watch you, Simonetta thought. Give Madison her due, the silly airhead was shaping up to be stiffer competition than Simonetta had originally thought.

chapter seventeen

'Well, isn't this nice?' said Madison, as she stretched out luxuriantly on Sapphire's king-sized bed. She eyed Sapphire like a cat watching its prey from a treetop. 'Is that a *guitar*?'

'No, Madison, it's a fork-lift truck.'

'Oh, LOL, Sapphire. You actually play that thing?'

Sapphire nodded. 'I've brought it out here so I can practise.'

'You're such a dork!' Madison propped herself up

on one elbow. 'Open the bubbles then, Little Miss Hostess. I'm literally *dying* for a drink.'

'Uh, OK.' Sapphire went next door to the fridge in the living-room, and came back with the champagne a few moments later. She looked at the label on the bottle. 'It looks really *old*. Do you think it's vintage?'

'Of course. Nothing but the best for our Bradley! He must have, like, *hundreds* of them,' said Madison. She exchanged looks with Simonetta, who was stretched out on the chaise longue at the end of the bed. Sapphire was too busy wrestling with the cork to notice.

'Here goes!' she said. Finally, and with a loud pop, the cork flew out, closely followed by a spray of champagne that went all over Madison. She screamed, and in her haste to escape getting wetter, tumbled head-first off the bed. Moments later, she popped up, hair wet and stuck to her forehead.

'O.M.G!'

All three girls looked at each other and burst into laughter.

An hour later, they'd polished off the bottle and had moved on to the vodka. Sapphire was feeling a little light-headed and asked Madison, who was in charge of the drinks, for just a tiny slug of spirit and a lot of mixer. She was sitting on the edge of the bed while Simonetta stood over her with a pair of tweezers.

'Ow!' She winced as Simonetta plucked out another stray hair.

'Oh, stop being a baby,' Simonetta said in a motherly way. 'Your eyebrows have been bugging me since you got here.' She did one final pluck and stood back, satisfied. *'Mamma mia!* So you *have* got eyes under those great hairy things!'

Sapphire got up, stumbling a little, and went to look in the mirror. Simonetta was right, plucking her eyebrows *had* opened up her eyes more. When she got home she was definitely going to invest in a pair of tweezers. She came back and sat on the bed, reaching over to get her drink from the bedside table.

'Whoa, look at the size of your boobs!' said Madison, getting an eyeful of Sapphire's cleavage. 'Are they real?'

Sapphire went bright red. 'Of course.'

'Oh, leave her alone,' said Simonetta lazily, reclining against the pillows. They all sipped their drinks before Madison sat up and looked at them both.

'So, girls, what will you do with the cash if you get the golden ticket to Brad's money?'

The air took on a sudden tension. No one had dared bring it up yet. It had been like a big, fat, white, trumpeting elephant in the room when they had all been together.

'Simonetta? You go first.' Madison's squeaky voice had taken on a steely tone.

'I would invest it – start up my own business. My own clothing line, then other things.'

Madison raised a dismissive eyebrow, 'Forget making money, how about *spending* it? I'm talking my own island, private jets…'

Simonetta shrugged nonchalantly. 'That as well.'

'How about you, Sapphire?' Madison asked, turning to her. 'Would it all go to Save The Arctic Snow Monkey or something totally lame like that?'

Sapphire ignored the jibe. 'Yeah, I *would* give some to charity. Then I'd redecorate our kitchen, buy my mum a new car…'

'Jesus, don't go too crazy!' Madison exclaimed. She sighed, raising a long leg in the air to admire it. 'I wonder where Cam is? We should have asked him along.' She shot a curious look at Simonetta. 'What happened with you guys anyway?'

Simonetta took a delicate sip of her drink. 'We kissed, that was it. He is too young for me.'

'Well, *I* wouldn't mind hooking up with him!' Madison rolled over to look at Sapphire. 'What do *you* think of our resident hottie?'

'I hadn't really noticed,' Sapphire said, trying to sound casual.

'A-ha! You have *totally* gone red! So our sweet little Sapphire has it bad for Cam.'

Sapphire threw a cushion at Madison. 'Shut up!'

'I wonder how... endowed he is...' Madison pondered. 'He's pretty built up top...'

'Eeew, Madison,' said Sapphire, pulling a face.

'Has anyone seen that other guy around, the one with the curly black hair?' Simonetta said, changing the subject. She found the way Madison talked about sex immature and tasteless.

'I think you mean Raphael,' Sapphire said. The

ceiling was doing funny swirly things above her. 'He's Brad's chauffeur.'

'Yet again, too young for me,' said Simonetta. 'But it is nice to have pretty things around to look at.' She laughed throatily.

'He looks a bit weird to me,' sniffed Madison.

The swirling above Sapphire's head was getting faster. She sat up, suddenly feeling rather sick. 'Madison, can you get me an orange juice?'

Madison jumped up. 'Of *course* I can,' she said and went over to the sideboard, where they'd put all the drinks. Once again she mixed Sapphire a super-strong vodka and orange, just as she had secretly been doing all evening. The stupid bitch hadn't even noticed the difference. Adding a few lumps of ice, she took it back to Sapphire.

'There you go honey, drink it all up!'

Sapphire took one sip and then everything went black.

Sapphire opened her eyes. The pounding in her head started immediately. It took a few seconds for her eyes to focus. Gradually, Madison's face came into view, her features set in a picture of concern. An upset-looking Maggie was standing behind her.

'Thank God you're all right!' Madison said. Sapphire flinched as Madison wiped her forehead with a damp flannel. She tried to sit up, but the room was still blurry.

'What happened?' she croaked. 'What time is it?'

'It's past midnight and you've had far too much to drink,' Maggie said sternly. 'Sapphire, I thought more of you. Why can't you be sensible like Madison and Simonetta?'

Madison smiled sweetly at Maggie, while from the other side of the bedroom Simonetta watched the proceedings silently.

'But I didn't have that much to drink...' Sapphire said. She managed to sit up and saw the empty vodka bottle by the bed. Maggie raised an eyebrow.

'Someone must have spiked my drink!' she cried. 'Madison, you were making them...'

Madison's hand flew to her mouth. 'Oh, Sapphire! How could you say such a thing? Simonetta and I told you to slow down.' She looked across at Simonetta, who gave a small nod, backing her up.

Maggie folded her arms. 'I want to know why you thought you could go and help yourself to Mr Masters' bar? He's been nothing but hospitable to you, and you act like this!'

Sapphire looked at Madison in confusion, 'But you told me Brad said we could!'

Madison widened her innocent blue eyes. 'No, I didn't, Sapphire! Whatever gave you that idea?'

'Simonetta!' pleaded Sapphire, but the model shrugged and looked away. Just then, there was a noise at the door. It was Brad, still dressed in his suit and tie.

'Is Sapphire all right? Tito said she was ill.' His eyes took in the empty bottles littering the room and his face lost its concern. 'I see. *That* kind of ill.'

'Madison and Simonetta have been looking after her. They came and fetched me.' Maggie told him. Brad saw the empty champagne bottle lying carelessly on the floor and his expression darkened.

'Is that my Dom Perignon?'

'We tried to stop her,' Madison simpered.

'You said we could drink it!' Sapphire shouted,

then she stopped at the sight of Brad's face. He looked furious.

'Sapphire, I've given you the free run of my house with your every whim catered for. Why the hell would you do this?'

'I don't understand...' Sapphire started.

Madison cleared the matter up for her. 'Michael Jackson gave it to Brad. He was saving it for his sixtieth birthday.'

The stitch-up became immediately obvious. 'You bitch!' shouted Sapphire. She lunged at Madison, but Maggie, surprisingly strong, stopped her.

'You've done quite enough for one night, young lady!'

Sapphire watched miserably as Brad stalked from the room, closely followed by Madison and Simonetta. 'Brad!' She heard Madison yell. 'Wait up!'

She lay back on the bed, eyes filling with tears. 'Maggie, I honestly didn't know. Madison said we could drink it. I didn't know it was a present from Michael Jackson!'

Maggie sighed. 'Well, pet, it's done now anyway. The best thing you can do is get a good night's sleep and go apologise to Mr Masters in the morning. He's fairly upset.' She patted Sapphire's hand and, with a command to drink lots of water, closed the bedroom door quietly behind her.

Sapphire stared up at the ceiling, a horrible taste of stale alcohol in her mouth. Why had Madison and Simonetta done this to her? But then again, she knew why. They were trying to get her into Brad's bad books. Tears of anger filled her eyes. Why had she gone along with this stupid idea in the first place?

The answer was clear. She had to leave Capri, as soon as possible.

chapter eighteen

Sapphire knocked on the door nervously. It was a few moments before Brad answered.

'Come in.'

Heart pounding, she pushed the door open and entered the room. Brad surveyed her from behind the desk, unsmilingly. Sapphire gulped. It felt like she was in a headmaster's office for doing something naughty.

'I just wanted to say how sorry I am about last

night. I had no idea Michael Jackson had given you that champagne. I feel terrible that you were saving it for your sixtieth birthday. Honestly, I would not have drunk it if I'd known...' She trailed off, miserable.

Brad stared at her hard for a few moments. Sapphire dropped her gaze; it was like his eyes were boring into her.

'Apology accepted.'

She looked up, astonished. 'Really? Honestly, Brad, I'm so sorry.' She contemplated telling him Madison and Simonetta had set her up, but he probably wouldn't believe it. After all, she was the one who had been drunk and not the other two.

'Sit down,' Brad said sternly. Sapphire slumped down in the chair opposite him. 'As I said last night, I'm surprised at you, but I have faith it won't happen again.'

Sapphire sighed. 'I've been thinking, Brad – I don't know if I should be here.' She was feeling homesick for her mum's cooking, the flat, Jerry and the shop. She hesitated. 'I think I might go home.'

Brad folded his arms and looked at her. 'Because of

this? It will make you a better person if you stay and face up to your responsibilities rather than run away from them.'

'I'm not running away, I just—'

'Look, Sapphire,' Brad's voice was gentler now. 'Despite what's happened, I really would like you to stay. Will you think about it?'

An image of Cam, suntanned and muscled, flashed through her mind. It stirred more feelings than the money.

'OK,' she said. 'I'll stay.'

Brad suddenly smiled, and relief rushed through her body. 'I'm pleased to hear it.' He looked down at the paperwork spread over his desk. 'Now, if you don't mind...'

She jumped up. 'I'll leave you to it.' Just as she reached the door Brad spoke again.

'Sapphire.'

'Yes?'

'Just stay away from the drinks cabinet, OK?'

Sapphire was making her way outside later when a voice called her name. She turned around. Her stomach did a back flip, then somersaulted over again. It was Cam, looking heartbreakingly gorgeous in a V-neck T-shirt and dark-blue jeans. A baseball cap turned backward was on his head, accentuating his dark, long-lashed eyes.

'Heading to the pool?' Cam asked. He came and stood unnervingly close to Sapphire, so close she could smell his aftershave and the washing powder on his clothes.

Sapphire nodded dumbly. In her bikini top and faded denim shorts, Sapphire suddenly felt very naked. Cam's eyes lingered on her body and instinctively Sapphire crossed her hands over her breasts.

'H-h-how about you?' she asked. *Oh great, now I've got a stutter!*

Cam didn't seem to notice her stumbling over her words. 'Needed to stretch my legs – I've been writing all morning.' Sapphire jumped as his hand suddenly brushed her collar bone. The very feel of him on her bare flesh made her skin prickle all over. 'Had a bug on you,' he said, smiling.

Approaching footsteps made them both look

round. Raphael was walking towards them carrying a guitar. Next to Cam's all-American good looks, Raphael's lean physique, pale complexion and startling eyes made him look almost supernatural.

'Hey, buddy,' Cam said. Raphael nodded coldly and swept past.

Cam shook his head. 'I can never work that guy out.' He reached across and tucked a stray hair behind Sapphire's ear. 'Gotta fly. Catch you later, babe.'

As he walked off, Sapphire touched her ear again in wonder. It was tingling as if he had physically branded her. As she caught another lingering waft of Cam's aftershave, Sapphire started grinning. Cam Tyler had just called her babe! Shallow as it was, at that moment nothing else mattered.

OK, she thought. *So I'm staying. Just for a little bit.*

chapter nineteen

Sapphire's euphoria didn't last long. She knew she had to confront Madison and Simonetta, but she wasn't looking forward to it. Two against one was always bad; especially when it came in the form of her newly found half-sisters.

'Hey, Tito, you seen Madison and Simonetta anywhere?' Sapphire had come up to the swimming pool to find them, but to her surprise they weren't there. They practically *lived* there usually. Tito was busy clearing up the remains of two breakfast trays, which had been left messily on the floor.

He grinned goofily. 'I think they are down the beach, *Signorina* Stevens.'

'Thanks, Tito,' she said gratefully. His eyes twinkled. 'How are you feeling after your little party?'

'Oh, not you as well,' she groaned.

He laughed. 'Hey, don't worry about it.' Tito dropped his voice and looked around. 'I shouldn't really say anything, but Maggie is on your side. I overhead her saying she doesn't trust *Signorinas* Vanderbilt and Mastrangelo.'

Sapphire smiled ruefully. 'Pity no one else agrees! But thanks, Tito, I appreciate it.'

Sapphire finally found Madison and Simonetta on the jetty, dangling their long legs over the edge. A speedboat with three hunky young men was zooming round showing off. Madison threw them flirty little waves every now and again. As Sapphire reached them, Simonetta looked up, her face expressionless.

'Oh. Hello.'

'Is that all you've got to say for yourself?' Sapphire demanded. *I sound like my mum!* she thought, cringing inwardly. She stood with her hands firmly on her hips, even though she was a nervous wreck inside.

'What else do you want us to say, honey?' Madison said, her eyes following the speedboat. She looked the picture of all-American innocence in a white Ralph Lauren sundress and a large-brimmed straw hat.

'You set me up with the champagne!' Sapphire said hotly.

Madison turned round, her pretty face alive with malicious glee. 'I really don't know what you're talking about. Have you been drinking again? God, you're like a frickin' alcoholic.'

'I said, "You set me up",' Sapphire repeated through gritted teeth.

Madison glanced at Simonetta. 'So what if we did? It's not our fault you were dumb enough to take the bait.'

Sapphire shook her head, angry little tears pricking the back of her eyes. 'Why would you *do* that?'

'Why not? It's time Brad started to see your true colours. Your sweet and innocent act might fool him, Sapphire, but I can *totally* see though it.'

'I'm not putting on an act!' Sapphire cried in frustration. 'Stop trying to shit-stir!'

Madison smiled nastily. 'Oh, there'll be plenty more where that came from.'

Sapphire said what she'd been wanting to, ever since she'd found out they were all Brad's daughters. 'I cannot actually believe we're *related*.'

'Oh, honey. And why's that? You thought as soon as we all found out we'd fall into each other's arms? As if. You're just some frumpy little freakazoid who I've got to put up with for a while.'

Madison turned back to face the sea as the speedboat zoomed up.

'Hey girls, you wanna come for a ride?' the hunky young men on board shouted.

Madison tossed her hair sexily. 'O.M.G, *totes*! Simonetta?'

The model looked confused. 'Totes?'

'Like, *totally*! Oh sweetie, we really are going to have to teach you the lingo.' Madison stood up and tossed a contemptuous look at Sapphire. 'You still here?' She turned her back on Sapphire. 'OK, guys, we're coming!'

As Sapphire stood watching, the white-hot rage that had been building inside her exploded. Without really thinking about what she was doing, she leapt forward and shoved Madison hard between the shoulders. Madison screamed and, as if in slow motion, toppled off the jetty, landing with a resounding splash in the waves below. The guys in the speedboat cracked up with laughter, as Madison came to the surface, coughing and spluttering. Her sunhat floated off like a bedraggled jellyfish.

'Sapphire, I am gonna frickin' kill you!' she shrieked.

Simonetta, her eyebrow raised in amused astonishment, looked down at Madison and then back to Sapphire. 'You really should not have done that. Madison is not someone you want as your enemy.'

'Seems like I've done a pretty good job already,' retorted Sapphire and, feeling a lot happier than she had in days, she walked off back up the jetty.

Sapphire half expected a bucket of water to be waiting on top of her door when she returned to her bedroom later, but there was nothing. She knew it hadn't been wise to piss off Madison, but the American bitch had wound Sapphire up so much she didn't care. She might be a nice person, but that didn't mean people like Madison could be a cow and walk all over her. Still, she'd have to watch her back – and her drinks – from now on.

In a funny way, Simonetta and Madison's nastiness had made Sapphire, for the first time, really *want* to be chosen as Brad's heir. She wasn't normally very competitive, but they had stirred something in her. *Anything to piss them off and stop them getting their sticky little hands on the money.* Sapphire grinned at the thought of Madison's face as she, Sapphire, wrote a cheque out for the entire inheritance to some random squirrel charity. That'd teach her!

She was roused from her daydream by the sound of a raised voice outside her window. Sapphire pulled the muslin curtains aside and looked out. It was Raphael, having a fierce argument in Italian on the phone. His hair was wild and his angry eyes seemed more penetrating than ever. Sapphire didn't know much Italian, but she did have a basic understanding from her GCSE course. She edged closer to the balcony to try to hear. Straining her ears, she could make out the words *morte* and *distruzione*. Sapphire frowned. Those words sounded familiar. As she racked her brain, Raphael glanced up, as if aware he was being watched. Sapphire jumped back behind the curtain, her heart beating so loudly she thought it would give her away. But a few seconds later his voice floated off down the garden. Sapphire leant against the wall, her mind whirling. *Morte* and *distruzione*, what did those words mean? Suddenly they came to her and her blood ran cold. *Morte* meant death and *distruzione* meant destruction.

'*Death and destruction,*' she muttered. What on earth had Raphael been talking about? Another chill went through her body. She'd thought Raphael was mean... but what if he was *dangerous* too?

chapter twenty

Madison speared a tomato viciously. She was still burning from Sapphire pushing her in the sea and making her look like a total idiot in front of those hot guys. And now, to her complete annoyance, it looked like Brad had forgiven Dorkface for the drunken episode. They'd been having some dumb love-in conversation about soul music for ten minutes and Madison was *bored*.

'Look at that sap kissing Brad's ass,' she hissed at Simonetta.

The model gave a secretive smile and surveyed Madison through half-closed eyes. 'You are going to have to try harder,' she told her. The more she encouraged Madison, the better. Madison was revealing her game plan to Simonetta without even realising it. There was no way Madison was going to trick *her*.

'What are you two girls whispering about?' Brad said, smiling over the table.

'Oh, girl stuff!' Madison said brightly. She smiled sweetly at Sapphire. 'Sapphire, me and Simonetta were just saying it is so cool you *can* be around alcohol and not act retarded.'

Sapphire went a dull red. Why did Madison have to bring that up? She looked down at her glass, which contained sparkling water. Alcohol was the last thing she wanted to think about at the moment.

Brad frowned, as if he didn't want to recall the events of the other night either. To Sapphire's relief, he changed the subject. 'How do you girls fancy a little day trip tomorrow?'

All three looked at him with interest. 'Yes, please!' trilled Madison. Brad grinned. 'Excellent. It'll be an early start so you'd better turn in early.'

'What time are we leaving, Brad?' Simonetta asked.

He turned to her. 'I'd like you to meet me at the heliport at five thirty.'

'In the *morning*?' gasped Madison.

Brad looked at her, amused. 'Yes, is that all right?'

'Perfectly,' Madison gushed. *It was like the middle of the freakin' night!* 'Where are we going?' she asked.

Brad smiled mysteriously. 'Ah, now that's a surprise. But pack your bikinis.'

It was still dark the next morning as the three girls made their way to the helipad. 'My ass is seriously going to freeze off,' grumbled Madison from under her Juicy Couture hooded top. 'And my ass is my best asset. I'm not swimming anywhere until it warms up.'

Her mutterings swiftly stopped when they saw the sleek red helicopter. It looked like a giant squatting insect, rotors resting on the ground. Brad was already there loading bags into the back, while a uniformed pilot sat at the controls, fiddling with knobs and buttons.

'This is *so* cool!' squealed Madison.

Brad turned round. 'Morning, girls! You didn't oversleep then?'

'I've been too excited to sleep,' Sapphire confessed. 'I've never been in a helicopter before.' She ignored the incredulous looks from Simonetta and Madison.

Brad gestured at the pilot. 'This is Santo. He'll be flying us to our destination.'

'Hi, Santa!' trilled Madison. 'Like, it is so cool that your parents named you after Father Christmas.'

Brad, Sapphire and Simonetta exchanged amused glances.

'Are we ready, Santo?' Brad asked. The pilot nodded. 'All right girls, you can climb in the back.'

Inside, the helicopter was small but snug. The three girls sat closely, their legs touching. Sapphire realised it was the first human contact she'd had with her half-sisters since she'd come to Casa Eleganza. To her surprise, Madison's skin wasn't ice cold.

Suddenly, the engine started up and the rotors began whirring into life. The noise was deafening. Sapphire felt a thrill of excitement as the helicopter slowly began to lift off the floor. They were flying! As they rose, the trees all around shook and waved with the down-draught from the whirring blades. Sapphire watched, her nose pressed against the window. Soon Casa Eleganza looked like a little toy house below, as they soared off into the distance.

As dawn approached, the sky began to lighten. Hundreds of feet below, the sea sat like a smooth glass surface, the occasional boat bobbing around now and again. It was like nothing Sapphire had ever seen before.

After half an hour, Brad turned round. He had to shout to be heard over the roar of the engine. 'We're landing in a minute.' He pointed out of the window to a small island in the distance. As they approached, a sweeping white sandy beach backing on to luscious green woods spread out before them. To her surprise, Sapphire could see the tiny figures of people standing on the beach. Who would be on an island this isolated at this time in the morning?

A few moments later they touched down on the beach, spraying sand everywhere. Brad turned to Santo. 'Nice work. You'll be back for us at four?' The moustached pilot smiled and nodded. Brad turned to the girls. 'We've got quite a welcoming committee.'

'Where are we?' Madison whispered. 'Who *are* all those people?' A smiling man dressed in a white shirt and linen trousers came to open the door. One by one, he helped the girls out. Already, more similarly dressed men and women were opening the back and getting the luggage out.

As Sapphire looked around, she could see palm trees fringing the beach. High above, a mountain soared up high, its peak heavily forested and alive with flowers. *This is paradise*, she thought to herself. Beside her, Simonetta and Madison were looking just as impressed. Brad walked over and waved his hand over the surroundings.

'Welcome to Charlotte Island.'

'This is so cool!' Madison gushed. 'Is it a new resort? I've never heard of it.'

'You wouldn't have. It's very exclusive,' Brad told her.

'Oh, I get it!' Madison exclaimed. 'It's like Richard Branson with Necker Island. He charges, like, zillions of dollars to stay there. So who owns this?' she asked.

Brad smiled. 'I do.'

Before it could sink in that there was a private

island up for grabs, Brad ushered them down on a little path through the woods. 'There's something I want to show you,' he told them. From where they'd landed it looked like the island was pretty much uninhabited, so the girls were astonished to be led to what looked like a luxury mini-resort, complete with sprawling bungalows, a swimming pool and gymnasium. In the middle of all this stood an amazing modern house with razor-straight lines and floor-to-ceiling windows.

'We've got to hurry,' Brad told them. They followed him inside and up a glass staircase to the next floor. There was a living-room running the entire length of one side of the house, with spectacular views out to sea. Brad opened a sliding door and led them out.

'We're just in time.'

Before them, on the crest of the horizon, the sun was just beginning to move skywards. The blue-black sky became filled with a brilliant, luminous light, changing night into day. *I wish Cam was here to see this*, Sapphire suddenly thought. The big orange ball continued its spellbinding journey, until it was hanging high in the sky, casting a sunny glow on everything under its gaze. In just a few minutes, the world had changed before their eyes.

'Pretty good, hey?' Brad said. 'That's one of the reasons I bought this island. You don't get a better view of the sunrise anywhere else in Italy.'

'It was bellissimo,' said Simonetta. Being a lover of beautiful things she was actually quite overcome.

Madison's gaze travelled back inside, already bored. It was just the sun – she'd seen it, like, a million times. 'So, is this your house? Who are the condos for?'

'Anyone I want to invite to Charlotte Island. They're all empty right now, though.'

Until now, Sapphire had been left speechless by the beautiful spectacle they'd just witnessed. 'Who runs the place when you're not here?' she asked.

'I've got a team of live-in staff.' Brad looked at his watch. 'Which reminds me, breakfast should be ready.'

Charlotte Island was also a nature reserve and the girls spent an idyllic morning being shown around by

Brad. It was clear how passionate he was about the place and even Madison couldn't fail to be impressed by the hundreds of species of exotic plants and birds. By lunchtime, they were sitting at a beautifully dressed table on the terrace by the pool. They ate fish caught that very morning off bone china plates, with discreet staff to cater to their every whim.

'I could get used to this,' Madison declared. Simonetta had excused herself to use the toilet and it was just her, Brad and Sapphire sitting round the table.

Brad chuckled. 'You can have too much of a good thing, believe me.'

By the look on her face, Madison clearly didn't. 'So was it called Charlotte Island when you bought it? Who named it?'

'It's named after my mother, actually,' Brad said.

Madison looked blank for a moment.

'Oh. So that would, like, make her my *grandmother*?'

'Yes.'

'Neat,' she said. 'Is she still alive?'

A sad expression crossed Brad's face. 'No, she died a long time ago.'

Madison shrugged, as if he'd told her he'd just lost on the fruit machines or something. 'Oh well.'

Sapphire gave Brad a sympathetic smile and resolved to ask him about his mother later. She wanted to know what her grandmother had been like.

Simonetta returned to the table and Sapphire noticed that her eyes were red, as if she'd been crying. She raised an eyebrow questioningly, but Simonetta shot her down with a dirty look. If she had been crying, she didn't want anyone to know about it. *What has Simonetta got to cry about?* wondered Sapphire, before realising that she actually knew very little about her two half-sisters. It made her feel sad and weird at the same time.

Brad put down his napkin. 'After this morning's activities I thought I'd let you get a bit of sunbathing in, before we head back later. I've got a few things to check up on anyway. Is that OK with you?'

'Super dooper!' said Madison.

'Actually, I might do a bit more exploring if that's OK,' Sapphire said.

Brad looked pleased. 'Of course. Just mind you stick to the path. We've had guests lost for weeks out there. In fact, I think there's a few still wandering about.' His eyes twinkled.

'Ha ha, very funny,' Sapphire said with a smile.

Brad grinned. 'Stick to the path anyway. Your mother would never forgive me if I lost you.' He stopped abruptly, as if he'd said too much.

'I'll get going then,' Sapphire said hastily. She didn't know if she liked it or not when Brad talked about her mum.

As she started off down a winding path, Sapphire thought about Brad's mum instead. Her grandmother. Sapphire wondered what she had been like, and if she looked anything like her. *I should ask Brad if he has any photos,* she thought.

Half an hour later, Sapphire found herself at a little cove with its own beach. The waters were turquoise blue with little twinkles of sunlight bouncing invitingly off them. She walked over the sand and stuck her foot in. It was as warm as a bath. Sapphire was beginning to regret not putting her swimming costume on when a thought struck her. There was no one to see her – why not just swim in her birthday suit?

Excitedly, she kicked off her flip-flips and pulled her dress over her head. Her underwear was next and, with a carefree whoop, she ran into the sea. The water rushed over her naked body, making her feel alive and happy. Sapphire swam out a few metres and then turned on to her back, gazing up at the cloudless blue sky above. *Life doesn't get much better than this*, she thought, remembering the crowded pool at the leisure centre she and her mum sometimes used, which was cold and festooned with hairs in the changing-rooms.

After staying in so long that her hands started to go wrinkly, Sapphire decided to head back. Wading out of the water, she made her way across the beach to where she'd left her clothes. But they were nowhere to be seen. She frowned. Where were they? She was sure she'd left them right there, by that rock. With a sense of rising panic, she scanned the beach. It was empty. She ran to where she thought she'd left her clothes and, with a lurch of shock, saw another pair of footprints leading back towards the wood.

Someone had stolen her clothes.

* * *

Brad had been on a tour of the island with his estate manager, Peppe. Despite its natural beauty, Charlotte Island needed a lot of upkeep and Brad was determined to keep the place looking its best. He was just telling the manager he thought the gym needed another coat of paint when there was a scream. He swung round to see Gloria, his elderly housekeeper, staring at something with her hands over her mouth. His eyes followed hers and, to his shock and dismay, Brad saw Sapphire running totally naked across the grass. 'Oh, *mio Dio*!' examined Peppe as he averted his eyes. Sapphire ran around in circles a few times, her long hair flying after her, before eventually disappearing into the gymnasium.

Brad turned to Peppe, who was a deeply religious family man with daughters of his own. The look of disapproval on the estate manager's face said it all. 'Peppe, I apologise for my guest's behaviour,' he said.

'It's nothing,' said Peppe, but he didn't look at all impressed.

Anger burned through Brad. How dare Sapphire embarrass him like this? Making his excuses, he went over to Gloria, who was still standing with a look of shock on her face. Trying to keep calm, he asked her to go into the gymnasium to find out what was going on. Gloria emerged a few minutes later, looking concerned.

'*Signor* Masters, she say someone stole her clothes.'

'What?' he said in annoyance.

Gloria held her hand out in confusion. 'I do not know.'

'All right,' sighed Brad. 'Thank you, Gloria, I'll take it from here.' He walked over the gym and opened the door a crack, careful not to look inside.

'Sapphire?'

'Brad!' She sounded panicky. 'I went swimming and someone stole my clothes!'

'*Stole* them? There are no thieves on this island. And what were you doing swimming nude in the first place? This isn't a naturist resort, Sapphire.'

'I'm sorry. I just thought…'

Brad's eyes travelled to a pile of something by the gym door. On closer inspection it looked like a pair of flip-flips and the dress Sapphire had been wearing earlier.

'Sapphire, your clothes are over there. What the hell are you playing at?'

Sapphire followed his gaze. Her jaw dropped. 'Madison must have taken them or something, that's just the sort of thing she'd do.'

Brad looked cross. 'Madison and Simonetta have been by the pool all afternoon, I've seen them myself! Stop flinging accusations around to try and save your own skin. I don't know what possessed you, Sapphire, but it was entirely inappropriate.'

There was a pause. 'OK,' she said miserably.

Brad picked up the bundle of clothes and threw them in the door. 'Now if you don't mind, get dressed.'

From her hiding place behind a large bush, Madison had listened to the exchange with a big smile on her face. All it had taken was for Simonetta to tell Brad that she, Madison, was in the toilet when he came to check on them, while she crept off to follow Sapphire. Madison hadn't been quite sure what she was actually going to *do* once she found Sapphire, but when the golden opportunity had presented itself she couldn't believe her luck. When Sapphire wasn't looking, she'd run down to the beach and taken the clothes, before hotfooting it back and leaving them somewhere obvious. There was no way Sapphire could talk her way out of this one! Rubbing her hands gleefully, Madison made her way back to her sunlounger.

While the journey to Charlotte Island had been full of excitement, the journey back was entirely different. Even though the sound of the engine made it difficult to talk, the atmosphere was strained. Brad had climbed aboard grim-faced and ignored Sapphire, who was now wedged uncomfortably between Madison and Simonetta. She knew they were behind it, but yet again, how could she prove it? From the sneaky little glances Madison kept giving her, Sapphire guessed Madison was the one who'd actually taken the clothes. On her other side sat Simonetta, silent and sphinx-like, staring out of the window.

Once they'd landed, Brad quickly jumped out and made his way up to the house. *He can't stand to be near me*, Sapphire thought. She watched as Madison and Simonetta started to slink up the path, looking as if they hadn't a care in the world. A sudden fury flashed through her and she ran to catch them up.

'Madison, I want a word with you!' Sapphire put her hand on Madison's shoulder, but the American girl pulled free violently.

'What, are you going to *beat me up* now as well?'

'I know you took my clothes!' Sapphire said angrily.

Madison opened innocent blue eyes. 'Er, excuse me? I was by the pool all afternoon. Simonetta will back me up.'

'I'm sure she will,' said Sapphire, glaring at Simonetta. 'Brad hates me now!'

Madison gave a nasty little smile 'What do you expect if you act like a slut and run around with no clothes on? I'd be surprised if Brad doesn't kick your skanky little ass out of here!'

Despite herself, tears welled up in Sapphire's eyes.

'Oh dear,' Madison said patronisingly. 'Is Little Miss Perfect upset now that her true colours are coming out?'

'You're an evil cow!'

'Ooh, don't get all bitchy. Anyway, I'm outta here. I've got more interesting stuff to do, like watching nail polish dry or something.'

She shot Sapphire a final triumphant look over her shoulder. 'All things aside, sweetie, you should know that *no one* pushes Madison Mercedes Melody Vanderbilt overboard and gets away with it!'

chapter twenty-one

Sapphire spent the next few days keeping out of everyone's way. Even Maggie seemed to be off with her, while Sapphire hadn't seen Brad since they'd got back from Charlotte Island. One of the few times she'd left her bedroom she'd overheard Simonetta saying to Madison that he'd flown to Berlin for another business trip.

To be honest, it was probably a good thing if she didn't see the other two for a bit. Right now Sapphire couldn't trust herself not to pour a whole swimming pool's worth of water over their heads. *I shouldn't have stooped to Madison's level*, she thought. Maybe if she hadn't pushed Madison off the jetty, she wouldn't be Public Enemy Number One right now. But then again, Madison seemed to have it in for her anyway. In some ways Simonetta was even worse. She might not be as obvious as Madison, but she was like a snake, silently watching everything from the sidelines. Sapphire couldn't work the model out at all, whereas at least she knew what Madison was.

A grade-A bitch.

Sapphire sighed and flopped back on her bed. She'd been trying to read, but was finding it hard to concentrate. Her thoughts kept wandering back to what had happened. She wondered why she was putting herself through the ordeal of sharing air space with such horrible people. But Sapphire was stubborn, and the nastier Madison and Simonetta were to her, the more determined she became to stick it out. It might not matter, if Brad had decided to send her home anyway, but as long as she *was* here, Sapphire knew she'd have to be extra-vigilant.

Not wanting to waste another second thinking about the Two Not-So-Ugly Sisters, as she had nicknamed them, Sapphire decided to go for a walk. It was late in the afternoon and the sun was just starting to bob down in the sky. The grounds of Casa Eleganza were so beautiful that Sapphire's mood lifted and she found herself thinking about new lyrics. This place would provide great inspiration for a song about a holiday romance, but, as she reminded herself, she had to have a romance first…

'Hey, Sapphire! What are you doing out here?' She turned to see Cam jogging towards her. He was topless, in just a pair of running shorts and high-tech trainers, iPod headphones in his ears. His tan was deeper than ever, making him look like some kind of bronzed statue.

Sapphire's heart stopped at the sight of him. 'Uh, I was just taking a walk.' As he came up to her she could see the droplets of sweat running down his perfect chest. Sapphire longed to reach out and touch that hard, muscular body. Just one touch would satisfy her for the rest of her life…

'Are you OK? You look kinda spaced out,' he asked.

Sapphire jumped, trying to pull herself together. Her tongue had probably been hanging out! 'I'm cool. I was just in a world of my own.'

'Mind if I walk with you? I'm done anyway.'

'No, that's cool,' she stuttered. *Stop saying cool, you saddo!* she told herself. They walked along in silence for a few moments. Even though Sapphire had her eyes fixed ahead, she was aware of the sheer strength and bulk of Cam's body. They were walking so close, arms touching occasionally, and she could literally *feel* the heat coming off him. He smelt of aftershave, fresh sweat and sheer testosterone. Sapphire thought she had never smelt anything so amazing in her whole life.

'Where've you been? I haven't seen much of you lately,' he asked.

Sapphire flushed. 'Just kind of doing my own thing,' she responded. She held her breath to see if he would mention what had happened on Charlotte Island, but Cam didn't say anything. He either didn't know or was being polite.

'What about you?' she asked. 'It must be really quiet out here, compared to what you're used to.'

Cam smiled at her, a flash of white in a brown face.

Sapphire's heart did a little skip. 'That's why I'm here, remember? I gotta say, I'm really vibing off it. No one hassling me for my autograph every time I go out, no cameras going off in my face. Here it's just *me*, y'know? It sounds kind of cheesy, but it's given me the chance to get to know myself.' Cam laughed. 'That *does* sound cheesy, doesn't it?'

'No. I know what you mean,' said Sapphire, smiling. 'When you're away from it all, you have time to stop and think about things differently. See things in a new way.'

'That's exactly it!' Cam studied her. 'Y'know, I think you really get me, Sapphire. Most girls just want a piece of Cam Tyler, world-famous R&B star, but you – you see beyond that. I like that.'

Sapphire realised she was holding her breath. She couldn't believe Cam was saying this stuff to her!

'You're different, Sapphire.'

'Am I?' she said, aware that her voice had suddenly gone very squeaky.

Cam stopped and looked at her. 'Yes, you are. Sapphire, I've been wanting to say this for quite a while…'

Sapphire's knees went rather weak and she took an involuntary step back. Instead of finding even ground, her foot went in some kind of rabbit hole. She fell back heavily, twisting it as she went. As she crashed to the ground, a sharp pain shot through her ankle. She yelped loudly. 'Oww, shit!'

'Are you OK?' Quick as a flash, Cam was crouching down at her side. 'Here, let me look at that.' With the outmost care, he gently lifted her ankle. Sapphire winced as another stab of pain went through it.

'I think you've got a bad sprain,' he diagnosed. Let's get you back to the house.' As he helped her up, the pain was agonising.

'I don't think I can walk on it,' she grimaced.

'No problem,' Cam said. 'I'll carry you.'

'You'll do *what*?' gasped Sapphire. But before she knew it, she'd been swept up into his strong arms.

Madison and Simonetta were lazing on the lawn in their bikinis. 'I wonder where that little runt is hiding?' Madison said, checking out her flat stomach for the fifth time in as many minutes. 'Mind you, if I were her, I wouldn't show my face round here either.'

At first she thought Simonetta hadn't heard her, until the model gave a low whistle. 'I can tell you exactly where she is.'

'Where?' said Madison, lifting up her sunglasses. She blinked once, twice, then three times before she could actually believe what she was seeing. Striding across the lawn, like something out of an action movie, was a topless Cam carrying Sapphire in his arms.

'O.M.G!' Madison sat bolt upright.

Maggie came rushing out of the house at the same time. 'Sapphire! Whatever have you done to yourself?'

'I tripped and twisted my ankle,' Sapphire said.

'Lord, girl, you've got two left feet!' Maggie exclaimed.

'I think she'll live, Maggie, don't worry,' Cam said, smiling.

The housekeeper looked relieved. 'Thank Mary and Joseph for that! Let's get you inside so I can get an icepack on it.'

'Did I just see that?' Madison asked Simonetta incredulously. 'The runt being carried across the lawn by *Cam Tyler*?'

Simonetta eyed Madison's furious face with amusement. 'You look so ugly when you go red like that.' She blew a long breath out, thinking. 'Sapphire, she is like, how do you say it… a cockroach, *si*? They always survive, no matter what.'

'Cockroach is about right,' muttered Madison. She wouldn't have put it past Sapphire to have made the whole goddamn ankle-twisting thing up.

chapter
twenty-two

Brad's private doctor was summoned and, after bandaging Sapphire's ankle heavily, told her to not put any weight on it. Maggie seemed to have forgiven her and was fussing round like a mother hen, bringing Sapphire soup and succulent bowls of fruit picked from the orchards.

'I'm not ill, I've just hurt my ankle,' Sapphire insisted after Maggie brought her yet another delicious homemade broth. 'I do appreciate you looking after me though,' she added with a smile.

'May as well have you where I can keep an eye on you. At least you won't get into any more trouble,' Maggie said, but her voice was kindly. A movement at the door made them both look up. Madison was standing there with a bunch of hand-picked flowers from the garden.

'Madison, what a lovely gesture!' said Maggie. She gave Sapphire a 'see, she's not that bad' look.

'I just thought I'd come and see how the patient is doing,' Madison said sweetly.

Maggie smiled. 'I'll go and put those flowers in a vase for you.' She got up and left them to it.

Madison didn't sit down immediately, wandering round the room instead, carelessly picking up Sapphire's things. 'I'll give you credit, you're better than I thought,' she said eventually.

'Better than you thought at what?' Sapphire asked in exasperation. She didn't like the way Madison was prowling round while she was stuck on the bed.

'Playing the helpless maiden as a way to get back into everybody's good books.' Madison came and sat down on the edge of the bed.

Sapphire looked at her fat, swollen ankle. It was aching in time with her heartbeat. 'You need your head examined if you think I did this deliberately,' she retorted irritably.

Madison looked down at the bandaged ankle. Very slowly and very deliberately she put her hand down, resting her whole weight on it. The pain was agonising.

'Get off!' cried Sapphire, pulling her leg away.

'Whoops! Sorry, my hand slipped,' Madison said breathily.

Sapphire rubbed her aching ankle. 'What is *wrong* with you?'

Madison leant in towards her, her pretty face a mask of hatred. 'Not half as much as will be wrong with you if you keep this up.'

'For God's sake, Madison! Keep up what? Can't we just see this as a bit of healthy competition? I'm getting sick of you acting like Cruella De Vil.'

Madison smiled. 'And I'm getting sick of your skinny little ass hanging around here like a bad smell. You don't even *want* the money, sweetie, so why don't you go back to Dweebsville and leave us big girls to sort it out amongst ourselves?'

'Well, unfortunately, you don't know anything about me and what I want, so why don't you leave it just there?' Sapphire said stiffly.

Madison sat and looked at her for a moment, her cold, ice-blue eyes boring into Sapphire's. 'Well,' Madison said lightly. 'Don't say I didn't warn you.' She jumped up. 'A word of sisterly advice, Sapphire. You ain't seen *nothing* yet.'

The next day Sapphire's ankle had gone down enough for her to walk round her bedroom on it. Even though she had a plasma television and an amazing sound system to keep her occupied, Sapphire was bored of being cooped up. If she took it slowly enough, she'd be able to go for a short walk. Grabbing her new Prada sunglasses off the bedside table, she opened her door and walked out.

As usual, the rest of the house was peacefully quiet, with just the occasional chatter or laughter from staff working somewhere on the grounds. Sapphire was struck, not for the first time, by how much like a museum Casa Eleganza was, with its cool marble floors and antique furniture. Although undeniably beautiful, it was also devoid of life. Silently, she padded in her Havaiana flip-flops past the Rembrandt and Picasso paintings and out in the sun-filled garden.

The light and warmth was a welcome relief. She was aware of a car crunching on the circular driveway behind her and turned to see a blacked-out Mercedes being driven in. The driver's window was open and music blasted out. To Sapphire's surprise, she saw Raphael in a chauffeur's uniform, singing along. His face was flushed, his eyes alive. He looked almost happy. Then the car disappeared from view behind the house, as if the image had been a figment of her imagination.

Sapphire hobbled to her favourite spot on the beach and gingerly sat down. For what seemed like the thousandth time, she replayed the scene of Cam carrying her up the stairs to her bedroom and laying her gently down on the bed. Sapphire had barely been aware of Maggie as she stared up at the wondrous sight of Cam Tyler, standing topless in *her* bedroom. Cam had just had enough time for a smile at Sapphire before Maggie had ushered him out. Sapphire had been left on her own – lying back on the pillows and wondering what Cam had been about to say before she put her stupid foot down that rabbit hole.

Sapphire, I've been wanting to say this for quite a while…

'*What?* What were you about to say?' she said aloud in excited frustration. She couldn't believe her bad timing! Talk about ruining the moment.

Her shoulders started to feel itchy and Sapphire realised she'd forgotten to put any suncream on. The last thing she wanted was to add bright-red lobster skin to a fat ankle. She was making her way back up the winding stone steps when suddenly a helicopter buzzed overhead. Stomach lurching, she looked up, but it wasn't Brad. The black helicopter carried on flying out to sea. Sapphire still hadn't seen Brad since the naked drama. The longer it went on, the worse she felt. Sapphire didn't know if she was avoiding him, or the other way round.

She had just started climbing the steps when she misjudged one and tripped, pitching forward.

Not again! she thought, bracing herself for the fall. But to her astonishment, someone caught her. Sapphire looked up to see Raphael holding her, his eyes glaring into hers. For someone so lean and sinewy, he had surprising strength. They were so close that Sapphire could see the strange gold flecks in his eyes. Suddenly, he shoved her away, as though he couldn't stand to touch her.

'Why don't you watch where you're going, English girl? I hear it's not the first time. No doubt your head was full of other, stupid things.'

Sapphire was tired of this guy and his weird moods. After her run-in with Madison, it was the final straw.

'Hang on a minute,' she said angrily. 'I don't know what your problem is, or what idea you've got of me, but you're wrong! And quite frankly, I'm sick of you having at go at me every time we meet. So just stay out of my way, OK?'

Raphael seemed surprised at her outburst. Something shifted behind his eyes. 'I saw you trip,' he said angrily. 'What was I supposed to do, let you fall?'

'I didn't ask you to rescue me! And I certainly don't need the knight-in-shining-armour routine, so just leave me alone,' she said. And with that, Sapphire turned and stormed up the path as fast as her sore ankle would allow her.

chapter twenty-three

Brad clicked off the screen and turned to the girls. 'That just about wraps it up. Do you have any questions?'

They were sitting in Casa Eleganza's private cinema and Brad had just shown them a short, slick company film on Brad Masters Enterprises. It was even more impressive than the three had thought. As well as BMM, the record label, Brad owned several multi-million-pound development companies and more real estate than a small African country. That wasn't forgetting the chain of luxury health clubs, the Michelin-starred restaurant just off the Champs-Elysées in Paris, and dealing in the most expensive, sought-after art in the world. Sapphire had to hand it to the bloke – he knew what he was doing.

Simonetta coughed. She had been taking notes on her BlackBerry the whole way through. 'Is it true you are looking to invest in brands like Giuseppe, to take them to a global level?' Giuseppe was an up-and-coming young Italian designer the fashion world was raving about.

Brad looked impressed. 'You've obviously done your research.'

Simonetta nodded regally. '*Si*, this is what interests me. Fashion is not just about clothes; it is a lifestyle. This needs to be communicated to badly dressed people the world over.' She looked pointedly at Sapphire. 'If people do not make an effort with their appearance, how will they get anywhere in life?'

Brad looked at her with interest. 'So it's all about image then, Simonetta?'

'Of course! Looking good is what matters.'

'Surely being talented, or being a nice person, counts as well,' Sapphire ventured.

Simonetta looked at her as if she were speaking in an alien language.

'I've got an idea!' announced Madison, not wanting to be outdone. 'Have you thought about, like, a puppy swap service? Me and my friends are always talking about it. You know how you get a dog and it's so cute and small at first and you can carry it around everywhere in your handbag? And then, like, it *grows* and gets all big and ugly. How about a company where as soon as your puppy isn't cute any more, you can go back and swap it for a new one?'

Even for Madison, this was a new one. 'And what happens to the dogs you take back?' Sapphire asked in disbelief.

Madison shrugged. 'I don't know. Let them loose in a park or something? There'll be loads of space to run about.'

'That's, er, very inventive, Madison,' Brad said. 'Thank you.'

'Hey, that's what I'm here for!' she said sweetly.

Brad gave Sapphire a hard look. 'Do you want to

ask anything?' Sapphire had loads of questions, like whether Brad donated any of his money to charities, but she couldn't bring herself to ask. She looked at the floor instead.

'No? OK then. I hope the film's helped you three see what Brad Masters Enterprises is all about.' The girls got up to leave. 'Can I have a word please, Sapphire?' Brad said. The other two looked exchanged glances.

Sapphire felt another sick lurch in her stomach. 'Uh, yeah.'

Madison and Simonetta left and Brad closed the door behind them. He turned round. 'How's the ankle?' he asked. 'Maggie told me about your mishap.'

'Better, thanks,' Sapphire mumbled.

Brad gazed at her. 'You seem to have a lot of mishaps. I must say, I'm surprised at how it's all turned out. I thought Madison and Simonetta would be... wilder. But they've been the perfect guests.'

Sapphire reddened. There was no point blaming them again, Brad would just think even less of her.

'Is there anything you want to tell me?' he asked suddenly. His voice was quizzical.

Sapphire hesitated. 'No... nothing.' There was a long pause. The walls seemed to be closing in on her.

'Now look.' Brad came to stand in front of her, his arms folded. 'We've been here with the alcohol and I gave you a second chance. You blew it. Despite all this, I think you're a good kid and I owe it to your mother. From now on, I want best behaviour. Do I make myself clear?'

At the mention of her mother, Sapphire felt a flash of anger. Who did he think he was, turning up after all these years and telling her what to do? *She* should be the one angry with *him* – he'd abandoned her and her mum in the first place.

'Yes, Brad,' she said, through gritted teeth.

He studied her perceptively. 'Do you find it hard to take criticism from me?'

Sapphire kept quiet, not trusting herself to speak.

Brad sighed. 'Look, I know it must be weird for you, and you probably think I've got no right to tell you what to do. But while you're staying here as my guest, there are certain ways to behave. Do you understand?'

Sapphire bit her lip with the injustice of it all. 'Perfectly,' she said quietly.

Brad stared at her. 'Good.' A smile beckoned at the sides of his mouth. 'How's the song-writing going?'

With a stab of guilt, Sapphire realised she hadn't picked up her guitar or written anything since she'd got to Casa Eleganza. 'OK,' she said, hoping her red face wouldn't give her away.

Brad looked at her closely. 'Keep practising, OK? It's the only way you'll get there.' He strode back across the room to pull the door open. There was a shriek as Madison and Simonetta fell in, from where they'd been spying through the keyhole.

'Can I help you ladies with anything?' Brad asked mildly. 'No, no!' said Madison. 'I'd, uh, dropped one of my false eyelashes and Simonetta was helping me look for it. But it's all right, we just found it.' And with that, the two of them beat a hasty retreat down the corridor.

'False eyelashes,' mused Brad. 'Well, I never.'

Sapphire left the cinema room feeling better. As long as she stayed out of Madison and Simonetta's way, they shouldn't be able to get her into any more trouble. She thought about what Brad had said about her music instead. It was almost as if he had a sixth sense. She had been avoiding it because she was worried she wasn't good enough. By not thinking about it, she didn't have to arrive at the gutting conclusion that she would never get the melody right. But in her heart of hearts, Sapphire knew Brad was right. She had to face her demons. Encouraged by their conversation, and the fact that he wasn't going to send her away, Sapphire decided to get her guitar and head down to the beach.

Ten minutes later she was sitting on the warm sand, strumming the strings gently. She had recently written a new song, "Boy", which Jerry said was her best yet, but as usual she couldn't make the leap from writing the words to picking up the guitar and actually *playing* them. It was beginning to frustrate her beyond belief.

'*Boy, you came along…*' Her voice stopped. It just sounded wrong. She rubbed her hands over her face. 'Aargh!'

Suddenly, she was aware of a shadow falling over her. Sapphire looked up and shielded her eyes. To her shock, she saw it was Raphael. She'd only just got over their last encounter. 'Look, if you've come to start on me about something else, I'm not in the mood for it,' she told him.

Raphael's striking face was like stone. 'You play the guitar?' It was more of an accusation than a question.

'Er, yeah,' said Sapphire. There was something about Raphael that unnerved her. She remembered what he'd been saying on the phone.

Morte. Distruzione. Death. Destruction. Had Raphael destroyed something? The thought she'd been trying to suppress came screaming into her head. Had he been involved in the *death* of someone?

She tried to control her shiver. Raphael put his hand up to shield his gold-flecked eyes from the sun – they looked more luminous than ever. Sapphire forced the dark thoughts out of her mind. *You're safe here anyway*, she told herself. Yet Raphael was watching her in a way that made her feel uneasy. She noticed that despite the scorching heat, his pale skin showed no signs of tanning.

'What?' she demanded, her nerves making her defensive.

His voice was cold and toneless. 'Maggie saw us

fighting. She said I should come and apologise for my behaviour.'

Sapphire's eyebrows shot up. 'Apologise? You?' she said disbelievingly.

'Yes. She says you are a *nice girl*.' Raphael accentuated the words sarcastically. 'She says I am acting on my presumptions.'

'And what are your presumptions?' Sapphire asked, getting more cross by the second. Why bother coming to find her if he was just going to be a rude git?

'That you are a spoilt little rich girl, just like your friends.'

'They're *not* my friends! We've only just met,' she added hurriedly.

Raphael stared at her. 'We'll see.' He turned and strode off, his tall, lean form gliding, rather than walking, over the golden sand.

Sapphire shook her head in confusion. What the hell had all that been about?

'What a weirdo,' she said wearily.

chapter twenty-four

Simonetta listened to the voicemail and promptly deleted it. It had been Lexi again, her agent at Models Italia. Lexi wanted to know what was happening with Brad and why Simonetta hadn't returned any of her calls. 'We have castings lined up for you – it's very unprofessional,' she had chided. Simonetta curled her lip; unprofessional was one thing she was not. She looked after herself and was always on time. Unlike most of her fellow models, Simonetta had made the effort to take courses in English and French to make sure she was well-equipped to deal with the catwalks of London, New York and Paris.

Things were just… different out here. Lexi was ignorant to the fact that she, Simonetta, was in a race to change her life completely. When Simonetta became Brad's heir, Lexi would rue the day she ever questioned her intergrity.

Throwing her bathrobe on the bed, she walked over to the mirror to scrutinise her body. The toned limbs, the fat-free midriff – these took time and effort. It was what set her apart, made heads turn, made her one of the beautiful people. Her love for *Mamma*'s homemade pasta had been abandoned long ago. But Simonetta knew it was worth whatever it took to get where she was going. Which was *everywhere*. With a final satisfied once-over, she turned and sashayed into the bathroom for a shower.

As hard as she tried to think about other things, images of Cam kept flashing across Sapphire's mind. The heat and smell of his body seemed to fill her head. Sapphire could almost *feel* the warmth of his touch, his naked, rock-hard chest pressed against her. In her imagination she visualised Cam carrying her off to the guesthouse, kissing her passionately with every step. And once they got there...

Sapphire shook her head. *You've got it bad, girl,* she told herself. It was time for a major reality check. Why would Cam Tyler, who could have any girl he wanted, be attracted to her? Even if he did like her freckles... He was probably just being nice – freckles weren't exactly sexy.

But even with the talking-to she gave herself, Sapphire's desire to see Cam grew stronger and stronger. It was like an itch she had to scratch. Despite keeping a look-out round the pool and down at the beach, there had been no sign of him. She knew there was only one thing left – to go to the guesthouse. The thought made her feel sick with nerves and excitement. At least she had an excuse – to say thank you for saving her. She hoped he wouldn't see through it.

Dusk was beginning to fall as she made her way there later. After what seemed like hours of deciding what to wear – she wanted to look nice but not too try-hard – Sapphire finally decided on the little flowery playsuit she had bought from Topshop. It showed off her shapely legs, but wasn't too low-cut. Her hair had been pulled into a casual ponytail so little bits fell round her face, and she had applied a subtle coat of mascara and lip-gloss. Heavy make up was not a good look in this heat.

To her disappointment the guesthouse was in darkness. He obviously wasn't there. Sapphire went up and knocked on the front door anyway. The doorbell clanged into silence. Heart heavy, she turned and started to walk back down the path. She'd only got halfway before a voice stopped her.

'Sapphire!' With a surge of excitement, she turned round. Cam was looking out of one of the upstairs windows, his hair ruffled.

'I fell asleep. Hold on and I'll come down and let you in.'

Smoothing her hair down and wiping her fingers under her eyes to make sure she didn't have any mascara smudges, Sapphire went back to the front door. Her heart was beating furiously. A few moments later, Cam pulled the door open, looking sleepy-eyed but as gorgeous as ever. He leaned forward and gave her a kiss on the cheek. Sapphire's heart went into overdrive.

'Hey, you. How's the ankle doing?' He looked down at her leg.

'It's much better, thanks,' she said. 'Actually, that's why I'm here, to say thank you for helping me.'

Cam was still looking at her legs. 'You've got a nice tan coming along, my little English rose. It suits you.'

His English rose! Sapphire's stomach did a little lurch of joy.

Cam smiled at her. 'You feel like a beer on the back terrace?' He shot her a mischievous look. 'Just don't tell Maggie I've got a fridge full of beers – she's big on the good ole USA's over twenty-one thing. And I thought the Irish *liked* a drink.'

'It seems stupid, when you're a credible international music artist, that you can't even have a drink in your own country,' Sapphire said. It was probably the longest sentence she'd ever said to him.

Cam grinned. 'One beer's not going to kill me, right? Luckily Brad is more relaxed about that sort of thing. Thanks for the compliment by the way,' he added.

'What complement?' she asked, puzzled.

'You called me a "credible music artist". Unless you're just buttering me up?'

Sapphire blushed. ''Course not. I meant it.'

Cam gave her a wink. 'I was just kidding.'

She followed him down a corridor into a big, open-plan kitchen. It was bare, apart from a collection of protein shakes stacked on one worktop. Cam saw her looking round and laughed. 'As you can see, I'm not the greatest of cooks. Luckily I get something brought over from the kitchen every night. Maggie wants to make sure I'm not wasting away. It's like she's my feeder or something.'

Sapphire giggled. 'I know what you mean.' The food at Casa Eleganza was gorgeous and plentiful. She was sure her clothes had got tighter since she'd arrived.

Cam reached into the fridge and pulled out two Budweisers. He popped the caps on the side of the work surface and handed Sapphire one. 'Let's head outside.'

A bewitching glow had fallen over the garden, giving it an almost otherworldly look. Little fairy lights swayed gently in the trees, while a firefly buzzed past and disappeared into the gloom. 'Pretty, huh?' Cam said. 'I like sitting out here at night, watching the world settle down.'

'Don't you get scared, being so far away from everyone else?' Sapphire asked.

Cam did a comedy flex with one of his arms. 'Hey, I can handle myself! Besides, Brad's got enough security patrolling the place to make sure no one's getting in.'

They sat down in two wooden loungers and stretched their legs out. Cam raised his bottle. 'Cheers, then. Isn't that what you English say?'

Sapphire laughed. 'Cheers.' For the first time, she was beginning to feel relaxed, like she wasn't holding her breath the whole time. Her heart still did a little skip every time she looked at him though.

'How's the music going, Sapphire?' he asked.

'Badly,' she said wryly. 'How about yours?'

He laughed. 'Hit that wall, hey?' He took a swig of beer. 'I've just finished something I've been working on. It's called "Ride".'

'What's it about?' Sapphire asked. She couldn't believe she was talking to Cam Tyler about music!

'It's about this dude meeting a girl who is like, so fly and hot. But she ends up pulling one on him, messing with his head and his wallet. He's got to decide whether he wants a good-looking chick on his arm or his self-respect.'

'So she's taking him for a ride, right?'

'You got it. It works on two levels; like, if he wants to go on this trip with her and just take it, or if he'll give her the flick and move on.'

'Speaking from experience?' Sapphire smiled.

Cam laughed. 'Kinda. You see plenty of girls like that when you're in my position. One of my buddies got wiped out pretty bad last year.'

He eyed Sapphire over his beer bottle. 'What kind of guys do you go for, Sapphire?'

She felt herself flush. 'Um, someone who's into music and has a good personality I guess.' She'd never really had a proper boyfriend, just a few ill-fated romances that had fizzled out after a couple of months.

'You're not into looks?' he said, as if he didn't believe her.

'I like nice eyes,' she admitted, realising she had been gazing into Cam's for the past five minutes. She blushed deeper and took a hasty swig of her beer. The cold liquid flowed through her, making her feel a bit light-headed. She'd stop after this one – there was no way she wanted a repeat of the last time.

She realised Cam was looking at her through the darkness.

'Uh, what kind of girls do you go for?' Her heart starting beating furiously as she said it.

Cam shrugged. 'I don't really have a type.'

Sapphire was plucking up the courage to ask what Cam had been about to say to her before she fell over, but he jumped up. 'Come on, I've got something cool to show you.'

Slightly breathless, she got up and followed him. Cam led her down to the end of the long, wide garden and pointed at something between the trees. 'You see it?'

Sapphire squinted and peered into the darkness. She could just make out what looked like a little gravestone. It had something written on it: *Badger, 1958. A true friend and comrade, never forgotten.*

'Is that an animal's gravestone?' she asked.

Cam nodded. 'Pretty cool, huh? Brad told me

about it, he's really big on the history of this place. Apparently the guy who used to own Casa Eleganza was some English fighter pilot dude called Charles Lightfoot. Brad said he was one of the most famous pilots of the time, fought in the Battle of Britain and all that. But his fiancée got killed in the Blitz and Lightfoot never recovered. Gave it all up and came out here, lived as a total recluse. His only friend in the world was, like, this three-legged stray dog he found half-dead on the side of the road. Lightfoot took him in and from that day on Badger never left his side. When the dog eventually died, Lightfoot buried him here. The next day, the guy just walks into the sea and drowns himself. When his body washed up three days later, they found Badger's name tag in his pocket.'

'That is so sad!' Sapphire said, her eyes brimming with tears. She was a sucker for any animal story.

Cam nodded gravely. 'They say on the anniversary of Badger's death, a strange howling can be heard across the grounds of Casa Eleganza.' His eyes widened and he looked at his watch. 'Oh my God, I think the anniversary's tonight!'

Suddenly, a bird squawked loudly overhead, making them both jump. 'Jesus!' Cam said, holding his chest. He started to laugh.

Sapphire felt like her heart was about to give out on her. 'You git! You were making that up, weren't you?'

He chuckled. 'You *git*? Is that another one of your weird British sayings?'

Sapphire play-hit his arm. 'I was really scared there for a second!'

They looked at each other and cracked up laughing. 'Your face was so funny,' Cam said. 'It was like you'd seen a ghost!'

'Yeah, well you were telling me there *was* a ghost,' retorted Sapphire. 'I really thought there was a dead dog running around—'

Her words were cut short as suddenly a spray of cold water hit them both. 'What's going on?' she shrieked.

'Shit, the sprinklers, they're on a timer!' he shouted. 'Run back to the house!'

By the time they had got back to the terrace, Cam had slipped over twice and they were both hysterical with laughter. 'I am drenched!' laughed Sapphire. 'What the hell are people going to think when I go back?' *At least I've got my clothes on this time*, she thought. Cam laughed and ran his hands through his wet hair, slicking it back. The white T-shirt he'd been wearing had gone completely transparent and was stuck to his six-pack. Sapphire saw his eyes travel over her body and she realised with embarrassment that her playsuit was completely stuck to her, highlighting every curve and the swell of her chest.

'I'll get you a towel,' Cam said, making a point of looking away from her. Suddenly, he took a step towards her. Sapphire held her breath. Oh my God, something was really about to happen!

'Hey, anyone home?' a voice suddenly called from inside the house. Cam snapped his head round. Tito was standing in the kitchen. 'The front door was open, so I just walked in...' He looked quizzically at Sapphire and their soaking wet clothes.

'Sprinklers kinda caught us by surprise,' Cam told him.

Tito grinned. 'Your mobile's switched off. Brad wanted me to let you know he'll be picking you up at seven o'clock tomorrow for your trip to see the A&R guys in Rome.'

Cam winced. 'An early night for me then.'

Tito looked at Sapphire. 'Shall I walk you back? As Maggie would say, you'll catch your death in that.'

At the word death, Sapphire's skin chilled. It wasn't just to do with the wet clothes. *Death and destruction* were the words Raphael had said in that phone call.

'Are you OK?' Cam asked. 'You're doing that weird, spaced-out thing again.'

'I'm fine,' Sapphire said quickly. She couldn't believe Tito had turned up! She was sure Cam had been about to kiss her. Suddenly she felt very cold, wet and unsexy. Tito put a brotherly arm round her.

'Let's get you back.'

Heart sinking, Sapphire followed him like a bedraggled poodle.

chapter twenty-five

Madison was bored. Bored of Simonetta, bored of Cam not paying her any attention and *definitely* bored of that stupid dork Sapphire, who was still here, hanging round like a bad smell. She'd deal with Sapphire later, but right now Madison needed a different game plan. She had to elevate herself above the competition.

Her friend Tiffani had started Facebooking her to see what she'd been up to. Madison had told her she was at a health spa in Europe, but Tiffani had a nose like a bloodhound and she wasn't buying it. There were only so many facials a girl could have.

After waving her cell around irritably – like, why couldn't Brad do something about the signal out here? – Madison finally found a bar by standing on a chair by the bathroom window. She dialled Tiffani's number and waited. The phone was snatched up after two rings.

'Madison! Oh my God. Chelsea and me were starting to think you'd *died* or something,'

'Oh, well, you know.'

'Stop being all mysterious. Where are you? Chelsea asked her mom about the place you told her you're staying at and it's, like, only five hundred dollars a night! *Total* Poorsville. So we know you're lying.'

Madison pulled a face. She'd plucked the name out of the air when Tifffani had asked her. She hoped it hadn't got out amongst too many of her friends.

'Tiff, can you keep a secret? I mean, a *big* secret? If it gets out it will be so, so bad!'

'Oh my God!' squealed Tiffani. 'You've totally just got a part in *The Hills*!'

'No, it's not that,' Madison said hastily. 'What I'm

about to tell you, you have to keep secret. Cross your heart?'

'Hope to die! Come on, Madison – tell me!'

'I *am* in Europe, but not Switzerland like I said. I'm in Capri.'

'In what?'

'Capri. It's an Italian *island*,' Madison said patronisingly, as if she'd known where it was before. She paused, milking the drama. 'The reason I'm here is because I'm staying at Brad Masters' private villa.'

Tiffani gave a sharp intake of breath. '*Brad Masters?* But why are you there?'

Madison savoured the moment. 'Because, dear Tiff, I've just found out he's my real dad!'

There was silence at the other end as Tiffani's brain struggled to take it all in.

'Shut *up*!'

'I'm, like, totally serious! I found out a couple weeks ago.'

'Oh my God, bitch!'

'Totally! But you have to swear not to tell anyone. If this gets out, it'll be, like, huge.'

'I'll take it to my grave. O.M.G, this is *way* beyond exciting!'

Madison crumpled up a page of her *Vogue*, making a crackling sound. 'Tiff, I'm losing you...' She pushed the red button and cut the call off. She gave a satisfied smile and looked out the window. Tiffani was the biggest rumour-slut on the Upper East Side. The story would be out there in hours.

Brad was in his study winding down. At the end of a long day he liked to flick through the news channels, check the markets and generally find out where he was at before starting all over again the next morning. Keeping tabs on Brad Masters Enterprises was a full-time job in itself.

He took another sip of his whisky and carried on channel-hopping. Sky, BBC, CNN... he'd just gone past Fox News when something familiar caught his eye. He switched back immediately. The blonde newsreader was standing outside Brad's New York offices with an excited expression on her face.

'*News just in that Brad Masters, the world's most famous bachelor, has a secret love child!*'

Brad went cold and put down his glass of whisky. The newsreader was in full flow.

'Fifty-year-old Brad Masters, one of the world's richest men, has always kept his private life away from the spotlight. But now we can reveal that he has a secret daughter. Nineteen-year-old Madison Vanderbilt was conceived when Brad, then a struggling producer, had an affair with her mother, Candy Vanderbilt, in the Eighties.'

The news programme cut to footage of Candy coming out of her apartment in huge sunglasses with a ratty dog under her arm. 'I've got nothing to say!' she shrieked, before adding, 'Make sure you get my best side.'

Brad groaned and covered his eyes. This was his worst nightmare. Someone was going to pay for it.

Madison wiped away the tear that had been trickling down her face. Her lessons with that acting coach had paid off. 'Honestly, Brad, I haven't told anyone anything,' she said, her voice wobbling convincingly. 'I have no idea how this happened!'

There was a loud buzzing noise outside and Brad went to look out the window. A Sky news helicopter was hovering overhead. His heart sank. He'd gone to every effort to make sure Casa Eleganza was his hideaway and it had been ruined in an instant. Anger burned in his throat. He pointed at the telephone on his desk.

'Ring your mother and find out what the hell is going on,' he snapped.

Madison went over to the phone and pretended to dial the number. 'Mom? It's me. Tell me you didn't do it!' She paused. 'Didn't tell everyone I was Brad's daughter, of course!' She waited another few seconds. 'I *cannot* believe you did that! I don't care how good the money was. I'm going now, Mother. Don't expect to hear from me for a long time.'

She slammed the phone down and turned and looked at Brad, eyes brimming. 'I'm so sorry, Brad. I don't know what to say.'

Another flash of anger went through Brad. That bloody Vanderbilt woman would do anything for money! Well, she'd broken the terms of their legal arrangement, so she wouldn't be getting another penny out of him. 'It's not your fault, Madison,' he said wearily. 'This does change everything, though.'

'Does it?' she asked hopefully. Brad nodded, grim-faced. He'd wanted this summer to get to know his daughters, without any interference or influence from the outside world. Now it had all been blown out of the water.

'I'm calling a meeting in thirty minutes,' he said grimly.

The atmosphere in the room was tense. Brad looked round at the three girls.

'I assume you all know what has happened by now.'

Madison blew into a handkerchief loudly.

'As you can guess, this is *not* an ideal situation. Not that I'm not proud to be Madison's father' – at this Madison lifted her eyes emotionally – 'but it just… complicates things. No one knows Cam is here either and that's the way I want to keep it. From now on, I don't want any of you having contact with the outside world. This may seem harsh, but it's the only way for the time being. Apart from your family, of course,' he added, seeing Sapphire's face.

He walked over to the window, where more

helicopters had appeared, whirring around like annoying mosquitoes.

'I've got security on to this, to sort out the press attention. It annoys me greatly, but we'll just have to deal with it. I've also asked all my staff to sign confidentiality agreements, to make sure nothing else gets out.'

He swung back to them. 'Simonetta and Sapphire, no one else knows that you are my daughters. I have every intention of protecting you as long as I can. I know how the press can turn your life upside-down and make it impossible to live normally. Pictures of Madison are already splashed everywhere.

Madison tried to look shocked. *Tiffani had better not put any of me out there with a double chin or I'll kill her!*

'Don't worry, I've got my press team on this to see how we can minimise it,' Brad assured her. 'But I would like you all to stay inside for the time being until we can make Casa Eleganza secure again. There are already boats full of paparazzi circling the harbour.'

He looked at them all. 'Is there anything you want to ask?'

'No, Brad,' they chorused.

Brad looked more kindly at Madison. 'I know it must be an awful shock for you, but we'll help you get through it.'

Madison put on a grateful expression. 'Thanks, Brad. I just can't believe my mom would *do* such a thing.' She wiped an imaginary tear away. 'Do you mind if I go now? I just need a bit of time to take it all in, y'know.'

'Of course, take all the time you want,' he said. Smiling bravely, Madison left the room. Once in the corridor, the smile turned evil. *Good work, bitch!* she congratulated herself. Now that it was out there, Brad would feel compelled to make her his heir. From now on, Simonetta and Sapphire had *no* chance.

chapter twenty-six

Maybe she was just being suspicious, but Sapphire had a feeling Madison was more involved with the news story breaking than she was making out. Madison had done a pretty good job of convincing Brad, though. Sapphire sighed. *However* it had got out, all this hoo-ha was a pain in the arse. Sapphire had already had to calm down her mum when Leonie phoned, panicking that Sapphire's identity was about to be revealed, and now to top it all off she was cooped up inside on a gorgeous day. The place had been swarming with security and it seemed they'd managed to get rid of most of the paparazzi hanging around, but Sapphire still wouldn't be surprised if someone got a long-lens picture of Madison 'accidentally' posing on a balcony or something.

Since she couldn't go outside, Sapphire decided to explore the rest of the house instead. It was so enormous, with so many sweeping corridors and rooms, she imagined it would take weeks to get to know every corner of it.

Half an hour later she had found an underground swimming pool, Brad's own private art gallery, and a sprawling air-conditioned garage that housed an amazing fleet of cars. Sapphire found herself wandering between the Rolls-Royce, the Bentley and the Ferrari, her eyes on stalks. There must be millions of pounds worth of stuff here! No wonder Brad had such tight security.

Sapphire tried the door of the Ferrari and, to her surprise, found that it wasn't locked. The temptation was too great. Looking round to make sure no one was watching, she climbed in. The leather seats were as soft as a baby's skin, and the mahogany dashboard gleamed like burnished gold.

'Sure beats the bus,' she told herself. The next moment she nearly jumped out of her skin when someone poked their head through the window.

'What are you doing in here?'

To Sapphire's dismay she saw it was Raphael, his chauffeur's hat and jacket off, his shirtsleeves rolled up.

'I, er…' In her haste to get out she banged her head on the door frame. 'Ouch!'

Raphael moved his hand as if to help her, but quickly dropped it again.

Shame-faced, she scrambled out. 'OK, you've totally busted me. I suppose you're going to tell Brad now, aren't you?'

'Why would I tell Brad?' he replied. 'Sitting in a car is hardly a crime, is it?'

'I just thought… oh, forget it.' Sapphire shook her head. 'I really can't work you out.'

Raphael stood watching her intently. Sapphire tried to outstare those hypnotic eyes, but she couldn't.

'Work me out?' he asked. His tone was still unfriendly, but not nearly as hostile as it had been. 'How could you work me out, English girl?'

Sapphire was getting tired of him calling her that. 'My name's Sapphire, actually.'

'Well, *Sapphire*,' he repeated, saying the name mockingly, 'how would you work me out?'

She shook her head again, unnerved by his sudden change in mood. 'I dunno.' Even though he wasn't as well-built as Cam, Raphael was taller and had a certain presence.

He cocked his head, those green eyes never straying from her face. 'And what am I to make of *you*, Sapphire?'

'I don't know and I don't care,' she said curtly.

Raphael's pale cheeks burned, as if she'd offended him.

'Anyway, I'd better be getting out of here,' she said hastily. But just then, something behind Raphael caught her eye.

'Is that a *Franklin* guitar?'

Raphael looked behind him. '*Si.*'

'That is so cool! Can I have a look?' Franklin

guitars were one of the most sought-after makes in the world, each one custom-made by hand. It was every musician's dream to own one.

Raphael hesitated. 'If you must.'

Sapphire rushed over to where the guitar was leaning against the wall. She picked it up as if she were handling priceless china, savouring the workmanship. 'I've always wanted one of these. Jerry, he's the guy whose music shop I work at, says they're really rare. Is this one old? It's in great condition.'

She looked up to see Raphael watching her, an odd look on his face.

'It was a family heirloom. From my father to me.'

'You've got a pretty cool dad,' she joked.

Raphael didn't smile. 'My father is dead.'

Sapphire's smile vanished. 'Oh, I'm sorry.' She'd had this with people all through her life – saying the wrong thing, offending them without meaning too. 'My dad's dead as well.' Then she remembered Brad Masters was her father and her stomach did a funny little drop. She had thought time would be a healer, but it still felt as raw as when she'd first found out.

Raphael stared at her knowingly, as if he could somehow read her mind. 'You want to play?' he asked. But Sapphire's face fell. Even with a guitar as beautiful as this she'd be no good. The words to "Boy" danced through her head. If she could just get them out... 'How about your song from the other day?' Raphael continued.

Sapphire started. 'How did you...?' *Has he been spying on me?* Uncomfortable, she gave the guitar back to him. 'I should be going.'

Raphael didn't reply. Once again his face was devoid of emotion. What was it with this guy? He didn't seem to care about awkward silences. Eventually he spoke.

'You are having trouble with your melodies.'

'Did Brad tell you that?' Sapphire asked, annoyed they'd been talking about her behind her back.

Raphael shrugged. 'It doesn't matter. I can help you, if you like.'

'Yeah, well...' Sapphire's pride was about to tell Raphael where to stick it, but Brad's voice came into her mind. *You should ask Raphael for help with your melodies, he's a rare talent.*

'Why do you suddenly want to help me?' she asked bluntly. 'After all, you haven't exactly been friendly up till now.'

Raphael's eyes flashed angrily. 'Do you want my help or not?'

'All right, I was just saying!' she said hurriedly. As unsettling as she found Raphael, she knew she needed him.

He flashed her a challenging look. 'Now go, and leave me to work. You know where to find me.'

As Sapphire walked out into the bright sunlight she was shaking with anger. That was the second time Raphael had dismissed her as if she were an inferior being. If they couldn't even communicate in a civil manner, how the hell were they going to make music together?

chapter
twenty-seven

Madison was feeling very pleased with herself. The story about her being Brad Masters' daughter was still huge in America, while thousands of miles away in Capri she could sit and play the wide-eyed innocent act and have everyone fall for it. She had seen Sapphire give her a funny look in Brad's study, but the runt wasn't stupid enough to cross her and start blabbing. Besides, if the worst happened and she did get found out, Madison would do what she'd always done. Completely deny it and point the finger of blame at someone else.

It was *killing* her not being able to call her friends and discuss how fabulous she was, but it was a small price to pay for the day that Brad revealed her as his heir. Her mother had been frantically calling, saying they were being offered good money for Madison to tell her story, but Madison was ignoring her. She was only interested in hundreds of millions now, not hundreds of thousands. She wasn't worried about her mom denying she'd leaked the story, either. Candy was such an attention-whore that nobody would believe her anyway.

Business taken care of, Madison decided to pay Cam a visit. Now that the news was out that she was the boss's daughter, she'd have no trouble hooking up with him. Maybe it could even be written into his contract or something? She gave a little self-satisfied smile. Oh my God, she and Cam would make, like, the *hottest* couple!

When she got to the guesthouse, loud rap music was blasting out of the window. She knocked on the door and got no answer, but decided to go in anyway.

She stood in the hallway, looking around. The music seemed to be coming from upstairs.

'Cam?' she called. 'It's Madison. Are you here?' There was no answer, so Madison started to climb the stairs, admiring her reflection in every mirror she passed.

Upstairs, huge bedrooms led off a mosaic-tiled landing. Madison poked her head into one and saw it had a sunken Jacuzzi in one corner. She smiled. She and Cam could *so* have fun in that.

The music was coming from the bedroom across the landing. Madison pushed the door open. It was even bigger than the first room, with clothes lying on the chaise longue, a pile of magazines by the bed and a huge sound system pumping so hard the room reverberated. Madison moved round, picking up bottles of aftershave and expensive skin products. This was obviously Cam's room. But where was he? She was finding it hard to think with this racket. As she turned the music down, Madison heard a voice singing from behind another door in the corner of the room. It must be the en suite…

Madison walked over and knocked. 'Cam? It's me, Madison.'

No answer. *He totally wants me to walk in on him.*

Slowly, Madison turned the handle and pulled the door open. Steam wafted out and suddenly the glorious sight of Cam, soaping himself in the shower, confronted her. He had his back to her and Madison stood and savoured the view. Cam's body was even better with all his clothes off. His butt was hard and firm and, as she watched, water cascaded down his muscular legs, running in between his inner thighs.

'My, oh my,' Madison said softly. Licking her lips, she walked over and tapped lightly on the screen. Cam swung round violently.

'Jesus H. Christ!' Cam peered through the screen. 'Madison, is that you? You nearly gave me a frickin' heart attack!'

Her eyes strayed downwards through the steamed-up glass.

'I just came to say hello.' She looked at him provocatively.

Cam shook his head in disbelief. 'Can you pass me a towel?'

She pulled a fluffy white one off the chrome towel rack. Cam opened the shower door slightly and stuck

242

his hand out. 'It's all right,' she said, turning her head away. 'I'm not looking!'

Now that's a lie.

Moments later Cam stepped out, the towel wrapped round his waist. He shot her an amused look. 'Do you normally come into a guy's bathroom like this?'

'Why, don't you want me here?' she pouted.

Cam laughed. 'It's not every day I get a hot blonde to pass me my towel.' Madison glowed at the compliment. Cam pulled another towel off the rack to dry his hair, before putting it round his shoulders.

The air was still hot and steamy. Madison leaned back on the marble sink unit and smiled. Her see-through Matthew Williamson kaftan covered about as much flesh as Cam's towel. 'Isn't this cosy,' she breathed. She moved forwards and trailed a long talon across Cam's chest.

He raised an eyebrow. 'Madison…'

'Don't say a word.' She stepped behind him and trailed another finger across his wide, muscled back. Their eyes met in the bathroom mirror. 'How about it, R&B boy?' she said. Cam turned round and Madison closed her eyes. Any moment now he was going to kiss her...

Suddenly, she heard Cam cough. She opened her eyes, to see him standing by the bathroom door. He looked at her apologetically.

'Madison, you're a sexy chick, but I don't think we should go there.'

'What?'

Cam shrugged. 'It would just be too... difficult.' *What I mean is it would be more hassle than it's worth.*

Madison put one hand on her hip. 'Er, hello? Haven't you heard the news? I'm Brad Masters' daughter!'

Cam had heard the news, but he had enough money of his own not to be impressed. He shook his head. 'Still no, sorry.' He wasn't stupid enough to get caught with the boss's daughter. Brad was a powerful guy and he could knock Cam down just as easily as he had made him. Cam knew how it worked.

Madison looked outraged. 'I can't believe you're blowing me off!'

'I'm sure you can find some other dude to blow

off. Jeez, I'm only joking!' he added as his electric toothbrush came flying across the room and he jumped to dodge it. Madison stood there, hands on her hips, face furious.

'Are you calling me a *whore*?'

'Madison, calm down! It was a joke.' He watched it compute through her brain. Then she smiled.

'I know what it really is, Cam. Don't worry, I won't tell anyone. It's our little secret.'

'Tell anyone what?' he asked, puzzled.

'That you're intimidated by me, of course! Not only am I hot, I'm about to become more loaded than Donald Trump. It's too much for you, isn't it? You don't want me to steal your limelight.'

Cam fought to keep the laughter back. 'Madison, what planet are you on? You just offered yourself to me on a plate!'

Her face became cross again. 'I did *not*! Like, in your *dreams*, Cam Tyler.'

Cam sighed. 'Whatever. Can you get out now, please?'

Madison looked scandalised. 'You're throwing me out?'

Cam considered. 'Pretty much, yeah. But it's been very pleasant.'

Madison stormed past him, leaving a trail of musky perfume in her wake. She'd got halfway across the bedroom before Cam called out, 'Madison, wait!'

She stopped in her tracks, smiling. She'd known he couldn't resist her. She turned round seductively. 'Yes, Cam?'

'Sapphire left one of her earrings here the other night – it must have fallen off. It's in the kitchen. Can you take it back and give it to her?'

'Sapphire was *here*?' Madison looked as if she'd swallowed a fart. 'What was she doing?'

'Same as you, visiting.'

Madison didn't want to even *know* how Sapphire had lost her earring. Probably making out on the sofa with Cam, the little slut! She gritted her teeth. There was no way she was going to show Cam how much Sapphire got under her skin. She gave a false smile. 'Sure, why not?'

Cam grinned. 'Thanks, Madison, that's good of you. And about us…'

'What us? I was only screwing with you.' She

started to make her way down the stairs, giving her butt a wiggle for good measure to let Cam see what he was missing out on. In the kitchen she saw the silver hoop earring lying on the worktop. Madison picked it up; it was complete crap like the rest of Sapphire's things. As she stormed out through the front door, Madison flung the earring as far as she could into the undergrowth. Who needed a boyfriend like Cam Tyler anyway? When she was rich and famous beyond her wildest dreams, she could have any goddamn guy she wanted.

chapter
twenty-eight

'Brad!' The confident voice made him turn round. Walking towards him in a flowing leopard-print dress was Simonetta. Her tall, lean form moved seamlessly, as if she were on a catwalk. Brad had seen a lot of beautiful women in his time, but Simonetta was on another level. *I wonder if I'm biased because she's my daughter,* he thought wryly. He felt an odd sense of pride and regret.

'Do you have a moment?' she asked.

Brad held up his headphones and briefcase. 'I haven't got long. I'm flying off to Milan for a conference. Can we talk later?'

'It is better like this, when you are on your own.' Simonetta gave a dismissive shrug. 'Otherwise there are too many *people* around.'

By 'people', Brad guessed she meant Sapphire and Madison. 'I can spare five minutes. What is it you want to talk about?'

Simonetta held up the folder she had been carrying under her arm. 'I have been thinking about ways we can make Giuseppe a global brand. With your business acumen and my contacts and profile, we could make a success of it. That I am sure of.'

'That's very encouraging to hear, Simonetta.' Brad paused delicately. 'But do you think you have the right experience?'

She shrugged, as if it were a minor detail. 'I have a good brain, you can teach me the rest.'

'What about your modelling?'

'What, do you think because I am a model I have no intelligence?'

'No, that's not it.'

Simonetta smiled dryly. 'I think the two go well together. Beauty is power, Brad.'

Brad was impressed by her self-assurance. He held out his hand. 'Let me have a look through your ideas. I'll let you know what I think.'

She surveyed him through half-closed eyes that were bright and intelligent. '*Si*, that is good.' She leaned over and straighten his tie. 'Now you can go. *Ciao*, Brad.'

Brad watched her walk off, feeling as if *he'd* been dismissed rather than the other way round. He gave a chuckle.

Sapphire lifted her hand to knock at the door, but it was suddenly pulled open. 'Oh!' She jumped back. Raphael stood in the doorway. She tried a tentative smile, which wasn't returned.

'Look, if it's a bad time I can come back,' she said. She'd *known* this was a bad idea! But to her surprise, Raphael stood back.

'Come in.'

Hesitating, Sapphire crossed over the threshold into Raphael's little house. He pointed to a door – the living-room door, she remembered, from the time he'd caught her snooping around. 'In there.'

Don't kill yourself with the niceties, Sapphire thought. Had this guy no manners? She swallowed the irritation Raphael always brought out in her. He would help her with the melody and then she'd be out of there. Sapphire wondered if Brad had specifically asked Raphael to help her. He was Raphael's boss, after all – it wasn't like Raphael could refuse. And he didn't exactly look over the moon that Sapphire was here.

The living-room was just as bare as it had been the last time – a few bits of furniture stranded in the middle of the floor and the Franklin guitar leaning against the wall. Raphael didn't ask her to sit down, so she hovered uncomfortably.

'You have some lyrics you want to start with?' he said.

With some reluctance, Sapphire handed over the words to "Boy". Raphael took the piece of paper and read it intently.

Sapphire blushed, embarrassed that he was reading some of her most intimate thoughts. But

Raphael didn't look at her. He just went and got the guitar. He sat down on the only chair in the room, an uncomfortable-looking stool.

'Sing the first line to me,' he commanded. 'The one you sang the other day.'

Sapphire suddenly felt *really* stupid. What she wanted to do was snatch the paper out of his hand and get out of there, but there was something compelling about Raphael that made her stop.

'It's not very good—' she started.

'I didn't ask if it was good. I asked you to sing it.'

'All right!' she retorted, stung by his rudeness. Hesitantly, she took a deep breath and opened her mouth. The first line flowed out of her mouth like it always did.

'Boy, you came along one day...'

Then nothing.

She stopped, feeling stupid. 'That's about as far as I ever get.'

'Sing it again,' Raphael told her. He seemed to be concentrating heavily, like he was in another world. Sapphire started again.

'Boy, you came along one day...'

Suddenly, Raphael started strumming gently, his voice cutting in over hers as he sang the lyrics from the page.

'Saw you from a distance...
Boy, you came along and changed my world
Without even knowing it.'

His voice was rich and knowing, transforming the words into something bluesy and beautiful. Despite herself, Sapphire clapped her hands together in excitement.

'That's it! You've totally got it.'

Raphael stared at her. 'It was there already. You just had to *hear* it. Now again.'

Waiting for his cue, Sapphire opened her mouth and started to sing, quietly at first, then stronger. Their voices seemed to instantly mould together.

'Boy, you came along one day
Saw you from a distance...
Boy, you came along and changed my world
Without even knowing it.'

The air had become electric, like they had discovered something special. They stared at each other. As usual, Sapphire was the first to break eye contact. She swallowed. 'Raphael, that was amazing. How did you just *get* it like that?'

'I've told you. Have confidence in yourself. Just *feel* the music.' His look turned slightly contemptuous. 'This boy, was he special?'

Sapphire went bright red. 'It was just someone,' she mumbled.

Raphael sighed irritably. 'You English. You are so uptight.'

She'd had enough of his little comments. 'All right, mate!' she shot back sharply. Was he trying to humiliate her on purpose or what?

Raphael looked at her with a faint gleam of amusement in his eyes. 'Are you angry with me?'

'Yes, I am!'

'*Finalmente*, we have some passion! From the start, one, two, three...'

chapter
twenty-nine

Simonetta deleted the voicemail and stared out of her bedroom window. It had been the lettings agency who looked after her apartment in Rome, complaining that the rent hadn't been paid for the second month running. They were threatening legal action and worse. Only yesterday, Simonetta had received another voicemail, this time from her bank about the size of her overdraft. Regretfully, due to her current financial situation they were unable to raise the limit as she had requested. And, the bank manager asked, did she know she had a large Visa bill that still had not been paid? As he had been unable to get hold of her and she hadn't replied to any of the letters he'd sent, he would be forced to pass the matter on to the relevant authorities. *Which, put another way, means he's calling in the debt collectors,* she thought.

At least she wouldn't be there if they did turn up.

It had been a trying few days. Lexi was threatening to cut Simonetta loose from Models Italia if she didn't get in touch and fulfil her contractual obligations. Quite the turnaround from her initial excitement about Brad Masters! It wasn't even as if the agency were getting her well-paid work. Simonetta sighed. Didn't these people get it? All she was doing was building a better life for herself and then she'd pay them back, ten times back if she felt like it. The bank manager, Lexi: they had probably come from nice, middle-class families where they didn't have to share a bedroom with their four sisters or get teased at school for wearing handmade clothes. *They* didn't have a mother who had been worked to the bone as a domestic slave, or a lazy, layabout father who'd been off work with a 'bad back' for years and given his family nothing.

Simonetta turned and looked round the room. The Hermès scarf draped over the dressing table chair, the Missoni maxi-dress hanging on the wardrobe door. If anyone came in now and had to guess what kind of person she was, they would say someone rich, beautiful and successful. One of the elite. Which was why Simonetta had to have the best apartment in town, the most expensive designer clothes.

She still remembered the day she had joined the modelling agency, when she had mispronounced a designer's name and two models in reception had made fun of her. *Listen to the country bumpkin*, they'd sneered. *You'd better sharpen up your act if you want to make it in this business.*

Si, the other had said. *Getting some new clothes would be a start!*

If they'd expected Simonetta to cry, they had been disappointed. Holding her head up with as much dignity as she could muster, she had walked out. It was only in the street that she let herself feel hurt and embarrassed. She had stopped and looked at herself in a shop window. The girls, bitchy though they were, had been right: Simonetta had looked exactly what she was – a small-town girl in a cheap dress.

Right then, Simonetta had got her Visa card out, the one her *mamma* had made her promise she'd only use in emergencies, and gone shopping. Soon her wardrobe was bursting with Valentino, Cavalli, four-thousand dollar YSL handbags. Her savings were soon gone. Another credit card followed, and then another. It was ironic – the more in debt she got and the more well-dressed, the more people wanted to give her things. When she'd swept into her exclusive apartment block, the lettings agent had practically begged her to take the keys off them. It was a different story now.

Simonetta stared, unseeing, into the distance. All this debt business, it was so *undignified*. The thought of having to return to her village, shamed and in debt, filled her with horror. There was no way she could go back now, it would kill her.

But Simonetta was a survivor. The quicker Brad announced she was his heir, the better.

It didn't even cross her mind that she wouldn't be chosen.

Madison eyed Sapphire through her Ray-Bans. She took in the cheap swimsuit, the long hair pulled back in a boring ponytail, the look on the English girl's stupid freckled face as she read yet another book. Sapphire's earring came back into her mind – the one Madison had thrown into the hedge. Did Cam *really* prefer the runt to her? Madison had to find out, it was killing her. Getting up from her sunlounger, she walked over to where Sapphire was sitting.

'Hi, Sapphire!' she said, in an over-friendly voice.

Sapphire looked up. 'Hi, Madison,' she said warily. The two had been treading very carefully around each other since the Charlotte Island incident and it had suited Sapphire just fine.

Madison looked at the chair next to Sapphire. 'May I?'

Sapphire shrugged. 'Please yourself.'

Madison sighed in contentment. 'Awesome day, isn't it?'

'Awesome,' Sapphire said. *What was Madison up to?* She soon found out.

'So I hear you and Cam are getting pretty friendly!'

Sapphire went red. 'Who told you that?'

'Oh, I was just round there the other night and he mentioned it, said you've been hanging out together.'

'I just went over to say thank you,' Sapphire muttered.

'Don't get all shy about it! Of course, he's not my type, otherwise we'd be dating by now.' Madison leaned in conspiratorially. 'So, do you want to hook up with him?'

'No!'

'Come on, we're sisters. You can tell me.'

Sapphire hesitated. It would be good to talk to someone about Cam. It was sending her crazy thinking about him the whole time. 'He is quite cute,' she admitted.

'You are *so* adorable! Do you think he likes you?'

Sapphire shrugged with embarrassment. 'I don't know.'

'So you guys haven't made out or anything?' Madison persisted.

Sapphire went even redder. 'No, of course we haven't!'

'Don't get your panties in a twist,' Madison replied. She was feeling a lot better. She might not have hooked up with Cam *this* time, but she'd got a far more important thing. Information. From now on she was going to make damn sure she knew everything the runt was getting up to. She stood up. 'Must get back to my sunbathing. Ciao for now!' Leaving a bemused-looking Sapphire, she sauntered off.

chapter thirty

Despite looking out for him, Sapphire hadn't seen Cam for a few days. She was too shy to go and see him again and instead consoled herself with imagining what could have happened if Tito hadn't turned up. Her stomach felt sick with nerves and desire at the thought of Cam slowly peeling off her wet clothes and taking her in his arms. Sapphire wondered what it would be like to kiss him, run her hands over his chiselled body, have him touch his lips to her neck…

But in between her dreams about Cam, Sapphire found Raphael creeping into her thoughts. Although she would never had given him the satisfaction, she had come away from her lesson on cloud nine. Despite his arrogance, Raphael had shown surprising patience in helping her get the melody to 'Boy' right. It was as if a light had been switched on and, for the first time in ages, Raphael had made her look forward to picking up her guitar. Now the floodgates of inspiration had opened, Sapphire found herself wanting more.

He took longer to come to the door this time. She took a deep breath.

'Er, hi. Hope I'm not disturbing you. I was wondering if we could practise a bit?'

Her words caught in her throat a little. Raphael's eyes were so green they were almost hypnotic. As the light caught them, Sapphire could see those strange golden flecks again. *They're like a lion's eyes,* she thought, with a shiver.

'No,' he said.

Sapphire's cheeks flushed a dull red. 'Sorry, I'll come another time,' she mumbled and turned away.

'No, I meant you are not bothering me. Come in.'

Sapphire stared at him in disbelief, but he disappeared back inside, leaving her to follow. This time he went into the little kitchenette that backed on to the living-room. He turned round abruptly. 'Can I get you anything? Tea, coffee? I am sorry, but I do not have any beer.' His lips curled into a sarcastic smile. 'I hear that is what you like to drink with Cam.'

Sapphire went numb. '*What* did you just say?' she asked. Raphael didn't answer. 'I'll just have water,' she said, not wanting to pursue the subject any more. How the hell did he know anyway?

'So what is it you want to do?' Raphael asked, when he returned to the living-room. Sapphire shrugged, suddenly feeling self-conscious. 'I thought we could practise "Boy" again.'

'You don't need me for that now,' he said bluntly. 'Do you have anything else to show me?'

'Anything else?' Sapphire couldn't help but smile. She handed him the notepad full of her lyrics from the last year. 'How about one of these?'

He flicked open the notepad and raised his eyebrows. 'OK, let's get started.'

Three hours later they were still going. Raphael was relentless, picking out different lyrics she'd written and bringing them to life. With music as their communicator, the unspoken tension between them seemed to disappear. As Sapphire watched Raphael, his long, elegant fingers moving deftly on his guitar, she couldn't help but be fascinated. All the hatred and moodiness seemed to be ironed out of his face, to be replaced by something calm and almost otherworldly. For the first time she noticed the fullness of his lower lip, the razor-sharpness of his cheekbones.

Raphael looked up, as if aware of her gaze. 'What?'

'Did Brad put you up to this?' she asked tentatively.

He frowned. 'Put me up?'

'I mean... did he ask you to do this?' She waved her hand round. 'To help me. I can't think why you would otherwise.'

'Then you are wrong,' he muttered.

'Hey, I didn't mean to sound ungrateful. It's just that...' Sapphire trailed off, not sure how to say it. In the end, she came straight out with it. 'Why did you hate me so much when we first met? Had I done something to offend you?'

If she'd thought Raphael couldn't get any paler, she'd been wrong. 'You do not understand,' he said abruptly. His face was suddenly back to its normal impenetrable self.

Sapphire stood up, feeling awkward. 'I didn't mean to upset you.'

Raphael gestured towards the door. 'We are finished for today.'

Sapphire gripped her guitar. This was so embarrassing! 'Raphael, I'm really sorry if you're offended.'

He looked at her in a way she couldn't work out. 'You may have got that impression, but I don't *hate* you. It is just... difficult.'

Sapphire didn't know what to say. *What* was difficult? They barely knew each other.

'Uh, OK,' she mumbled eventually. 'I should get going.'

Wordlessly, Raphael followed her to the door. As he towered above her, she realised once again how tall he was. How *powerful* he was, under that pale skin and lean muscle.

'As you wish,' he said. He sounded so offish that Sapphire was about to tell him to get stuffed, when a familiar voice greeted her ears.

'Well *hi* there, Sapphire. You do get around!' Madison was walking up the path in wedge heels and a tiny bikini.

'Who do we have here, then?' She'd seen the weirdo boy around, but up close he was quite attractive. In a kind of Edward Cullen, undead way. She fluttered her eyelashes but got no response. Offended, she turned her attention to Sapphire instead. 'So, what are you guys *up* to? It all looks very cosy.'

Sapphire flushed. 'Raphael is helping me with my music, that's all.'

Madison smiled knowingly. 'If you say so! I'm off to the pool. I *swear* I'm not as brown as I was yesterday. I'll leave you two to enjoy... your privacy.'

Sapphire stared at Madison's retreating back in

disbelief. Why did she always have to stir up trouble?

She turned back to Raphael. 'Thanks for today. I really enjoyed—'

She stopped. The front door had been shut in her face. Madison stopped, and turned to cock her head at Sapphire patronisingly.

'Lovers' tiff? I just can't keep up with you, Sapphire.'

'I told you, he's just helping me with my music!' Sapphire resisted the urge to smash her guitar over Madison's head. Even if it wasn't a Franklin, it was the only one she had.

It was a baking-hot day, the kind of day that turned tarmac to treacle and swimming pools into gigantic warm baths. Even the birds had stopped their chirping and retreated away from the heat, as Madison lay round the swimming pool motionless under a layer of Kiehl's factor 15 sunscreen. Her body glistened with a fine layer of oil and perspiration.

To anyone watching, it might have seemed that she was sound asleep, but behind the huge Chanel sunglasses her brain was scheming furiously. She thought about Sapphire's earring in Cam's kitchen, about her so-called 'guitar lessons' with that moody Italian boy with the Edward Cullen cheekbones.

Suddenly Madison sat up, disturbing the stillness of the afternoon.

'I have, like, *totally* got it!' Grabbing her sarong, she jumped up to go and find Simonetta. *That Sapphire bitch is history*, she thought.

chapter thirty-one

Simonetta raised an eyebrow. 'You're crazy. It will never work. By the way, do you know you've got horrible sunglasses marks?' They were sitting in the coolness of one of the terraces. It was here Madison had found Simonetta, reading the latest Italian *Vogue*.

For once Madison didn't run screaming to the toilet to look. She had far bigger things on her mind. 'We'll never know unless we try,' she urged. 'C'mon,

Simonetta! This will deal with the runt once and for all. It's an *awesome* plan.'

Simonetta eyed Madison carefully. As long as Madison did all the dirty work and Simonetta didn't get implicated, she didn't really care. And once Sapphire was out of the way, there would be only Madison to remove from the game. Simonetta wasn't stupid enough to think that Madison wouldn't turn her attention to her once Sapphire was out of the picture, but she'd deal with that when the time came. She had no doubt she would be chosen as Brad's heir, but it was better to be safe than sorry.

She sat up, interest taking hold. '*Si,* I will help. Tell me once again what I have to do.'

Madison's eyes gleamed. 'You betcha.'

After the disastrous end to their last session, Sapphire didn't reckon on seeing Raphael again. But to her surprise, he came and sought her out on the beach the very next day. Without saying hello he dropped down next to her on the sand, his long legs folded in front of him. He was wearing shorts and a faded linen shirt rolled up at the sleeves. Sapphire noticed that despite being about the same age as Cam, Raphael didn't seem to go in for fashion or labels.

Raphael looked out to sea, his dark curls ruffling in the breeze. He didn't seem in a hurry to say anything so Sapphire thought she should.

'Uh, I never got the chance to say thank you yesterday,' she said. 'It was really good of you to take time out to help me.'

Raphael shrugged dismissively. 'It is not just for you. The practice helps me as well.'

Sapphire felt a bit stung by his words. Even if it was true, he didn't have to say it like that.

Raphael seemed to pick up on her silence and glanced sideways at her, before looking out to sea again. 'So who was this boy you wrote about in your song?'

'Just some guy I knew.'

'Tell me about him,' Raphael said. It was more of a command than a request.

Sapphire blushed, out of irritation as well as embarrassment. 'I'd rather not, actually.'

Raphael turned to her, eyes mocking. 'What, did

he steal your little English heart and run away with it?'

'No, he didn't, actually!' she snapped. A look of triumph crossed Raphael's face, as though he actually *enjoyed* winding her up.

They sat in silence for a while, until Sapphire spoke. 'OK, it was someone I fancied.' She sighed. 'You want to know the funny part? I never even said hello to him. It was this guy I used to see on my way home. I called him Trainer Boy because he was always wearing these really cool trainers.' Sapphire sighed. 'I kind of became a bit obsessed with him, but I never even had the guts to go and say hello.' She paused. 'You probably think I'm really weird.'

'Perhaps we are all weird in our own way,' he said mysteriously.

Death and destruction, the words came back into her mind. Was that what he was talking about? She had to stop thinking about it, it was freaking her out! Instead, encouraged by this almost-conversation with the usually monosyllabic Italian, Sapphire decided to ask a more personal question. 'How about you? Do you have a girlfriend?'

Instantly, she knew she'd said the wrong thing. Dark storm clouds rolled into Raphael's eyes and his jaw clenched like granite.

'No.'

From the tone of his voice, Sapphire knew not to push it any further. She wondered what had happened. Had he fallen for some Italian beauty like Simonetta and had his heart smashed to pieces?

'I should go,' Raphael said. He jumped up.

'Raphael, wait!' Sapphire got to her feet and faced him. He was head and shoulders above her, his pale face and body at odds with the golden sunlight and sand.

'Can't we just be friends?' she said awkwardly. 'We seem to argue every time we meet and it's getting stupid.'

'Stupid?' he repeated, in a not-unfriendly tone.

Sapphire bit her lip. 'Yeah, you know what I mean. It's just that…' She trailed off, feeling uncomfortable.

'Just that what?' he asked.

Sapphire laughed. 'Are you going to repeat everything I say?'

A faint smile tugged at the corner of Raphael's

mouth. Sapphire shook her head self-consciously, not knowing where to start.

'This is going to sound really cheesy,' she said, 'but you've really inspired me. I thought I had fallen out of love with music, but you've made me believe in myself again.' She swallowed, working up the courage. 'If you don't mind, I'd really like to carry on our sessions.'

He was silent.

Cringe, thought Sapphire. *He's going to tell me to get lost.*

His golden eyes looked down at her. 'Come and see me tomorrow. Five o'clock.'

'Really?' Sapphire broke into a huge smile. 'That's great! I have loads of new ideas to show you already.' She stuck out a tentative hand. 'Are we friends then?'

For a moment she didn't think he was going to take it, but then Raphael reached out and took her hand in his. His hand was cool and firm, like shaking hands with a marble statue.

'Until tomorrow.' He started to walk away across the sand.

'Bye!' Sapphire called after him. Without turning back, Raphael lifted his hand briefly and then dropped it again.

Well, she thought, *I can't say we're best buddies yet, but it's a start.*

chapter thirty-two

Sapphire was in the kitchen of the huge villa. Even though Casa Eleganza was beautiful, she somehow preferred the back rooms of the mansion, where staff worked and lived together. The enormous kitchen, with freshly baked bread sitting on the counter and cooks bustling around, reminded Sapphire a bit of home. It made her feel warm and comforted.

Today she and Maggie were perched at the big wooden table in the middle of the room, drinking tea and eating delicious homemade biscuits. Maggie looked across the table at her.

'Are you sure you wouldn't rather be out in the sun with Madison and Simonetta? Us oldies aren't very interesting, you know.'

Sapphire smiled. 'I'd much rather be in here with you.'

Maggie gave her a perceptive look. 'How are you all getting along? I know what girls can be like!'

Sapphire shrugged. 'To be honest, I don't think we're each other's kind of people.' *That's putting it mildly.*

'It's going to take some getting used to, my dear. Don't expect it to come overnight.'

'What, the fact that we're sisters?' Sapphire still felt funny saying the word; she'd spent most of her life assuming she was an only child. 'How long have you known, Maggie?' she asked. 'About us, I mean.'

Just then, one of the cooks came over, frowning. 'Maggie, that tiramisu I made tonight for dinner has disappeared!'

Maggie frowned. 'What do you mean?'

The cook shrugged helplessly. 'I left it in the fridge

overnight, and now it has gone. Someone must have taken it!'

Maggie looked cross. 'I bet it's the gardeners – they've got the devil of a sweet tooth. I'll be having a word with them.' The cook nodded and scurried back to the stove.

'We've got a food thief round here,' Maggie told Sapphire. 'Things keep going missing – the other day it was a whole lump of cheese Cook was going to use for the lasagne.' She took a sip of tea. 'Anyway, I digress. Where were we?'

'You were about to say how long you'd known about Brad being my father,' Sapphire told her.

Maggie sighed. 'A long time, my love. Too long, probably.'

'Why didn't he tell us before?' Sapphire asked.

Maggie smiled. 'I think he wanted to wait until you were a bit older, so you could cope with it better. Turning fifty was a big milestone for him. At that age in life you start to reassess things.'

Sapphire looked thoughtful. 'Does he talk to you, Maggie? About emotional stuff and things?'

'Brad tells me what he wants to.' She smiled again.

'He's very private, always has been. I know enough though.'

Sapphire wondered if they'd had any discussions about her. The thought made her feel a bit sick. Maggie would *definitely* not approve of the Charlotte Island drama. She dunked her biscuit in her tea, waiting until it got really soggy.

'I haven't seen much of Brad lately,' Sapphire said hesitantly. 'I thought we were getting on really well at the start, but now I don't really know.'

Maggie's eyes were sharp and intelligent. 'He's a very busy man, Sapphire.'

'I know that,' she sighed. 'It's just that…' She shook her head. 'Forget it.'

'Is money important to you?' Maggie asked suddenly.

Sapphire was a bit taken aback by the question. 'Um, not really. As long as I've got enough to get by, I suppose.'

Maggie took another sip of tea. 'It'll be a big responsibility, Sapphire, taking on all that money. Would you be ready for it?'

Sapphire decided to be straight with her. 'Honestly,

Maggie? I just don't know. I know that's probably not the right thing to say, but that's how I feel.' She gave a small smile. 'Don't tell Brad, will you?'

The housekeeper smiled back. 'My lips are sealed. And for what it's worth, I think you're a very sensible young woman.'

Sapphire didn't feel very sensible, though. Her longing to see Cam was growing by the day. She'd started the journey to the guesthouse so many times, only to bottle out halfway there. She was *sure* there had been chemistry between them last time, but what if she had imagined it? What if she was making a total fool of herself going round there again?

Finally, her brain could take no more. She had to go and see Cam otherwise she would drive herself crazy thinking about it. If it was obvious she was interrupting, she would say she'd just been passing. Passing on the way to what, she didn't want to think about.

There were a few clouds in the sky now, giving a brief respite from the scorching sun. Sapphire had to admit she was looking pretty healthy. Her skin was tanned to a light caramel, while her hair had little blonde streaks round her face. She had far too many freckles, in her opinion – but hey, Cam had said he liked them. She'd even taken the plunge – literally – and was wearing a pretty little sundress with a low-cut front. As she approached Cam's, Sapphire thought she would have never have had the confidence to wear something like this in London. The thought made her feel good.

To her disappointment the house appeared quiet and lifeless. Sapphire tried the doorbell anyway and heard it clang into silence. She turned to go and noticed Cam had left one of his tops lying on the terrace. Sapphire went over and picked it up. Without really thinking, she brought it up to her nose to smell it. Her tummy did a funny little flip as Cam's aftershave filled her nostrils. She breathed in again, this time more deeply. Just smelling it was doing strange things to her...

'Hello there! Who are you then?'

The voice made her jump a mile in the air. Sapphire swung round guiltily and dropped the top. A thirty-something man was walking towards her, a smile on his face. Sapphire noticed he had a high-tech camera hanging round his neck.

'I'm Sapphire.'

'Sapphire who?' said the man, grinning. He had an English accent.

'Sapphire Ste—' She bit her tongue. Not that she had much experience of them, but Sapphire thought the man looked like a paparazzi.

'Er, I'm just staying here. I'm a guest.'

'Madison about, is she?' the man said, his eyes darting all over the place.

Sapphire started to feel uncomfortable, like she was doing something wrong. 'Look, I don't mean to be rude, but I don't really think you should be here. It's private property.'

Flash! The bright light took her by surprise. When it faded from her eyes Sapphire blinked. 'Oi, you can't take my picture!'

'I just did,' grinned the man. *Flash!* 'Just a few more,' he called.

'I said STOP!' she shouted.

The man held his hand up. 'All right! Didn't mean to upset you.' He fumbled in his pocket and brought out a card. 'If you see Madison, give her this, will you? Tell her I'll be expecting her call.'

Sapphire looked at the business card he'd handed her. It had the words *Terry Blake, freelance photographer* across the middle, and a mobile number in the corner.

'I think you'd better go,' she said.

Brad sighed irritably. 'Where did you say this guy was again?'

'By Cam's house. I was just passing,' Sapphire added hastily.

Brad stared at her for a good five seconds before turning away. 'And you say this guy was looking for Madison?'

'Yeah, he gave me that business card. But I didn't give it to her. I came straight to you.'

Brad glanced up from the card. 'I suppose that's one good thing. At least we know who we're dealing with.'

They were in Brad's private living-room, which Sapphire hadn't been in before. To her surprise it was quite small and cosy, very different from the rest of the house. A black-and-white photograph of a young woman hung on the wall. It looked very old-fashioned and Sapphire guessed it must be Brad's mother. She had been very beautiful, with the same dark hair and refined face as Brad.

Brad noticed her looking. 'My mother, Charlotte,' he said abruptly.

Of course. Charlotte as in Charlotte Island.

'She's beautiful,' Sapphire said. 'She looks very happy too.' *That's my grandmother*, she thought. It was a weird idea.

'Hmm,' said Brad. It was obvious he didn't want to talk about his mother, and Sapphire fell quiet.

Not wanting to meet Brad's eyes, she continued to scan the walls. There was another picture of a young woman, standing by a huge sunflower. This one was in colour but, by the style of the clothes, Sapphire reckoned it must have been taken in the late seventies or early eighties. The woman was throwing back her head and laughing, long brown hair tumbling down her back. There was something vaguely familiar about her – was she an actress or something? *I know I've seen that woman before…*

But just then, Sapphire felt Brad's eyes on her and quickly looked away.

'I'll get straight on to my lawyers and make sure no pictures of you get out. And then I'll get him to give Mr Blake here a phone call.' Brad looked at her, scrutinising her face. 'Sapphire, are you sure you didn't tell him anything? It just seems strange that he got through the perimeter fence. We made sure that thing was impossible to climb.'

Did he think she'd let the photographer *in*? 'Of course not!' she replied hotly. 'I told you I was just out taking a walk. I don't know where he came from.'

There was an awkward silence. 'OK,' Brad said. 'Well, thanks for letting me know. You can go now.'

As Sapphire left the room, Brad stared after her for a few moments, before reaching for the phone. Before he phoned his lawyer, his head of security was going to get a right bollocking.

chapter thirty-three

The next morning at breakfast, Maggie came to tell the girls that Brad was holding a special dinner party. They were to meet in the drawing-room at seven o' clock, dress code formal.

Madison's ears were up, twitching like a rabbit's. 'What's the special occasion?'

'You'll have to ask Mr Masters that,' came the housekeeper's enigmatic reply. Madison could burst with excitement; she had been *dying* to wear her new Hervé Léger bandage dress.

Shortly before seven, Sapphire was making her way downstairs. As she passed a full-length mirror in the hallway, she did a double-take. The person looking back at her was a million miles away from the girl she'd been in London. Her hair was sun-kissed and tousled, tumbling round her tanned shoulders. She was wearing a sparkly black dress from H&M, which she normally wore with leggings to tone down the look. Tonight, however, her legs were bare, the dress stopping midway down her tanned thigh. In a sudden fit of self-consciousness, Sapphire tugged it down.

Maybe you should go and change…

A low wolf whistle sounded from downstairs. She turned to see Cam standing in the hallway, hands in his pockets. He was wearing a dinner jacket, bow tie casually undone around his neck. Sapphire's stomach turned upside-down. He looked utterly gorgeous.

'Hi, Cam!' Her voice did a really embarrassing wobble on his name. 'Er, I was just wondering if I should go and change.' She blushed. 'Do you really think I look all right? I was thinking it was a… bit much.'

'Don't you dare go and change! You look really hot.' He grinned up at her and Sapphire almost burst with happiness. *Cam said I look hot!* Concentrating hard to make sure she didn't ruin the effect and trip in her heels, she made her way down the staircase holding on to the banister for balance. She got to the bottom and Cam looked her up and down appreciatively. 'You look even better up close.'

He leaned in to give her a kiss on the cheek and Sapphire caught a waft of his aftershave. Just his smell did peculiar things to her. Cam held out his arm and gave a little bow. 'Shall we?' Sapphire smiled and took it. They made their way down the wide hallway, Cam like a broad-shouldered, muscled protector at her side. They passed another mirror and Sapphire caught sight of their reflection, walking along together like a regular couple. She did a little inward jump of joy – if only her mates at college could see her now!

They stopped outside the drawing-room. 'After you,' Cam said. He pushed the door open and gently steered her in, one hand lightly on her back. Sapphire's whole body tingled at his touch. The occupants of the room turned to face them. Brad, in black tie, stood with Simonetta, who looked tall and sleek in a long, black evening dress. To Sapphire's surprise, Raphael was there too. Even though his jacket didn't have the obvious luxury of Brad and Simonetta's clothes, he still looked cool in an offbeat way.

'Sapphire, you look beautiful,' Brad said approvingly. She felt her cheeks burn again as everyone looked at her. 'Oh, this old thing,' she mumbled jokingly.

'Moschino?' asked Simonetta, giving her an expert once-over.

'Something like that,' Sapphire replied, thinking Simonetta would probably collapse and die of horror if she told her the dress had cost all of £19.99.

'Now all we're waiting for is Madison,' Brad said.

As if on cue, the door burst open and Madison made her usual dramatic entrance. 'Hi, guys!' she said breathlessly. 'Sorry I'm a bit late. I had a *complete* nightmare; I couldn't get my hair straighteners to work.' She tossed her ice-blonde hair anyway, clearly fishing for a compliment.

'You look lovely,' Brad told her dutifully. He looked round at everyone. 'Shall we?'

The dining-room looked even more exquisite than usual, with chandeliers twinkling above and a huge display of exotic lilies on the table, their scent filling the air. There were little place cards at each setting and Sapphire realised with a stab of disappointment that she would be sitting between Brad and Raphael, not next to Cam. The R&B star took his place opposite, with Madison and Simonetta either side of him. Madison was quick to lean in, giving him the full benefit of her cleavage, while she pretended to brush something off his lapel. Sapphire felt a burn of jealousy. She turned to her right, where Raphael was sitting upright and still. His face was paler than ever, green eyes penetrating the low light of the room.

'So, how come you're here tonight, Raphael?' she asked.

His lips curled sarcastically. 'What, do you think the hired help shouldn't attend such events?'

Sapphire frowned at him. 'That's not what I meant and you know it,' she told him.

He raised an eyebrow. 'Do I?'

Frustrated, Sapphire shook her head. Why did he always have to do this? Two of the waiting staff entered the room, carrying bottles of champagne in thick white linen napkins. They moved round the table discreetly, filling each of their glasses. As they finished and left the room, Brad spoke.

'I want to make a toast to you all tonight. You're all great kids and I'm thoroughly enjoying having you stay with me at Casa Eleganza.' He raised his glass. 'Here's to you all.'

They all followed suit and raised their glasses. 'To us!' As Sapphire took a sip, she saw Cam looking directly at her. He gave a little grin. Sapphire's heart quickened and she smiled back. She realised Madison was eyeing her beadily from across the table. Sapphire took another sip of champagne and looked away, the fizzing liquid running down her throat.

Despite the underlying tensions in the room, the evening passed well. Brad was a great host and made sure none of them were left out. But despite his best efforts, Raphael remained virtually silent, only saying the odd word or sentence when he really had to. *It's almost as if he thinks he's above us,* Sapphire thought.

By ten o'clock the meal was finished. 'I have a headache coming on,' Simonetta announced suddenly. 'Would you please excuse me?' She stood up.

'Shall I send Maggie up with some painkillers?' Brad asked. Simonetta waved a hand. 'I have some in my suitcase, thank you.' She left the room in a haze of heavy perfume.

Strange, thought Sapphire. She could swear Simonetta had been having a really good time. *There's more to that one than meets the eye.*

The remaining guests retired to the drawing-room. Raphael went and looked moodily out of one of the windows, while Madison prattled on to Brad about some New York clothes shop she'd been, '*Like*, the first to discover!'

Sapphire had just kicked off her heels and was curled up in one of the big chairs when Cam came and sat down on the arm. He'd taken his dinner jacket off and Sapphire could see his wide arms nestled under the white shirt he was wearing. Huge diamonds glittered in his cuff links. Suddenly, to Sapphire, it was as if no one else was in the room with them. His hand brushed her bare arm, sending little shockwaves through her body

'What are you up to after this?' he asked.

'Er, just going to bed, I guess,' she said, trying to sound casual.

Cam gave a slow, lazy smile. 'It's too early for bedtime. Meet me on the beach in, say, half an hour? The moon is real pretty tonight.'

Sapphire found it hard to swallow. 'That would be great,' she managed.

Cam gave her a secretive wink. 'See you then.' He got up and went over to Brad. 'Brad, I think I'm going to turn in. It's been a cool night, thanks.'

'My pleasure,' Brad said. 'I've got some correspondence to catch up on, so I think I'll leave you guys to it.' He called over the room. 'Raphael.' The Italian boy turned round. Brad grinned. 'Your new stuff sounds great, I'd love to hear it.'

To Sapphire's surprise, the three of them had enjoyed a surprisingly animated conversation about music during dinner. Sapphire had been secretly impressed with the breadth of Raphael's knowledge and his ideas for songs, and it was obvious Brad thought the same.

Raphael nodded, even allowing himself a little smile. '*Si, Signor* Masters.'

As Cam and Brad left, only Madison, Sapphire and Raphael remained in the room. Sapphire thought Raphael would be desperate to get out of there, but to her surprise he walked over and stood by the window again. Madison came and threw herself in the chair opposite Sapphire.

'What am I supposed to do now? I'm still wide awake.'

'You could always go and play Scrabble or something,' Sapphire said, keeping a straight face.

Madison rolled heavily made-up eyes. 'Scrabble's for *total* dorks.'

Sapphire ignored the jibe. Her throat felt tight with excitement and nerves, just as it had been since Cam had asked her to meet him on the beach. She took a sneaky look at her watch.

Madison turned her attention to Raphael, who still had his back to them, looking out the window. 'So what's this music you've been working on? It is any good?'

Raphael did a good job of ignoring her.

Madison's mouth screwed into a petulant sulk; she wasn't used to men giving her the cold shoulder. 'How rude!' she said to Sapphire.

Sapphire shrugged.

Seeing that she wasn't going to get a rise out of either of them, Madison got up. 'I'm going to paint my nails. I've got the perfect shade to go with my new Matthew Williamson bikini. I'm gonna look *awesome* round the pool tomorrow!'

The door slammed behind her. Across the other side of the room Raphael made a scornful noise. Sapphire was about to get up and put her shoes on, when suddenly he was standing in front of her.

'God, Raphael, you made me jump!'

He looked at her, his angular face softened by the dimmed lighting. With his razor-sharp cheekbones and perfect, almost feminine lips, Sapphire thought – not for the first time – how striking he was. Pity he was such a grumpy git.

'You want to practise?' he asked.

'What, now?' Sapphire looked at her watch. She was due to meet Cam in a few minutes. 'I'd love to, but I've got to go and phone my mum. She's expecting me.' She dropped her eyes under his penetrating gaze – it was as if he could see into her soul and knew she was lying. 'How about tomorrow?' she asked, anxious to get out of there. 'I'm free all day.'

There was a long pause, in which all that could be heard was the *caw caw* of a seabird circling high above outside. 'Tomorrow,' he agreed eventually.

'Great!' Sapphire said, edging away. 'I'll see you then.'

Raphael stopped her as she was opening the door. 'Sapphire.' The tone of his voice made her turn round. He looked at her, something working behind the impenetrable face.

'Yes?'

His face wore a strange expression. 'Nothing. Just…' He hesitated. 'Just be careful.'

She frowned. 'What do you mean?'

But Raphael was already walking back towards the window.

Sapphire quickly forgot Raphael's weirdness as she left the room. She was going to meet Cam! Quickly, she ran upstairs to put on another coat of mascara and a fresh squirt of perfume. She was so nervous she almost dropped the bottle of Daisy by Marc Jacobs she'd saved up for weeks to buy.

Calm down, she told herself.

But it was hard to remain calm when the fact was she was about to go and meet Cam Tyler for a moonlight walk on the beach. How much more romantic could it get? *Millions of girls would kill to be me right now,* she thought. It was a *nice* thought.

It was a still, almost noiseless night when she walked on to the beach a few minutes later. All Sapphire could hear was the gentle roll of the waves and the violent beating of her own heart. The full moon cast a ghostly pallor on the sand, making it look almost spooky. Sapphire shivered and rubbed her arms; she wished she'd brought her jacket.

'Here, take this,' Cam said out of the darkness.

Sapphire swung round to see him walking towards her. He was barefoot like her, his dinner jacket slung over his shoulder. Wordlessly, Sapphire let him drape it round her. She could feel the silk lining against her skin, the smell of his aftershave stronger than ever. She was still shivering with an intensity that had nothing to do with the chill of the night air. For a few moments they walked in silence.

'Did you have a good time at dinner?' Cam asked.

Sapphire nodded. 'Yeah, it was good to get us all together. All the young people in the house, I guess.'

'I was kinda surprised Raphael was there,' remarked Cam. 'I wouldn't have thought it was his thing. The guy hardly said two words the whole night.'

'I don't think Raphael is a people person,' Sapphire admitted. 'He seems happiest when it's just him and his guitar.'

Cam turned to look at her. 'You seem to know more about him than anyone else does.'

'We've been hanging out a bit. He's been helping me with my melodies,' she said.

Cam gave her a crooked grin that made her heart melt. 'Well, just as long as you don't spend too much time with him. I might get jealous.'

Sapphire's throat seemed to have constricted again, robbing her of the powers of speech.

They walked along to a rocky outcrop. Cam climbed up on a large boulder and held his hand out.

'Here.' Sapphire took his hand and he pulled her up easily, as if she were as light as a feather. 'Pretty cool, huh?'

Sapphire had to agree. On the far side of the rocks, a line of lights shimmered against the dark water. They came from an exclusive resort several miles down the road – the nearest thing Casa Eleganza had to neighbours. They stood looking across the bay at them, but all Sapphire was aware of was how close Cam was standing to her, and the solid, powerful lines of his body.

'Sapphire.' He said her name so quietly that at first she thought it was the whisper of the waves. Slowly, hardly daring to believe, she turned to face him. They were only inches apart now. Cam was so broad and sculpted that to Sapphire he seemed as unbreakable as the rocks they were standing on. He reached a hand out and stroked her cheek.

'You're very special to me, Sapphire. I guess you could say... what was that English phrase of yours? I guess you could say that I fancy you.'

Sapphire felt as if she was having an out-of-body experience, like Cam was saying these words to another person and she was an outsider, looking in. Then, suddenly, as if in slow motion, Cam pulled her to him and kissed her softly on the lips. Sapphire literally felt her knees buckle. His mouth was dry and warm, the faint smell of toothpaste lingering even as he pulled away. He looked down tenderly and ran his hand through her hair.

'Wow, I could get used to that.'

Sapphire managed a smile. 'Me too,' she said, suddenly shy. Her whole body felt alive, euphoria rushing through every vein and nerve ending.

'I've got to go away for a few days,' Cam said, gently playing with a strand of her hair. 'But I'd really like us to spend some proper time together when I get back.'

This isn't happening, she thought. *Things like this just don't happen to girls like me.* 'I'd really like that, Cam,' she said, trying to keep the massive cheesy grin from spreading across her face.

Cam smiled. 'Great.' He leaned in to kiss her again and Sapphire's heart started flailing wildly in her chest. She shut her eyes in anticipation…

Suddenly, a light was flashed in their faces. 'What's going on here?' a gruff voice shouted.

Cam squinted into the spotlight being shone on them. 'It's me, Cam. Is that you, Billy?'

Brad's head of security turned his torch off. 'Sorry, Cam, I didn't realise it was you. We've had a few problems lately.' He saw Sapphire standing beside Cam, but if he was surprised, he didn't show it.

'Can I offer you folks my assistance on your walk back? I don't think Mr Masters would be happy if I left you out here alone in the dark.'

'I think he means Brad wouldn't be happy if he left *me* with *you* in the dark,' Cam whispered to Sapphire. She giggled and Cam held his hand up. 'All right, Billy, we're coming down!'

I am never, ever, going to come down from this, Sapphire thought ecstatically. She wanted to run screaming along the beach and shout it to the world.

Cam Tyler just kissed me!

chapter thirty-four

'Your mind is elsewhere.' Raphael frowned at her critically over his guitar. Sapphire was brought out of her daydream with a snap.

'Sorry, Raphael, I'm just a bit tired.' They were in his living-room again, practising. She'd hardly slept a wink all night, replaying everything that had happened. All she could think about was Cam – their kiss, how lovely his mouth felt on hers, what would happen when he got back…

'You want to stop?' Raphael asked abruptly.

'No, of course not.' Sapphire gave herself a mental shake. For some reason, the last thing she wanted Raphael to do was ask about Cam. She rested her chin on her own guitar and looked at him. 'Did you have a nice time last night?'

Raphael shrugged dismissively. 'It was all right. *Signor* Masters is an interesting man.'

Sapphire smiled. 'He seems to like you.'

Raphael didn't reply.

'Do you miss home?' she asked suddenly. They were all so far from anywhere here. For the first time, he looked vulnerable.

'I have no home.'

Sapphire was shocked. 'Surely you have someone to go home to? Your mum…'

'She died last year,' Raphael said brutally. 'I am an orphan.'

Sapphire was quiet for a moment. 'I'm really sorry, Raphael.'

He turned on her, eyes suddenly blazing, 'Why? Why should you feel sorry? She wasn't *your* mother.'

His angry tone made her eyes well up. Why was

he so horrible to her? Sapphire looked away, so Raphael couldn't see that he'd upset her. When she turned back, he was staring at her, a dark expression on his face. Not for the first time, it made Sapphire shiver. What hid behind those fathomless eyes? Was he capable of harming someone?

Just as quickly as he had flared up, his voice softened. 'I have a brother, Gabriel.' He hesitated, his long fingers picking away at the seam on his trousers. 'Sapphire, I am sorry if I upset you. It's just...' He stopped and looked away.

This bloke is all over the place, she thought. Wasn't it girls who were meant to be so moody? Even so, his stilted apology made her feel a bit better. She tried to make light of the moment; being on such uncertain territory with him unsettled her. 'It's all right, I don't mind being used as an emotional punch-bag.'

He looked puzzled. 'Punch-bag?'

She shook her head, smiling. 'Forget it.'

The strain seemed to have drained out of the air. 'I have something for you,' Raphael announced. He pulled a notebook out of his back pocket. 'I have written some lyrics. I want you to find the melody.'

Sapphire gulped. It was fine when Raphael was helping her along, but this was different. 'I don't know if I can do it without you.'

'Yes, you can,' he said firmly. He handed the notebook to her. 'Read, see what you think.'

Sapphire looked down. Raphael's sprawling handwriting was quite hard to make out. '*Jewel*,' she read out. She looked up. 'That's a lovely name for a song.'

'Just read it,' he commanded. 'I am going to get a drink of water.'

Is he nervous? Sapphire suddenly thought. Left alone, she started reading the first verse.

'*The brightest star, the richest sunrise, is nothing compared to your glitter*

Jewel

Colours fade away when you walk into a room, birds lose their chatter

Jewel

But amongst the brightness, you bring with you dark

Your raven hair, raven heart

Jewel.'

The words almost flowed off the page into her.

Verse after verse, it was spellbinding. *Who was Jewel?* It was a heart-rending love story and Sapphire wondered if it was based on a true-life experience. No wonder Raphael was so up and down. Not that she would dare ask him.

After a few minutes, Raphael came back in. 'So?' His voice was almost challenging.

Sapphire looked up, her eyes full of tears. 'Raphael, it's one of the most beautiful things I've ever read.' The last line about bringing colour back into a lonely existence had almost finished her off.

The intensity lifted from Raphael's face. 'You like it?'

'I more than like it,' she cried. 'I love it!' Sapphire's face dropped. 'There's no way I can do this justice. My melodies are rubbish.'

'So we are going to work on them to make them better,' he said, handing Sapphire her guitar. 'Don't worry about being perfect. It will come.'

Sapphire took a deep breath. 'Here goes!'

The only reason Sapphire knew it was lunch-time was that her stomach rumbled. She looked at her watch and was surprised to see they'd been sitting there for nearly three hours. After a frustrating start, in which her head had been filled with the usual silence when it came to thinking up melodies, it was as if a light had been switched on. It was like she could *hear* the words for the first time, not just see them. With Raphael's encouragement she had finally brought the song alive, her voice stronger and sweeter than ever. It sounded stupid, but the last time Sapphire had felt like this was when she'd ridden her bike for the first time without stabilisers. It was like entering a whole new world of exciting possibilities and adventures.

'I think we should stop now,' Raphael said. 'I have to work this afternoon.'

Sapphire looked at him, her eyes sparkling. 'Raphael, I can't believe I've got it!' She got up and did a little jig of joy on the spot. 'I've *got* it!'

For the first time since she'd met him, Raphael laughed. It was a deep, throaty sound – melodic, warm and rich. It was a sound she never expected to come from him, like it belonged to someone else. Sapphire found herself laughing back in surprise, but then Raphael stopped abruptly. It was as if he suddenly remembered that he shouldn't be doing something as frivolous as laughing.

'What is it?' Sapphire asked.

Raphael shook his head. 'Nothing. I must get ready for work.'

It still hadn't spoilt the moment. She grinned up at him. 'Raphael, I don't know how to thank you. This whole thing has been amazing!'

For the first time, he smiled at her. It was like a ray of sunlight peeking through on a cloudy day, and Sapphire almost gasped as his carved looks were transformed into something radiant and beautiful. Then it was gone, and Raphael's marble-like features settled themselves again.

'You want to thank me? Then practise. Practise, Sapphire Stevens, practise!'

Sapphire had got halfway down the path before she realised Raphael had used her surname. She was sure she hadn't told him it. Her phone beeped and Sapphire dug around in her bag to retrieve it. It was a number she didn't recognise. She opened it. The message was short but sweet.

Can't stop thinking about you. Cam X

Sapphire let out a squeal of joy and did another little happy dance on the spot. She didn't care if anyone saw her. Things couldn't get much better at the moment and she didn't want anything to spoil it.

'*Someone's* in a good mood,' Madison remarked. The three of them were sitting round the pool, basking in the sun. Sapphire had been humming 'Jewel' merrily to herself as she stretched out, arms behind her head. Every now and again she would think of something Cam had said or done, or remember the way he'd kissed her, and a secret smile would break out across her face.

'That's it, you just did it again!' Madison exclaimed. She turned to Simonetta. 'Did you see Sapphire? She keeps doing that weird goofy smile to herself.'

Simonetta peeled open one eye and shut it again.

'*I* know that smile!' Madison jumped up and came to sit on Sapphire's sunbed. 'It's a boy, isn't it? Oh my God, have you hooked up with Cam! You have, I can tell by your face!'

'Ssh, Madison!' Sapphire pleaded, but she couldn't help grinning.

Madison bounced up and down excitedly. 'Have you kissed him?'

'Madison!'

'O. M. G! You totally have.' Madison leaned in. 'What was it like? You have to tell me.'

Normally Sapphire wouldn't share her confidences with a girl like Madison in a million years, but she was bursting to tell someone. 'You have to promise not to tell anyone,' she said, 'but yeah, we did kiss.' She couldn't contain herself. 'Madison, it was amazing!'

Madison clapped her hands like an orgasmic seal. 'That's *awesome*!'

'Thanks, Madison,' Sapphire said. For once Madison seemed genuinely pleased for her. Maybe a human heart did beat under the grade-A bitch exterior.

Madison gave her a little wink. 'What about Raphael? I thought you guys looked pretty hot together.'

Sapphire laughed. 'What are you like? Raphael is just helping me with my music.'

'Like, whatever! If you spend so much time

practising' – she made quote marks with her fingers – 'then where are the songs? You can't prove it, can you?' She gave a wicked smile.

Sapphire sat up. She had recorded her and Raphael singing 'Jewel' on her mobile phone. It was a bit crackly, but Raphael told her it would be good for reference. 'Actually, I can. This is me and Raphael singing this new song, "Jewel".'

'Well, let's hear it then!' Madison motioned to Simonetta. 'Come and listen to this! Sapphire's going to play us a song she's come up with, all by herself!'

'It was Raphael as well,' Sapphire said hastily. 'It's only really a rough version,' she said as Simonetta wandered over.

'Oh, don't get all shy on us now!' Madison said brightly.

'I'm just telling you,' Sapphire said, scrolling down. 'Here we are.' She clicked on play and waited. A few seconds later, her voice sang out, Raphael's guitar strumming gently in the background.

'The brightest star, the richest sunrise, nothing compares to your glitter
Jewel'

Colours fade when you enter a room, birds lose their
chatter
Jewel

Raphael's voice merged in seamlessly with hers, bringing a rich intensity.

But just as there is light, you bring with you dark
Taking all around down with you
Raven hair, raven heart
Jewel…

Sapphire saw Simonetta and Madison exchange looks. She switched the phone off. 'What do you think?' she asked self-consciously.

Madison had actually thought it was quite catchy, but there was no way she was telling the runt that. She might get too full of herself. 'It was OK,' she shrugged. 'If you like that sort of thing. I mean, like, that schoolkid MySpace kind of vibe.'

Sapphire's face fell. 'Oh.'

'I liked it,' Simonetta said, and wafted off back to her sunbed.

'She's only being nice, I can tell,' Madison said sympathetically. 'Still, practice makes perfect, hey?'

The happiness had suddenly seeped from Sapphire's day. *Maybe Madison is right,* she thought. *Maybe I will never be good enough.*

Even the thought of seeing Cam again couldn't lift her sudden despair.

chapter thirty-five

The collision came from nowhere. One minute Sapphire was walking out the front door, the next Simonetta came flying into her. It was a surprise to see the Italian model in such a hurry as she normally didn't move faster than a catwalk crawl.

'Watch it!' Sapphire said, as they narrowly avoided banging heads.

Simonetta jumped back, her normal sleek mane wild around her face. 'You should be more careful!'

'You're the one who was going like a bat out of hell!' Sapphire protested. She stopped, noticing the shadows under Simonetta's eyes. She looked tired, and for the first time her complexion had lost its glowing hue. 'Are you all right?' Sapphire asked.

Simonetta looked annoyed. 'What do you mean?'

'You just look a bit stressed.'

Simonetta tossed her hair back angrily. 'Of course I am all right! Why wouldn't I be? What have *I* got to worry about?'

'I was just asking!' Sapphire said. Someone had got out of bed on the wrong side!

Simonetta gave her a filthy look. 'If anyone has anything to worry about it is you. Have you seen the split ends on your hair recently?'

Sapphire held her hands up. 'OK, I give up. I don't know what's put you in such a bad mood, but don't take it out on me.' She walked past Simonetta out into the garden.

Face tight, Simonetta watched her go. The tiny twinge of guilt she felt at being nasty to Sapphire was quickly forgotten. No matter how much she tried to quash it, worry was starting to build inside her. Lexi had just left her a cold voicemail, saying they were suspending her contract with Models Italia, and both the bank manager and the estate agency were phoning daily now, to find out where their money was. The last message from the estate agent said that if she didn't pay her outstanding rent within forty-eight hours, they were going to evict her.

There won't be much to evict, she thought bitterly. Besides a beautiful face and a Louis Vuitton suitcase full of designer clothes, she had nothing in the world.

Nothing.

Suddenly, her indestructible self-belief seemed to be slowly slipping away.

Even worse, The Problem had found her again. At the time, she had been naïve and young, but by the time she realised what a terrible choice she'd made it had been too late. It had been an abusive love-hate relationship and Simonetta had fought hard to get out. From experience, she knew the pattern. Clever and manipulative, The Problem would try to coax her back, pretending things would be different this time. Panic momentarily gripped Simonetta. Was she strong enough to resist? Did she *want* to resist?

Ironically, The Problem had given her some of the best times, as well as the worst times, of her life.

Calm down. Focus, she told herself. She could deal with it, just as she had before. Gradually, her breathing became calmer. She fixed an indifferent look on her face and stepped out into the sunlight. She wouldn't, *wouldn't* let herself be won back. Not this time.

Her life depended on it.

As she wandered round the garden, Sapphire felt a thrill of excitement. Cam would be back later. Despite her previous gloom, the world had suddenly become a more exciting, colourful place. She gazed dreamily up at the sky. It had never seemed so blue, or the sun so bright. She wanted to go and write pages and pages of lyrics about a gorgeous, funny, laid-back boy who made her whole body go into explosions every time he even looked at her. She could write a whole song about Cam Tyler's abs. Forget Taylor Lautner – Cam's body was a million times better.

Not only that, but his lips were so soft and his eyes so deep…

You've got it bad, girl, she told herself. She mustn't get too carried away – looking too keen was definitely not the way to go.

'If you keep staring at the sky like that, you're going to fall again,' a voice said. Sapphire looked round to see Raphael walking towards her. He was carrying some apples in his hand. He threw one to her and Sapphire caught it. 'Nice catch,' he said.

'Netball captain at school.'

Raphael came up to her, his skin whiter than ever, green eyes burning in his face. 'Netball?'

'It's a bit like basketball. It's an English thing.'

He shrugged. 'Very well.'

Sapphire studied his pale skin. 'Being Italian, aren't you meant to be a bit more... I don't know... tanned?' she teased. She was in such a good mood she didn't mind if he ignored her.

To her surprise, Raphael smiled back, showing off perfect white teeth. 'We don't all have the luxury of lying by the pool.' He took a huge bite of his apple, chewing vigorously.

Sapphire cocked her head to one side and looked at him.

He stopped chewing. 'What are you looking at?'

'You. It's nice to see you smile for a change.'

Raphael finished the apple and threw the core in a bush. 'I suppose I have to take a break from being a... moody git, as I think you call it?'

Sapphire laughed. He was actually quite funny if he tried.

He looked at her. 'Would you like to walk? We can go through the orchards if you like, that's where I got the apples.'

'Been pilfering, have we?'

Raphael frowned. '*Pilfering?* Is that another of your strange English sayings?'

They made their way through the gardens towards the orchards. Although Raphael still wasn't much of a talker, the silence between them was companionable rather than strained. Sapphire walked with a spring in her step, gently humming.

'You are very happy today,' he observed.

Sapphire stretched her arms out. 'What's not to be happy about? The sun is shining, we're in a beautiful place.' *And I'll be seeing Cam in approximately six hours, fourteen minutes and twenty-one seconds!*

Raphael touched the side of his head. 'I think the sun has made you *matto*.'

He was calling her mad? Cheeky bugger. Sapphire play-punched him on the arm.

'*Ahi!*' he exclaimed, pretending to rub where she'd hit him. 'I think you've broken it.'

'Ha ha,' she said, smiling lazily. 'You're quite the joker today.'

'Better than being a git, no?'

She laughed. '*Definitely* better than being a git.' She didn't know what had caused the change in his mood, but she sure as hell wasn't going to ask. Better to enjoy it while it lasted.

'How are your friends?' he asked suddenly. Sapphire couldn't help but give a little start. There was something about his question that seemed loaded. 'Fine… but I wouldn't exactly call them friends.' She stopped. This was a subject they'd better not get on to.

Raphael raised an eyebrow. 'Oh? And what are they?'

'Just holiday companions, I guess,' she said hurriedly.

'Do you have any brothers or sisters?'

'S-sisters? Sapphire stuttered. 'No, why do you ask?' .

Raphael shrugged again. 'You seem very at ease around people.'

'I guess I'm just a people person!' she said in an overly cheery voice.

Raphael gave her a faintly amused look. 'Your parents must be nice people.'

'Actually, it's just me and my mum.' As she said it, she realised this wasn't strictly true any more. It made her feel really weird, so she directed the conversation back to him instead. 'What about your brother, are you close?'

For a moment, Raphael's expression darkened. 'We were, once.'

'Sibling rivalry, eh?' she joked, but Raphael didn't smile back.

'No cousins, aunts, uncles or anything?'

'No,' he said shortly. 'You?'

It's like we're playing a conversational game of ping-pong, Sapphire thought. For whatever reason, Raphael seemed as unwilling to open up as she was.

'I've got a great aunt – my mum's aunt Beattie.

She's funny. She comes to stay with us and smokes like a trooper and drinks all my mum's brandy.'

Raphael shot her a mischievous look. 'I see a love of alcohol runs in the family.'

Sapphire felt herself go red. Someone must have told him about her getting drunk, after all. 'Yeah, well, the less said about that the better,' she muttered.

'I was pulling your arm,' he said.

Sapphire smiled, pushing aside the embarrassing memory. 'I think you mean leg, Raphael,' she told him. And he said she had a way with words! They continued their walk in easy silence.

For once, everything's going all right, thought Sapphire.

chapter thirty-six

The text came through at six o'clock, when Sapphire had just emerged dripping wet from the shower. It was short but sweet.

Back at 9. C U on beach? Cam xx.

Hands shaking, she replied.

Gr8. C U then. S.

She wondered for ages how many kisses to put and in the end settled for two as well. Taking a deep breath, she pressed 'Send' and watched as it disappeared from the screen. Her stomach filled with butterflies again – she was going to see Cam again!

'*You're* twitchy tonight,' Madison said, eyeing her over the dinner table.

'I am not,' Sapphire said quickly, as Brad and Simonetta turned to look as well.

'You've looked at your watch, like, ten times in the last minute!' Madison said.

Shut up, Sapphire thought. *Stop drawing attention to me.* She looked at Brad. 'Actually, I'm feeling a bit tired,' she said to him. 'Would you mind if I skipped dessert?'

'Of course not,' he said. 'Are you all right?'

Sapphire forced a smile. 'Just a bit too much sun probably.' She felt bad lying, especially to him, but there was no way she would get out of this meal otherwise. She was sure Madison was dragging it out on purpose.

The velvet sky was alive with stars as Sapphire slipped down the winding stone path to the beach several minutes later. There was a slight breeze that ruffled the hem of her skirt, making it ride up her thighs. For the umpteenth time she smoothed down her blow-dried hair, praying it wouldn't revert to its normal, tumbling mess in the wind.

She stepped out on to the sand and looked left and right. The beach was deserted. Curling her legs underneath her, she sat down to wait. Her heart was pounding so much it almost drowned out the sound of the waves.

Every second ticked by painfully. Sapphire checked her watch for the umpteenth time – it was nine twenty-four. That was not a good sign. Five minutes, yes, even ten, but nearly half an hour? The realisation hit her.

He's stood me up.

She could almost taste the bitter disappointment in her mouth. Stomach churning unpleasantly, she started to get up.

'Sapphire!' The shout came from somewhere behind her. Instantly her spirits lifted. Jogging over the sand towards her, in baggy jeans and a Diesel T-shirt, was Cam. He looked so bloody gorgeous that all Sapphire's negative feelings melted away in a moment.

'Hey, I am *so* sorry,' He threw himself down next to

her, kissing her on the cheek. Her stomach flipped upside-down, but she managed to keep a calm smile on her face. Cam ran his tanned hands over his face, as if tired. 'We got held up in a meeting.' He rolled his eyes. 'My manager loves to do meetings! Sometimes I forget I'm actually a musician.'

'Anything exciting?' Sapphire asked. Cam's leg fell against hers and, even though he was wearing jeans, she could feel the warmth of his body melting into hers.

'I'm not really supposed to talk about it until it's all been decided.'

'Sounds very mysterious,' Sapphire said, smiling.

Cam laughed. 'Well, when I can tell people you'll be the first to know.' He turned to her and Sapphire took in the square jaw, the long-lashed eyes, the sheer symmetry of his face. *Guys like Cam aren't real,* she thought. *They're almost too perfect to walk amongst the human race.*

He cocked his head, smiling. 'What are you thinking about?'

Sapphire's heart started thudding even faster. 'Nothing, really.'

Cam held an arm out, his bicep rippling under his

T-shirt. 'Come and snuggle up with me. I don't want you getting cold.'

Slightly dazed, Sapphire inched down the sand to sit next to him. His arm wrapped round protectively, warming her and making her shiver all at the same time.

'So whatcha been up to?'

'Nothing much,' Sapphire mumbled. She was suddenly finding it hard to speak again.

'Sunbathing?'

'Uh, no. I leave that to the experts.' Cam smiled at this, making her feel calmer. 'I've been practising a lot with Raphael, actually,' she said. 'We've just written a really cool song together.'

Cam frowned. 'That guy is weird. I don't like you spending so much time with him.'

Sapphire felt a tingle of joy. Was Cam *jealous*? 'I'm not really,' she said hastily. 'It's more of a favour he's doing for me.'

'Hmm, well.' Cam didn't sound convinced. 'I've seen the way he looks at you.' A slow smile spread across his face. 'Then again, I don't blame him. I can't take my eyes off you either, Sapphire.'

As Cam lifted her chin up and moved to kiss her, Sapphire started to have that out-of-body feeling again. *I can't believe I'm kissing Cam Tyler!* But the moment his mouth crushed down on hers, Sapphire realised just how real it was. Cam's tongue found its way into her mouth, moving gently against hers. Gradually his tongue got more persistent, kissing harder. Sapphire felt herself melt into his arms as he pulled her into him, running his hands through her hair and down her arms. His mouth moved on to her neck and instantly Sapphire's whole body went on red alert, delicious little thrills running through her. Cam pushed her down on the sand, his hands holding her arms above her head. She couldn't go anywhere even if she wanted to.

'My English rose,' he whispered into her ear. He started kissing her again, their bodies pressed together. Sapphire could feel every muscle, every part of his hard, warm flesh against hers. His hand moved down her stomach and on to her leg. Sapphire stiffened as one of his hands started creeping up her inner thigh. 'Cam, I don't think…'

'Hey, it's OK,' he whispered back. 'You just turn

me on so much, sexy Sapphire. But we can go as slow as you want.'

He started kissing her again, his hands running through her hair and across her face. As a cloud rolled across the moon above, the beach was plunged into darkness. Sapphire lay back on the sand, wanting the moment to last for ever.

chapter
thirty-seven

'Morning, girls.'

All three of them looked up, surprised to see Brad. He never normally joined them for breakfast. It had been a quieter affair than usual today; Madison was happy to gabble on about herself as normal, but Simonetta was more aloof and uncommunicative than ever. As for Sapphire... she hadn't slept a wink all night, replaying the events with Cam over and over in her head. Already it almost didn't feel real, like it had been a scene from the most romantic film ever. She could still *feel* his hands on her, running over her body. It was all she could do to shove a few bits of toast down, her mind whirring with the memories. It was her glorious secret, a barrier between her and the rest of the world. *I could take anything that was thrown at me now,* she thought happily. *Life is bloody brilliant!*

Brad sat down opposite her and smiled. Sapphire dragged herself out of her daydream, flushing slightly as she remembered lying to him about feeling tired last night. Brad looked like a proper Italian gent with a fresh white shirt and a cashmere jumper tied over his shoulders.

'How are you feeling, Sapphire? You still look a bit tired.'

She flashed a smile back. 'Oh, I'm OK. I'll probably just take it easy today.' She was looking forward to a day by the pool, dreaming about Cam. She couldn't wait until she saw him again.

'Actually, I've decided to take the yacht out today,' he said. 'I was wondering if you girls would like to join me.'

'That would be awesome!' Madison said.

Simonetta nodded and smiled. '*Si*, Brad.'

He looked at Sapphire. It was the last thing she felt like doing, but it would look rude if she said no. Besides, Madison *had* been slightly more bearable lately. She forced a smile. 'Count me in.'

An hour later, the *Spirito Libero* was gliding through the deep, blue waters of the Mediterranean. All four of them were on the sun deck, drinking freshly squeezed mango juice that had been brought out to them by the staff. Sapphire was pleased to see Tito on board; she hadn't seen his smiling face for ages. He was busy in the galley kitchen, helping the chef prepare what would no doubt be another mouth-watering lunch.

'Well, this is nice isn't it?' Brad said. He looked round at them. 'So what have you all been up to?'

For once, Sapphire was grateful of Madison jumping in first and monopolising the conversation.

'Oh, like, really cool stuff!' She stretched out a brown arm. 'I think I'm more tan than ever.'

Brad stifled a smile. In her own funny way,

Madison did make him laugh. She was also brighter than people assumed, her sharp eyes roaming everywhere, missing nothing.

'How about you, Simonetta?' In contrast to Madison's bubbliness, he thought Simonetta looked rather drawn and washed-out. As she shrugged he saw the sharp jut of her collar bone.

'Oh, this and that.' She eyed him keenly. 'Have you had a chance to look through the proposal I gave you?' To Simonetta's satisfaction, Madison looked confused and then annoyed at the realisation she'd been excluded from something.

'I have, actually, and there's some really good stuff in there,' he told her. 'We'll talk later.'

Simonetta smiled; she knew it would score points against the other two. Not, she noticed, that Sapphire even seemed part of the conversation, as she stared out to sea with a faraway look on her face. Brad followed Simonetta's eyes.

'Earth to Sapphire.' Brad waved a hand in front of her face. She jumped. 'You still with us?' he asked with a smile.

She flushed. 'Sorry, I was just thinking what a nice

day it is.' *I'm getting quite good at this lying thing*, she thought.

Brad looked round at them all expectantly. 'I have some rather exciting news. How do you fancy spending some time at my mansion in the Florida Keys?'

They all sat up. 'That would be so cool!' squealed Madison. She was literally *dying* for a Yogiberry frozen yogurt.

Simonetta felt similarly pleased. The further away she was from Italy at the moment, the better.

'When are we going?' Madison asked.

Brad smiled. 'In a few days, once we can get everything tied up.'

A few days! Sapphire's heart sunk like a stone. America was thousands of miles from here, and more importantly, Cam. 'Can I ask the reason?' she said, trying not to sound too gutted.

Brad grinned. 'We've had some rather exciting developments here. Cam has got on so well with his song writing that he's ready to record his debut album. I thought it would be good for all of us to go to Florida, where my recording studio is. I'd like to show you girls another part of my life while Cam is working.'

In a matter of seconds Sapphire's spirits had gone from zero to off the scale. 'Oh, wow!' she exclaimed. 'That would be amazing!' At the same time she realised that she and Raphael wouldn't be able to practise any more and her face fell slightly. They'd been coming along so well together.

Brad seemed to read her mind. 'I thought it would be good for you, Sapphire, to come in and see how the recording process works. Cam's got some talented people working with him, the best in the business.'

Sapphire felt like all her Christmases had come at once. Two of her favourite things: Cam *and* music. This must have been the thing Cam couldn't tell her about. The thought of spending time with him and watching him work made her fizz with joy.

'Count me in!' she said excitedly.

Brad grinned. 'Excellent! I'll be sorry to leave Casa Eleganza but there is work to be done. I think you girls will have a lot of fun out there.'

After a blissful afternoon on board the yacht, they returned to the villa. Sapphire was dying to phone her mum. She knew Leonie would be over the moon; Sapphire had never been to America before. She bade a hasty farewell to the others and was the first to run up the path towards the house. Of course, there was another reason Sapphire wanted to call her mum. To tell her about Cam. Not *everything* of course. One part of her had wanted him to go further last night, but in the cold light of day Sapphire was glad they hadn't. She knew Cam respected her for it and besides, this was just the beginning.

She practically bounced into her room and went to get her phone from her bag. After a quick rummage around, she realised it wasn't there. Sapphire frowned. Had she used it after getting the text from Cam? A quick look around the room revealed it wasn't there either.

'Bollocks!' she cursed aloud. She hated mislaying her phone. *Think. When did you have it last?* A thought occurred to her – maybe it was by the pool. After sticking her head under the bed one final time, she went to have a look.

The phone wasn't by the pool either. Sapphire sighed. It had to be *somewhere*. Maybe she'd left it in the house. She decided to go back and have another look. Maggie would know if someone had handed it in.

As Sapphire headed back to the house, she was surprised to see Simonetta coming down the path from Raphael's place. She stopped and stepped behind a bush, not wanting to be seen. She watched as Simonetta looked left and right, before sashaying towards the house.

Sapphire stood, wondering. Why would Simonetta be going to Raphael's? She had already said he was too young for her. Sapphire was surprised to feel a little stab of jealously. What she and Raphael had was a complete breath of fresh air, away from all the rivalry and bitchiness here. She didn't want Simonetta muscling in and ruining it.

Then again, what did it matter? They would be leaving here soon to go to Florida. Sapphire sighed and continued her journey back to the house to find Maggie.

chapter thirty-eight

Maggie handed the mobile to her. 'Looking for this, young lady?'

Sapphire took it gratefully. 'Thanks, Maggie. I've been tearing my hair out. Where did you find it?'

'One of the gardeners found it by the terrace.' Maggie's eyes twinkled. 'Sometimes I think you'd forget your head if it wasn't screwed on.'

Sapphire smiled ruefully. 'I must be going mad. I don't even remember going in the garden with it in the first place.' She stopped and looked at the housekeeper. 'I suppose you know about us going to Florida?'

Maggie nodded. 'You must be very excited, my dear. What with Cam recording his album and everything.'

Sapphire looked at her suspiciously, but Maggie's face gave nothing away. Did she know about them? Maggie seemed to have eyes in the back of her head. With her kind, wrinkled face and fussing manner she was like the grandmother Sapphire had never had. Her mum's own parents had died when she was young.

'I'll miss you, Maggie,' she said.

'Oh, away with you,' the housekeeper replied, but her eyes looked sad. She put on a mock stern face. 'I'll still be keeping my eye on you from here!'

'I'm sure you will,' Sapphire laughed.

Simonetta was in her bedroom getting ready for the pool when there was a knock at the door. She went to answer it. Clara, one of the housekeeping girls, stood there.

'*Signorina* Simonetta? Your mother is on the phone. She says it is urgent.'

Simonetta's eyebrows shot up in shock. Her mother? But why would she call her? How did she know how to get hold of her?

'You can take the call on your bedroom phone,' the maid told her.

'*Grazie*,' Simonetta said curtly and shut the door. She went and picked up the phone by her bed. '*Mamma?*'

'Simonetta!' Her mother sounded panicked. 'I have had people calling, asking after you! They say you owe them money!'

'Ssh, *Mamma*!' Simonetta hissed. 'Wait until the maid has put the phone down.' Moments later, there was a click. Simonetta strode over to the window and pulled it open. She was in sudden need of fresh air.

'What is going on?' her mother demanded. 'I've had debt collection companies threatening me. What kind of trouble are you in?'

Simonetta cursed inwardly; they must have got her family's telephone number from her references. 'How did you get this number, *Mamma*?' she asked angrily. She didn't want her mother ringing her, panicking and blabbing her mouth. The last thing she needed was Brad thinking she was bad with money.

Her mother hesitated. 'Brad's secretary called after you left to give me this number. She said Brad wanted to make sure I knew where you were staying, in case of an emergency. *This* is an emergency, Simonetta! These people, they frighten me, and we cannot repay your debts.'

'Have you told Papa?'

'Of course not! What, do you think I want to bring shame on the family? Oh, Simonetta, I knew this was a bad idea. You should never have left for Rome in the first place!'

Anger surged through Simonetta, brought on by days of stress and worry. 'What, *Mamma*, so I could stay at home and get old and fat like you? To spend my days working myself into the ground just to keep that hovel? I *needed* that money, if I was going to have any proper chance in life. If it's anyone's fault I'm in debt, it's yours!'

Her mother went quiet and Simonetta knew she'd gone too far. When she eventually spoke again, her voice was flat and hurt. 'We always tried to do our best by you.'

Simonetta sighed. '*Mamma*, I didn't mean it like that.'

'I am going now, Simonetta. Why do you always do this to me?'

'*Mamma!*'

She was met by a dialling tone. '*Merda!*' she said and threw the phone across the room. Simonetta raked her hands through her long black hair. She *had* to be chosen as Brad's heir before her life was destroyed, taking her family along with it.

Next door, eavesdropping by Simonetta's window, Madison smiled. So, snooty Simonetta was up to her stupid, kohl-rimmed eyeballs in debt. This was a turn-up for the books. Madison was sure she could turn it to her advantage. Gleefully, she admired her reflection in the dressing-table mirror. First Sapphire and then Simonetta. Honestly, if they *insisted* on offering themselves on a plate to her, what could she do but take them up on it?

To Sapphire's disappointment, she hadn't been alone with Cam since that night on the beach. His whole management team seemed to have descended on Casa Eleganza, getting him ready to start recording. Cam's manager, a sinister-looking man who wore all black and had a mobile phone clamped to his ear constantly, never let him out of sight. They had exchanged a few texts, but that was about it. Sapphire literally felt like she was having withdrawal symptoms from him. Seeing Cam and his entourage across the courtyard one morning, she grabbed the opportunity to speak to him.

'Cam!'

He turned round, smiling when he saw her walking towards him. 'Hey, Sapphire! How are you doing? You look really pretty,' he added softly, as she got up to him and no one else could hear.

'I'm good. I just wondered if we could hook up soon.'

Cam raised an amused eyebrow. 'Hook up?'

Sapphire blushed as she remembered that hooking up to Americans meant the same as getting off with someone.

'Oh! You know what I mean.' She blushed even deeper. 'That's not to say I wouldn't want to hook up again.'

Cam looked into her eyes and smiled. 'Me too, my little English rose. Sorry I haven't seen much of you, things are crazy.' He looked at his manager, who tapped his watch pointedly.

'We need to get going, Cam!'

'I see what you mean,' she said with a sympathetic smile. He looked so gorgeous that Sapphire wanted to throw her arms round him and start kissing. It was agony being this close and not even being able to touch him.

Cam grimaced. 'Yeah, my manager is kinda overprotective. I guess he doesn't want my image to come undone.'

Sapphire felt her stomach turn over unpleasantly. 'You don't want to disappoint all those female fans,' she tried to joke.

Cam sighed. 'I don't know. It kinda gets frustrating being told what to do the whole time. I'm not a kid.' He looked at Sapphire meaningfully. 'I do want to spend more time with you.'

She felt a kick of happiness. 'Me too, Cam.'

'Cam!' This time the manager looked really cross.

Cam looked at her. 'I'm back tonight; I'll try and

catch up with you then.' He smiled his slow, sexy grin. 'Stay with me, Sapphire.'

She watched as Cam was bustled towards a waiting car by his manager.

chapter thirty-nine

Sapphire was feeling restless. She still hadn't heard from Cam so she decided to go and see Raphael instead. Maybe they could practise together. Picking up her guitar, she walked out of her bedroom and set off.

As she made her way outside, night had fallen and the little lights on the pathway had come on, casting a warm glow over the grass. The air was heavily scented with blossom and in the distance she could hear the waves lapping gently against the shore.

It is so gorgeous here, she thought. Despite the promise Florida held, she would be sorry to leave. She realised in a funny way that she would miss Raphael too. Not just because of how much he inspired her with the music, but because they were finally starting to get along. Raphael intrigued her, but now she would never really get to know him. It was a shame.

When she reached his little bungalow, however, it was in darkness. Disappointed, Sapphire looked around. She wondered where he could be. Brad hadn't said he needed driving anywhere tonight. It was such a beautiful evening she had an inkling that he might be on the beach, so decided to try there instead.

As she climbed down the stone steps and stepped on to the sand, Sapphire could see some kind of bonfire in the distance. Taking her flips-flops off, guitar in the other hand, she started to make her way towards it. A lone figure was sitting cross-legged beside it. As she approached she could see it was Raphael, his own guitar at his side. He looked up and saw her, raising his hand briefly in welcome.

'Hey there,' she said. Raphael had built a circle of little stones around the fire, and was busy throwing driftwood into the flames. It brought welcome warmth to the cool night air. Sapphire settled herself down opposite him.

He nodded at her guitar. 'You want to practise?'

'In a minute,' Sapphire said. 'It's such a beautiful night, I thought we could talk a bit first.'

Raphael glanced up, from where he had been gazing into the fire. In the shadows, his angular face looked even more carved than ever. *He's like a beautiful statue*, she suddenly thought. 'What is it you want to talk about?'

Sapphire shrugged. 'I don't know, just stuff.' She didn't want to bring up the subject of going to Florida because she wasn't sure if Raphael was going. She had a sudden weird feeling, like they were running out of time together. It was like that they had unfinished business, but she didn't know what. For some reason the thought made her feel panicky. *What is wrong with me?* she wondered.

Raphael's green-gold eyes fixed on hers. 'Let's play first, talk second,' he announced. Strumming softly, he started the first line of 'Jewel'. Sapphire picked up on the second line, following him.

'The brightest star, the richest sunrise, is nothing compared to your glitter

Jewel

Colours fade away when you walk into a room, birds lose their chatter

Jewel

But amongst the brightness, you bring with you dark

Your raven hair, raven heart

Jewel…'

For some reason, the words had a whole new meaning tonight. As they sang and played their guitars together, Sapphire felt her whole body tingling, as if they'd discovered something really special. The words of the final verse sang out into the night:

'Once where there was darkness, there is now light

Jewel

For all that glitters is not gold

Jewel.'

Raphael put his guitar down. 'I think this is good. You should record it.'

'But they're your lyrics,' Sapphire said.

Raphael shrugged. 'It doesn't matter.'

Sapphire studied him over the flickering flames. 'Can I ask you something? Who *was* Jewel? I mean, all the stuff about the darkness – she must have really hurt you.'

For a long time they sat in silence, the only sound the crackle and hiss from the burning driftwood.

Suddenly, Raphael got up and came to sit beside her. 'Jewel was a girl I once knew. Actually, her real name was Jessica.' He shot a glance at Sapphire. 'She looked a lot like you.' Raphael gave a twisted smile. 'In fact, when I first laid eyes on you I thought the devil herself had come back to haunt me.'

Sapphire felt the hair on the back of her neck stand up. 'Is that why you hated me so much?' she whispered.

Raphael shook his head. 'It wasn't that I *hated* you, Sapphire. It was just that seeing you stirred up all the memories, the feelings. Jessica was English too, a spoilt little rich girl with no thought of anyone but herself. So when you turned up…'

'You thought I was exactly the same,' Sapphire said.

Raphael nodded. 'Yes, but it was more than that. There are things that have happened that you cannot understand.'

Sapphire stared at him. 'Try me.'

Raphael took a long time before replying. 'Jessica was a university student, in Rome on her gap year. I met her when I was working as a caretaker at the college she was studying at. Even though she was several years older than me, I fell head over heels in love with her. Not that I would have ever told her that; Jessica was far too beautiful and sophisticated for me. We struck up a kind of friendship. Looking back now, I am sure it was only because she was in a foreign country, away from everything she knew.' His lips curled up bitterly. 'In England, she would have never given someone like me the time of day.'

Raphael sighed. 'We hung out, I showed her round Rome. I think I knew she saw me as some kind of plaything, but I didn't want to admit it. I really thought I had a chance.' He laughed derisively. 'Then she met my brother Gabriel.'

'Oh,' Sapphire said. She had a feeling she knew where this was going.

'All the girls loved Gabriel,' Raphael said. 'He was older than me, handsome, charming. Of course, the moment Jessica saw him, she had to have him. And what Jesssica wanted, Jessica got. For his part, Gabriel felt the same. It was the first time I had ever really seen him fall for someone. And it was real love, not the puppy dog infatuation I felt for her. My *mamma* was delighted too, she treated Jessica like the daughter she'd never had. There was only the three of us before, as my father had died some years before. Jessica seemed to breathe new life into our home. I saw my mother laugh for the first time in years.' He stopped, his face suddenly bleak. 'And then Jessica fell pregnant.'

Sapphire was spellbound. She could see the emotions running through Raphael's face as he spoke. He looked so anguished, so alone, that she had an urge to reach out and touch his face, tell him it would be all right.

'What happened next?' she asked softly.

Raphael's jaw tightened. 'Gabriel was overjoyed and even though my mother was shocked – it is not how we do things here in Italy – she was so excited at the thought of being a grandmother. I can still hear her voice, "*Bella mia,* Jessica, you have made our family whole again!"'

He shook his head bitterly. 'Gabriel didn't have much money, he worked in a shop, but he took out his whole life savings to buy Jessica an engagement ring. My brother was so happy the night before he did it. "Raphael," he said to me, "I am going to be the best father in the world! I have finally found my calling in life." The next day, he went down on one knee and proposed to her.'

Raphael's head suddenly snapped up, his face full of undisguised anger. 'And do you know what that, that, *girl* said? She laughed in my brother's face, while he was still kneeling at her feet, and said if he thought she would ever get engaged to a nobody like him, then he was a fool. Especially with a ring that looked like it had come from a market stall.'

Raphael shuddered, reliving the memory. 'Jessica told him that it had just been a holiday fling and she was flying back to England for an abortion.'

Sapphire felt terrible for Raphael. It was horrible to see him looking so broken. Raphael gave a twisted smile. 'And you want to know the best thing? When Gabriel asked Jessica why she'd gone out with him in the first place, she tossed back her hair and said, "When in Rome, darling! Every girl's got to try an Italian."'

'What a total bitch,' Sapphire said feelingly.

Raphael sighed deeply. 'Gabriel was too much in love with her to see what she was really like. He begged her not to have the abortion, but she flew home two days later without leaving any contact details. Gabriel tried desperately to track her down, but it was no use.'

Sapphire felt her eyes well up. 'Oh, Raphael.'

His voice was flat and void of emotion. 'Gabriel started drinking after that and pretty soon he lost his job. My mother, she drove herself to distraction worrying about him. When he lost his home and went missing, she walked the streets night after night until she found him living like a dog under a railway bridge. It was too late by then, the heroin had found its way to him.'

What he said next shocked Sapphire to the core. 'My mother died of a heart attack last October.'

Raphael's voice wavered momentarily. 'She died of a broken heart, Sapphire, after what that girl did to our family. How could someone treat people in such a way?'

A solitary tear rolled down his face. He wiped it off and looked away, as if embarrassed. Sapphire put her hand on his arm, fighting back tears herself. 'Raphael, I really am so sorry.' She couldn't bear the pain he had been through. She wanted to hold him in her arms and tell him it would be OK. 'What about Gabriel?'

'The last I heard he was selling drugs,' said Raphael tonelessly. 'Every time I have tried to reason with him, he has turned on me and told me to leave. I fear he is lost to me forever.'

Poor, poor, Raphael. Sapphire suddenly felt terribly guilty. She had been thinking he was hiding some dark and dangerous secret, and all along it had been something completely different. She didn't deserve to be so happy when Raphael had been going through such an awful time. He was completely alone in the world, through no fault of his own. She sighed; no wonder he'd had such strong feelings when he'd first seen her.

'I overheard you on the phone once,' she admitted. 'You were talking about death and destruction.'

Raphael looked contemptuous. 'I never thought I would hear from that girl again, but she had the cheek to ring me and ask if I could act as a tour guide to one of her friends who was visiting Rome.' He looked angry, incredulous. 'I told her exactly what she had done to my family and said to never contact me again.' Raphael gave a tight smile. 'It gave me a little pleasure, but it won't bring my family back to me again.'

Sapphire couldn't bear for him to go through life carrying such an awful burden. 'You talk about seeing the light at the end of "Jewel", Raphael. What is the light? Have you managed to find some happiness?'

He turned to look at her, eyes burning with a look she'd never seen before. 'You, Sapphire. *You* are the light! You are the *real* jewel in the song. There was nothing more to Jessica than a pretty shell, but you... you are beautiful on the inside *and* out.' A tender smile crossed his lips. 'Sapphire by name and Sapphire by nature.'

Sapphire was so shocked, she couldn't speak. Slowly, as if it were the most natural thing in the world, Raphael lifted his hand to her face.

'You are so much like her, but then also you are not. There is such warmth in you, Sapphire, such beauty in unexpected places.'

His hand continued to caress her face, hypnotising her. His touch was cool, and as he bent his head towards her she could feel his breath on her cheek.

'I should go,' she stammered, but her body seemed to have a mind of its own. Very slowly, Raphael leant in and kissed her. If Cam's lips were soft, Raphael's seemed to actually *melt* into her own. It was as if she could feel every nerve ending, every heartbeat between them. Despite herself, Sapphire started to kiss him back. There was such a passion, yet such a sweetness about it, that she felt powerless to resist. Suddenly, it was as if the whole world had stopped and they were the only two people who existed.

'What the hell is going on here?'

She sprang back from Raphael like a scalded cat.

To her absolute horror, Cam was standing over them. He looked furious.

'I can't believe you're hooking up with him, when you were only with me a few days ago!'

'Cam, it's not what you think!' She jumped up, blood draining from her face. 'I mean, it just happened, I wasn't—'

'Like it just happened with us?' Cam sounded really upset.

Raphael stood up, his face confused. 'But I thought...' Instantly, the wall went up again and he stared at her with undisguised hostility. 'You have kissed Cam as well?'

Sapphire stared at the ground, not knowing what to say. This was awful! Raphael made a disgusted sound and, grabbing his guitar, stalked off. Cam looked at her and shook his head. 'I thought you really cared about me.'

'I do!' she cried. 'Oh God, I can't explain what just happened. I'm so sorry.'

'I'm sorry too, Sapphire. I thought we had something.'

'Cam!' she shouted, but he'd already stormed off in

the other direction. Legs shaking, Sapphire collapsed on the sand and burst into tears. A slight noise made her look up.

A few feet away, across the sand, Brad was standing with Madison and Simonetta. His face looked totally shocked. With another jolt of complete despair, Sapphire realised they'd witnessed the whole thing.

chapter forty

Madison let out a scandalised laugh, 'Oh my *God*, Sapphire. You've really done it this time!'

'Be quiet, Madison,' Brad snapped. He looked at Sapphire sternly. 'What's this? Have you really been carrying on with Cam and Raphael under my roof?' Sapphire looked away, tears of shock and upset fighting their way up her throat. Brad took her silence as confirmation. 'I see.' His voice was cold. 'Well, Sapphire, I have to say I thought more of you. You've totally abused my trust, young lady.'

'It wasn't like that,' she tried to say, but Brad cut her off. 'I could see exactly what it was like.' He stepped forward. 'Look at me, Sapphire.' She tried to meet his harsh gaze.

'Listen, I have given you more chances than you probably deserve, but this is the very last time, do you hear me? Any more bad behaviour from you and I'll be putting you on the next plane home.'

It was all Sapphire could do to nod miserably. 'Yes, Brad.'

Brad nodded curtly. 'Now get out of my sight. I think you've got some apologising to do.'

Sapphire wept the entire way back to the house. Brad obviously thought she was a total slut now. She'd seen the looks on Madison and Simonetta's faces as well, like she was just a piece of dirt. Madison was probably in seventh heaven about her getting caught like that. A fresh wave of tears came; she hadn't meant to hurt anyone. Her stomach clenched as she thought of Cam's face, looking down on her and Raphael kissing. And now Raphael hated her as well.

It was like some kind of awful nightmare. She had to try and *do* something.

She desperately knocked at his door for a few minutes before Raphael finally opened it. He stared down at her like she was a stranger, eyes almost black in the dimness of the corridor. 'What do you want?'

'Raphael, I'm so sorry,' Sapphire gulped. 'I truly never meant for this. Ruining our friendship is the last thing I want to happen.'

His face tightened with anger. 'Our *friendship*? I was just about to…' He stopped himself and glared at her. 'I was wrong about you, Sapphire. You are just like the rest of them. Playing your stupid games that hurt other people's feelings and ruin lives!'

Sapphire was confused. What did he mean, playing games? 'Raphael, I don't understand—'

'Oh, I think you understand perfectly,' he said coldly. 'Why don't you get back to your rich, little world and carry on having fun? That's all that matters to girls like you, isn't it? *Fun.*'

'Raphael!' she pleaded. 'I'm not like that.'

'Leave now,' he said, his voice a dangerous growl. 'I never want to lay eyes on you again.' The door slammed violently in her face. Sapphire put her face in her hands and started to weep.

The evening got even worse. After failing to reach him on his mobile, Sapphire went over to the guesthouse to try and explain to Cam. A bulky minder with a shaved head wouldn't even let her past the front door. Not that it would have made much difference. As she forlornly made her way back to the main house, Sapphire received a text from Cam.

It's over. Forget it. Just leave me alone.

Fighting back tears, Sapphire ran straight to her bedroom. No one came to see if she was all right, not that she expected them to. She was even too upset to phone her mum. After hours of sobbing, she eventually cried herself to sleep.

She was woken by a knock at the door. Sapphire's eyes were still so swollen she could hardly make out the time on her wristwatch. She only knew it was morning from the sunlight streaming in through the curtains. 'Who is it?' she called out croakily.

'Maggie.' Her tone was no-nonsense. 'Let me in.'

Sapphire's heart sank; she couldn't face another person having a go at her. Reluctantly she got up, still dressed in her clothes from last night, and went over to the door. Bracing herself, Sapphire pulled the door open and waited for the telling-off to start. To her surprise, Maggie was standing there looking worried.

'What have you got yourself into this time?' Her kindly voice set Sapphire off again.

'Maggie, everything's gone wrong,' she cried, throwing herself into the housekeeper's arms.

'Oh, darlin',' Maggie said a few minutes later. They were sitting on Sapphire's bed, Maggie holding a box of tissues. Sapphire had eventually stopped crying; she didn't think she had any left to shed anyway.

Sapphire had just told Maggie what had happened. 'I'm really not that kind of girl, Maggie,' she said. 'It's all been a horrible misunderstanding. And now Brad hates me as well.'

'Hate is a very strong word,' Maggie told her. 'I'm sure Mr Masters doesn't feel like that.'

'Cam hates me, that's for sure,' Sapphire said gloomily. 'And Raphael. I've made such a mess of things.'

Maggie sighed. 'I don't know, you young people.' She put a hand on Sapphire's knee. 'Come on now, pull yourself together. You must hold your head up high and prove to everyone what you're really like.'

'I think it's too late for that. Even if I did try to talk to them, they'd probably just tell me where to go.'

'I have faith in you, Sapphire,' Maggie told her.

Sapphire tried to grin. 'At least someone does.' She exhaled shakily, feeling the tiniest bit better. 'Maybe I will give it a go.'

The housekeeper shifted on the bed. 'There is another reason I'm here.'

Sapphire looked at her. 'Oh?'

'Brad asked me to come and tell you the private jet is ready to fly to Florida.'

Sapphire felt sick; in all the drama she'd totally forgotten about the trip. 'When are we going?' she asked apprehensively. If she just had a few more days, she could talk to both Cam and Raphael and try to bring them round.

Maggie looked at her, face serious. 'If you want to make amends, Sapphire, you'd better do it quickly. You're flying out this afternoon.'

* * *

It was the weirdest experience of her life. Here she was, flying on a private jet, the stuff of dreams, yet Sapphire had never felt more miserable or lonely. As she glanced across the narrow aisle to where Brad, Simonetta and Madison sat talking and laughing together, Sapphire felt like they were deliberately excluding her. She hadn't missed the sly little glances Madison kept shooting her way, either. Brad had hardly said two words to her since they'd been on board.

Sapphire sunk down in the soft leather seat, wishing she had an Invisibility Cloak to pull around her. Raphael hadn't even bothered to answer the door when she'd gone around again to try and talk to him, and there was no way she could get through Cam's impenetrable entourage. To her relief, he was flying separately with his team. Until she had climbed on board at Rome airport, she'd had no idea that the space inside private jets was so *small*. It might look fantastic and be worth millions of dollars, but there was barely room to swing a cat. To sit so close to Cam in these circumstances would have been agony.

The glamorous flight attendant, her uniform the

same silver and blue colours as the aircraft, appeared in front of her. 'Miss Stevens, can I get you anything?'

'No, thank you,' Sapphire said. She looked out of the window and tried to prepare herself for what was ahead.

chapter forty-one

Key West, Florida

Madison stretched out in bed and smiled. Now that she was back on home turf she felt even more invincible. Homelands had turned out to be even more awesome than she'd imagined. It was a sprawling mansion with huge white pillars flanking the front door and acres of gardens, complete with swaying palm trees and a lake full of these weird, pink birds. Madison had thought they were flamingos, but on their tour last night Brad had called them spoonbills or something. Like, whatever! As if she was here for a *nature* lesson.

Throughout the tour last night, Madison had slipped her arms through Brad's and walked with him slightly ahead of the other two. As they took in the swimming pool and mini-golf course, the fleet of shining cars in the garages, Madison had never felt so truly at home. This was where she belonged, amongst all the wealth and glamour. She could just imagine herself living in a place like this and reclining poolside in a killer one-piece, snapping her fingers at the staff to bring her a freshly squeezed pomegranate juice. When she got her hands on Brad's money, she could have, like, hundreds of places like this!

Madison was also suitably satisfied to see that Sapphire was moping around with a face like a wet weekend. As far as Madison was concerned, the skanky slut had had it coming to her. She so wasn't Little Miss Perfect *now*. As far as Madison was concerned, it was all working out just fine. Forget needing any help from her – Sapphire had gone and stitched herself up good and proper. As if she'd really had any chance with Cam Tyler! Now Madison had to think about how to get rid of that skinny ho, Simonetta. And she had the perfect plan for that.

'Madison, honey, you're one clever bitch,' she told herself. Reaching across the bed, she picked up the phone to demand breakfast in bed.

Three days later

If Sapphire had thought Casa Eleganza was something, Homelands was in a different stratosphere. With its countless turrets, huge arched windows and sprawling verandas running along four sides of the house, it reminded Sapphire of an upmarket Disneyland castle. The views were even more spectacular, reaching the turquoise waters of the Florida Keys. Sapphire had never seen an ocean coloured like it. Brad had mentioned last night that Florida was famous for its alligators, and that one of his neighbours had even found one sitting in his swimming pool one morning. Sapphire had shivered at this – it seemed like a good metaphor for the place.

Beneath the luxurious beauty, tensions were running high.

Brad had been polite but distant to her since they'd got there. Every time Sapphire looked into his eyes, she knew she'd disappointed him. She hadn't seen Cam since they'd got there, either. Homelands was the size of a small town and Cam and his team were camped out in guest bungalows on the other side of the estate. Sapphire had half-heartedly tried his mobile a few times, but it was always off. Her constant checking of her own phone wore off as she realised she wasn't going to hear from him.

As much as she yearned after Cam, funnily enough the person Sapphire felt the worst about was Raphael. In some way, she felt like she *had* let him down, that she'd been the only person he'd ever reached out to and then it had all gone wrong. Cam had an open, confident manner, a solid warmness to him that made him easy to read. But with Raphael, it was different. Sapphire found herself wondering what was behind those mesmerising eyes, what made him tick. When Raphael had told her about Gabriel, she had seen a chink, but now Raphael's defences were drawn up even tighter than ever. There was no way she would ever be able to get past them, not now.

I totally blew our friendship, she thought miserably. *And now I'll never see him again.*

The next morning the three girls were sitting on the south-facing veranda, eating breakfast. While the other two made conversation, or rather Madison talked and Simonetta looked bored, Sapphire ate her waffles in silence. She had avoided seeing the other two as much as possible since the night on the beach, but with Brad busy at the recording studio with Cam, they had pretty much been thrown together again. Sapphire very much doubted the invitation to watch Cam work would stand. The only positive result out of all this were the new lyrics that had been pouring out of her. It felt like she was trapped in a five-star prison and writing songs was her only release. To her surprise, the melodies were coming thick and fast as well. *Guess it's true that musicians produce their best work when they're going through some kind of trauma*, she thought wryly.

Madison took a dainty bite of the kiwi fruit she was eating. 'Mmm, this tastes sooo good! At least we're away from all that pasta and cheese. I swear I put on, like, *half* a pound in Italy.'

'You do look a bit fatter round the face,' Simonetta said maliciously. With her idiotic chatter and constant sucking up to Brad, Madison was seriously getting on her nerves.

Madison shot her a death stare over the table. 'Yeah, well at least I'm not like…' Her eyes roamed over Simonetta, looking for some imperfection.

Simonetta raised a threatening eyebrow. *Just you try it.*

'At least I'm not, like, a *giant,*' Madison finally sniped, in reference to Simonetta's statuesque height.

The model snorted. 'Better to be tall than stupid.'

Madison's mouth dropped open. '*What* did you just call me?'

Simonetta stared at her insolently. '*Penso che lei è una ragazza stupida.*'

Madison turned to Sapphire. 'What did she just say?'

Sapphire shrugged. 'No idea.' She was sure she'd

heard the words 'stupid' and 'girl', but there was no way that she was getting drawn into this stupid argument. Sapphire knew she wasn't perfect, but she just couldn't believe that she was related to such awful people. She wondered whom they had got their personalities from. The idea that they'd all inherited some kind of negative trait from Brad was a worrying thought. If she suddenly started wearing head-to-toe pink and talking in a baby voice, she was going to kill herself.

Unaware of her thoughts, Madison looked at her with fake concern. 'Bumped into Cam recently?'

Here we go, Sapphire thought. She thought Madison had been far too quiet on the subject. 'No,' she said shortly. She was suddenly sick of being made to feel like Public Enemy Number One. It wasn't as if she'd murdered someone. Sapphire threw her napkin down on her plate. 'Was there anything else? I can tell you're practically wetting yourself with glee about it all. So come on, if you've got any other snide comments, let's get them out in the open. I'm fed up with these sly little looks you keep giving me.'

Madison's eyes widened. 'Ooh, the runt *has* got a

temper on her! Mind you, I'd be pissed off too if Cam Tyler dumped me. Not that he would, obviously.'

Sapphire tried to stay calm. At this rate Madison was coming very close to being stabbed with her own fork. 'You really don't know what you're talking about.'

Madison gave a nasty little smile. 'Oh, I think I know a slut when I see one! And that poor boy, Raphael – you didn't just lead him down the garden path, sweetie, you took him all the way down the path into the ocean!'

Sapphire jumped up, her fists clenched. 'You leave Raphael out of this! That's not how it bloody happened!'

'Sapphire, calm down,' said Simonetta. She was aware that a passing staff member had stopped to stare.

Sapphire remained where she was, hot angry tears springing into the back of her eyes. 'You can think what you like of me. I really don't care.'

'Er, obvious much?' Madison said. 'If you cared about anything, you wouldn't be running around like a bitch in heat.'

Sapphire looked into her pretty, hate-filled face.

Stay calm, she told herself. *Don't let her get the better of you.* She took a deep breath. 'You know what, Madison? I actually feel really sorry for you.' With a superhuman effort not to squash the rest of Madison's kiwi in her face, Sapphire left.

Madison looked at Simonetta in outraged astonishment. '*She* feels sorry for *me*? Girls would chop off their hair extensions to be Madison Vanderbilt and that runt knows it!'

'If you say so,' Simonetta drawled. 'Talking of hair,' her eyes swept critically over Madison's own tresses. 'I assume you know yours is going green. It must be all that chlorine.'

Madison narrowed her eyes at the Italian. 'Yeah, well, at least green is better than witch black! I didn't *realise* Halloween had come early.' They glared at each other over the table.

From his office on the edge of the lawn, Brad sat back in his chair and thought about what he'd just seen. He had no idea what they'd been talking about, but Sapphire had looked pretty upset. All three of them looked ready to blow up at the moment and Brad had a bad feeling Sapphire would be the first.

chapter forty-two

Later that day, Sapphire had calmed down enough to face the outside world. She knew she should rise above Madison, but she was just so evil. Once again Sapphire wondered why she was putting herself through this when no one wanted her here, but then Maggie's words came back to her. *'Hold your head high, and show them what you're really like.'*

Not that Sapphire gave a hoot what Madison or Simonetta thought. But she did want to make amends with Brad, even though it was pretty obvious she'd blown her chances of becoming his heir.

Then, of course, there was Cam. Sapphire hadn't wanted to admit it to herself until now, but there was still a little piece of her holding out hope. Her mind cast back to their night on the beach, Cam's kiss and his warm, brown hands on her body. It was starting to feel like a snapshot from a film that she'd never been in. *I have to make it up with him*, she thought desperately. The most exciting thing that had ever happened to her had been wrenched away, and Sapphire was shocked to find out how much it hurt.

She needed to clear her head and decided to go for a walk. She'd only got a few yards outside when her heart stopped. Cam was walking straight towards her, Larry his manager in tow, talking on his mobile. Cam looked surprised to see her and, unless Sapphire was imagining it, a little bit guilty. What did he have to be guilty about? It was meant to be the other way round.

'Hi, Sapphire.' Cam managed an unenthusiastic smile. He was in a hooded top and jeans slung low enough to see a flash of his stomach. Sapphire felt a rush of longing.

'Cam, I need to talk to you,' she said.

He sighed. 'Sapphire, it's kind of difficult right now. I'm sorry.'

Larry came up behind him. 'Cam, we've only got thirty minutes for lunch. Move along, please. I need a word with this young lady.' Cam gave an apologetic shrug and walked off.

Larry looked at Sapphire like he'd just found her on the bottom of his shiny Gucci slip-on. His eyes were mean and nasty, like a ferret's. 'Now listen here, sweetheart,' he said in a strong New York accent. 'Cam's got enough girls like you throwing themselves at him normally, but I won't have it when he's recording his debut album, you hear me?'

There was that expression again. *Girls like you*.

'I'm not trying to distract Cam,' she said tightly. 'We're friends.'

Larry looked at her. 'Yeah, right. I know just what you'd like to be, honey, and friends it ain't. There's no way I'm gonna let you get your hands on his money.'

'I'm not after his money!' Sapphire exclaimed. 'What do you take me for?'

Larry's mobile started ringing again. 'Exactly what I

said, sweetheart. Now you stay out of Cam's way or I'll make sure you regret it.' He walked off to take the call. 'Ari! My main man. How ya doin'?'

Sapphire stared after him, open-mouthed. She couldn't quite believe people could be so rude. Did Cam know how awful his manager was? *Then again*, she thought with a sinking realisation, *he probably employed Larry for that exact reason*. Larry made sure no one could get to Cam unless he wanted them to. Sapphire was starting to think she didn't like the world he operated in very much at all.

That evening there was a big dinner party, to which Brad invited several of his friends and work colleagues. They were a very glamorous, sociable bunch and Brad made sure that all three girls were included in the conversation. Madison was talking nineteen to the dozen and holding court as normal, while Sapphire was placed next to a female executive from Brad's record company. They had all been instructed to say they were family friends. Aside from having to keep up that pretence, Sapphire actually had quite a good evening. The food was delicious and the woman she was sitting next to was really nice. It was such a relief to have a normal conversation with someone who didn't know what had happened.

By contrast, she noticed Simonetta getting more and more withdrawn as the evening went on. Even though she was wearing a stunning black dress and had piled up her hair elegantly, her eyes looked flat and lifeless. It seemed like Brad had noticed too. When Simonetta announced she had a headache and wished to go to bed, Sapphire found herself exchanging glances with him. After the meal, when they had all retired to the veranda for coffee, Brad took her aside.

'Do you think Simonetta's all right? She seemed very subdued tonight.'

'I know,' Sapphire replied. 'To be honest, I don't think she's been herself for a while. I think I should go and talk to her, if that's OK. I mean, I don't want to leave your guests in the lurch…'

Brad smiled at her. 'I totally agree. Take as long as you want.' In that moment, it was like the old days, when he'd liked and trusted her. It gave Sapphire a nice feeling inside.

*   *   *

Sapphire still hadn't found her way round Homelands, so it took a few wrong turns and trips down several long corridors before she found Simonetta's bedroom. The door was slightly ajar, as if it hadn't been closed properly. Sapphire knocked softly on it.

'Simonetta?' Sapphire could hear strange noises coming from inside, as if someone was gasping and choking. 'Simonetta?' she said more loudly, alarm starting to build up. Slowly, she pushed the door open. Her mouth dropped open at the sight that greeted her.

Food was everywhere. Well, the remains of it anyway. Crumbs of bread were scattered across the floor, empty crisp packets lay scrunched up, the remains of a huge chocolate bar was smeared across the duvet cover. Sapphire didn't understand, where had this come from? Simonetta had the smallest appetite of anyone she knew.

Suddenly, there was a loud retching sound from the en-suite bathroom. Sapphire rushed over and pulled the door open. 'Simonetta, are you ill?' She stopped dead in her tracks. There, hanging over the toilet, her hair in soggy rats' tails, was Simonetta. She had her fingers down her throat and was so intent on making herself sick she didn't see Sapphire for a few moments. Sapphire wanted to move, run away so Simonetta didn't see her, but she found herself transfixed to the spot.

Then, as Simonetta's skinny shoulders heaved again, she looked up and saw Sapphire. Her beautiful face was blotchy and red, mascara running down from her watery eyes. Sapphire remembered when she had bumped into Simonetta outside the toilet at Casa Eleganza and thought she had been crying. Had she been making herself sick? How long had this been going on?

'Simonetta. I didn't mean to—' she started to say, but Simonetta cut her off.

'Get out!' she hissed, trying desperately to wipe the sick away from her face. 'This is my bedroom, how dare you come in?'

'I'm sorry, I—'

'You will be if you don't get out!' she shrieked. 'Leave me, GO!'

'All right, all right!' Sapphire said. Backing out, she turned and left the room quietly. The last thing she heard was another retch, followed closely by a sob.

chapter forty-three

Simonetta found Sapphire the next morning, reading by the pool. Madison was nowhere to be seen and the place was quiet apart from them.

'We need to talk,' Simonetta announced. She sat down on the sunbed next to Sapphire. She looked pale, but beautiful, with a hint of defiance in the way she held her chin. 'You will tell no one about last night, or you'll be sorry.'

Sapphire put her book down. 'Simonetta, I

wouldn't say anything anyway. You can trust me.'

In truth, Sapphire hadn't stopped thinking about it since. She had been piecing together the evidence – the food thief Maggie had talked about in the kitchen at Casa Eleganza, the sweet wrappers Sapphire had found stuffed down the back of the sofa. Katie, a friend of hers at school, had had bulimia, and Sapphire knew how unhappy and ill she'd been. She hated the thought that Simonetta was going through this by all herself.

'*Trust* you,' Simonetta said with a mocking laugh. 'There is little trust in this place, that is for sure.' She shot Sapphire a challenging look. 'So you have found out about my little Problem. That was what my *mamma* called it, "The Problem". You know, even when I ended up in hospital, when the doctor told me if I carried on I could *die*, she told people I was just suffering from a stomach complaint.' Simonetta smiled bitterly. 'She didn't understand, you see. I think it embarrassed her.' She shook her head. 'I've always been an embarrassment to my mother. Nothing I do is right.'

'I'm sure that's not true,' Sapphire said.

Simonetta laughed emptily. 'Sweet little Sapphire, always seeing the good in others! Sorry to shatter your illusions, but my mother criticised me from the day I was born.' She began to mimic her mother's voice. *'Why are you so naughty, Simonetta? Why can't you be like your brothers and sisters?'* Simonetta looked disgusted. 'As if I want to be like them. Fat, lazy and tied to my mother's apron-strings.'

'When did all… *this* start?' Sapphire asked gently.

Simonetta flashed her a look. 'What, my *bulimia*? You can say it, you know. My mother never would. She thought it was a dirty word, that she'd somehow failed to bring her family up properly.'

She stared moodily into the distance. 'As if our *family* were anything! There were eight of us, in one small house, and my papa' – she stopped, smiling scornfully – 'at least the man I *thought* was my papa, was lazy and cruel and picked on me. *Mamma* worked hard to try and make things better – always in the kitchen, cooking, cooking, cooking. She thought as long as we sat down as a family at every meal, it meant everything was all right. But it wasn't all right. *She* wasn't all right and she tried to mask the problems with food. Always there was food! I started to copy her. I ate when I was happy, which wasn't very often, when I was sad, lonely, stressed...

'People had started to comment on how beautiful I was, how I could make it as a model. I was stuck between two worlds: one where I would fill myself with food to hide the pain, and another, where I would panic about not being thin enough to be a model. I had started to gain weight and had to do something about it.'

Sapphire felt terrible for Simonetta. No wonder she was such a defensive, shut-off character. 'Did you tell your mum?' she ventured.

'*Si*. She found me one day in the toilet, just as you did. I think it frightened her, because she didn't know how to handle it. She told me to stop being so stupid, that Papa would be back soon and she didn't want him seeing it.' Simonetta laughed harshly. 'It didn't even *occur* to her that she and Papa might have something to do with it.

'It got better for a while,' she continued. 'When I left home and went to Rome, I felt more… in control of my life, like I was allowed to be me for the first time.'

Sapphire hesitated. 'What made it start again, Simonetta?'

'I *don't* want to talk about it.' There was no way Simonetta was telling Sapphire about her debts. To her surprise, however, Sapphire leant across and held one of her hands. For some reason, Simonetta found her eyes filling with tears. She blinked them away furiously.

Sapphire gave her a little smile. 'My mum always tells me that we don't have to let our past control our future.' She squeezed Simonetta's hand gently. 'All the stuff that happened at home, you can move on from it. I can help, if you like.'

'Help? You have no idea about my life!' Simonetta retorted. 'You, sweet little Sapphire, you have it all!'

'That's where you're wrong,' Sapphire said quietly. 'My dad Bill – and I do still think of him as my dad – died when I was little. It's just been me and Mum ever since and we've never had much money. We've had to struggle for things.'

Simonetta looked at her, in cross frustration. 'How are you so goddamn *happy* all the time then?'

Sapphire sighed. 'I'm not always happy, believe me. But I don't think being rich or being beautiful can bring you happiness. It might sound cheesy, but it's about finding out who *you* are and being happy with yourself.' She hesitated. 'You can get help, you know. There are people you can talk to. And if I can do anything—'

'Why?' Simonetta interrupted rudely. 'Why would you want to help me?'

Sapphire looked at her. Simonetta was deliberately challenging her, trying to push her away. 'No matter how much you hate it, Simonetta, we are flesh and blood. I care what happens to you.'

A funny expression came over Simonetta's face. 'Believe me, I am the last person you want to help. You are too nice for your own good.' She put her fingers to her lips warningly. 'We never had this conversation, remember.'

Sapphire watched as her half-sister shimmied off, looking as though she hadn't a care in the world.

That afternoon Brad had organised a sightseeing trip for the three of them on his luxury yacht. Sapphire had been half looking forward to it, half dreading being under Brad's radar, but just before lunch she started to get painful stomach cramps. Her period, always erratic, had come a whole six days early. Not sure whether to be upset or relieved, Sapphire told one of the maids that she was feeling unwell and went back to her bedroom to try and sleep it off.

A few hours later she opened her eyes. Sleep normally helped and her period pains had completely gone. She put aside the hot water bottle one of the staff had kindly brought up for her and sat up. Through the open window, she could see the sun was still high in the sky. Sapphire decided to get changed and take a walk around the estate to stretch her legs. *Maybe I'll see Cam*, she thought, hopefully. He hadn't seemed as angry the last time they'd bumped into each other.

As Sapphire set off, she wondered if her head had ever been so full of concerns before. As well as her upset at what had happened with Raphael and Cam, there was now Simonetta to worry about. Her half-sister had seemed so poised, so sure of herself. Never in a million years would Sapphire have thought she was suffering from bulimia, but then who knew how people were behind closed doors? Even though she had promised Simonetta not to say anything, Sapphire felt torn. Simonetta was clearly too proud to ask for help, but there was no doubt she needed it. *You gave her your word, Sapphire. She'd never speak to you again if you told someone.* For the time being, Sapphire had to respect Simonetta's wishes. At least Simonetta knew she could come and talk to her if she wanted, not that she expected her to.

Weirdly, Raphael was creeping into her thoughts more and more. As she didn't have his mobile number, she'd even thought about ringing the main house at Casa Eleganza and asking Tito to get him to contact her. She was still desperate to explain that she wasn't like Jessica, that she'd never meant to hurt him. Memories of their kiss kept flooding into her mind – his cool lips against hers, the electrifying feelings that had run through her. She still couldn't believe Raphael had made her feel like that. *Raphael?* But she was totally, one hundred per cent head over heels for Cam. Wasn't she? 'Aargh!' Sapphire said aloud, running her hands through her hair. What a horrible mess!

'Sapphire!' a voice called out. She turned to see

Madison tottering towards her on ridiculously high wedge heels. 'There you are! I've been looking for you.' She flashed a smile. 'I told Brad I'd come see how you're feeling.'

Sapphire had a feeling Madison had really come to impress Brad and not out of the goodness of her heart, but she didn't say it. 'Yeah, I'm feeling a lot better, thanks.'

'Time of the month?' Madison asked, putting on a sympathetic smile. 'You have seemed really moody the last couple of days.'

Sapphire shook her head, smiling; Madison couldn't help but be a bitch. You kind of had to hand it to her for consistency.

'So, where you off to?' Madison asked.

'Just for a walk,' Sapphire said.

Madison's eyes twinkled. 'Would that walk include going past *the recording studio*?'

'No!' Sapphire said hotly. How did Madison *know* these things?

Madison tinkled with laughter. 'Oh come on, sweetie! It can't just be a coincidence you're heading that way.'

'I told you – I'm going for a walk.'

Madison gave her a knowing smile. 'Well, if you *were* planning a little visit, I'd go now. I've just seen Cam's manager and his flunkies drive off somewhere. I mean, that guy *never* lets Cam out of his sight, does he?'

Sapphire tried not to show her sudden surge of hope.

Madison smiled. 'I'll leave you to it! I can go and sunbathe in peace now that I know you're OK.'

Don't lay it on too thickly, love, Sapphire thought as Madison tottered off. She wouldn't put it past Madison to have set her up, making her walk right into the lion's den. Still, no harm in trying...

As she approached the studio the coast was clear, no gorilla-type minder guarding the door. Maybe Madison was telling the truth after all. Looking left and right, Sapphire ran up the steps, adrenalin pumping. She found herself in a small reception area. Still no Larry. Leading off to either side were two glass-fronted rooms with signs saying "Studio One" and "Studio Two" on the outside of the doors.

Studio One was in darkness, but Sapphire's heart

did a little flip when she saw Cam, standing in a little booth adjoining Studio Two. He had headphones on and was singing into a large microphone hanging down from the ceiling. Next door, in the actual studio, two men nodded their heads and fiddled with buttons on a complicated-looking mixing desk.

Sapphire edged closer. Cam looked different – his dark, spiky hair had been shaved to a grade two all over. It showed off his bone structure and strong, muscled neck, making him look sexier than ever. Sapphire suddenly felt an intense yearning for him, wanted him to take her in his arms again and kiss her.

The booth was soundproof, but Sapphire's curiosity got the better of her. She wanted to hear Cam. Quietly, so as not to disturb them, she opened the door to the studio and stood in the dim light at the back. Cam's voice, husky and raw, filled the room. The track he was singing along to seemed oddly familiar to Sapphire.

One of the men waved his hands. 'OK, good, Cam! Now let's try the chorus again. One, two, three…'

As the beat started up again, it all started to fall into place.

*'Yo girl! Now listen up. The brightest star, the richest
sunrise, nothing compares to your glitter*

Jewel. Hey Jewel

*Colours fade when you enter a room, birds lose their
chatter*

Jewel. You listening to me honey?'

Even with the changes, it was obvious. She didn't
know how, or why, but Cam had stolen her and
Raphael's song. There was no way it could be a
coincidence. He started singing the next line and
blood started rushing through Sapphire's ears.

But just as there is light, you bring with you dark

Taking all around down with you…

Sapphire leapt forward, anger flooding through
her. 'You stole it! This is our song, mine and
Raphael's! We wrote it, not you!'

Both sound engineers spun round in their chairs.
'Jesus, what is this?' exclaimed one, who had a gingery
goatee beard. 'Cliff, call security.' Ignoring him,
Sapphire ran over and banged on the glass partition.
Cam looked across, the shock clear on his face.

'You stole our song, Cam!' Sapphire yelled. 'Why
would you do such a thing?'

Cam paled for a moment, and then he recovered himself. He shot her an uneasy grin. 'Hey, Sapphire,' he said. 'Is this some kind of joke? I really have *no* idea what you're talking about.'

chapter forty-four

Brad frowned. 'You're making a very serious allegation.' Sapphire had found him in his study, a massive room with floor-to-ceiling windows looking out over the ocean.

'Brad, I swear to you it's true!' she said. 'Raphael and I wrote "Jewel" together at Casa Eleganza. Cam must have overheard it somehow and decided to use it.'

Brad stared hard at her. 'Cam's one of the biggest

up-and-coming music artists in the United States. Do you realise what you're saying here? That he stole a song from you?'

Sapphire nodded miserably. 'I wish it wasn't true.' She was absolutely gutted. Cam hadn't even run after her to try and apologise. Why would he *do* such a thing? He must have plenty of great songs of his own. He was just one big fake and she'd fallen for the whole famous pop star thing. She'd been so stupid!

Brad sighed and ran his hands over his face. 'I've spoken with Cam. He says "Jewel" is his song and he wrote it months ago.'

'Then he's lying!' Sapphire said furiously.

Brad looked at her. 'Be careful who you call a liar, Sapphire.' She stared at the floor, not trusting herself to speak. 'Raphael's not here to vouch for you, unfortunately,' Brad said.

A thought popped into Sapphire's head. 'Madison and Simonetta! They heard it. I recorded it on my mobile and played it to them afterwards. Simonetta even said she liked it.'

'Do you still have the song on your mobile?' he asked.

Sapphire's heart sank. 'I looked for it the other day and I couldn't find it – I thought I had saved it, but…' She trailed off, a sudden sick feeling in her stomach. When her phone had gone missing that time at Casa Eleganza, one of them must have stolen it and deleted the song! Those complete *cows*. Sapphire's shoulders slumped in defeat. She could tell Brad, but what was the point? She'd been stitched up yet again.

From the look on his face, Sapphire could see Brad didn't believe her anyway. 'We need to sort this out once and for all,' he said. He picked up the phone on the desk. 'Hello, Tracie? Can you get someone to find Madison and Simonetta and bring them to my study? Immediately please, it's urgent.'

The minutes ticked by. Eventually the sound of footsteps could be heard down the corridor and, as Sapphire breathed out, she realised she'd been tense the whole time. Would Madison and Simonetta tell the truth? Did they really hate her that much? She glanced at Brad, but he was already walking towards the door. They hadn't said a word to each other. He opened it. 'Come in, girls.' The two girls walked in, wearing kaftans over their bikinis.

Madison smiled sweetly. 'Hi, Brad, we got here as quickly as we could! We were just by the pool. Hi, Sapphire!'

'I'm sorry to interrupt your afternoon,' said Brad. 'This won't take a minute. We have a rather, er, delicate situation here.'

The two girls looked from Brad to Sapphire with interest. 'Oh?' said Madison.

Brad came round from his desk and leaned on it, arms folded. 'Sapphire says that Cam has stolen a song that she wrote. She went to the studio and heard him singing it. However, Cam maintains the song is *his*. As I'm sure you are aware, Cam is about to release his debut album and any suggestion of plagiarism would be disastrous.'

Madison's eyes widened. 'Oh, my!'

Sapphire spoke, desperate to get this cleared up. 'Madison, you heard me play "Jewel" to you by the pool, remember? I told you Raphael and I had just recorded it. You didn't like it very much.'

There was a deadly silence in the room. *Prove me wrong*, Sapphire willed. *Tell Brad you heard it.*

Madison gave a sad smile. 'Oh, Sapphire, I can't believe you'd make up such a thing.'

'I didn't make it up!' Sapphire exploded. 'I played it to you! By the pool!'

Madison looked at Brad, her face a mask of concern. 'We were afraid of something like this happening. Ever since Cam dumped Sapphire, she has been talking about getting revenge.'

Sapphire laughed in despair. It was outrageous. 'I don't believe this! I've never said such a thing!' She turned to Simonetta. 'You heard me play "Jewel" to you by the pool! Just after Raphael and I had finished it! Remember? You said that you liked it.'

Simonetta's face was completely blank. 'You must be mistaken, Sapphire.' Something uncomfortable shifted behind her eyes, but then it was gone again.

Sapphire stood still, the blood draining from her face. She just couldn't believe this was happening. How could one human being be so awful to another? 'Simonetta, how can you do this?' she asked. 'We're sisters. After everything we talked about yester—'

'After what?' said Simonetta, a hard look in her eyes.

Sapphire swallowed. A small part of her wanted to reveal Simonetta's secret, but that wasn't her style. She'd made a promise, and she was going to keep it. Even now. Maybe Simonetta couldn't be trusted, but *she* was different. She looked away, tears welling up.

Brad cleared his throat. 'I think I've heard enough. Thank you, girls, you can go now. Sapphire, you stay behind.'

'Brad, I—' she started, but Brad held up a hand. His face was like thunder.

'Sapphire, you've pushed it too far this time. I've given you so many chances, but you've thrown them back in my face. You've left me no solution but to send you home. I'll get Tracie to organise your plane ticket back to London tonight.'

Sapphire went to open her mouth, but shut it again. What was the point? She was sick of trying to prove herself. She was sick of this whole stupid thing. She just wanted to be a million miles away from this whole place, away from Brad, Madison and Simonetta. It had been a total disaster and she wanted to be home again, with people who knew and loved her.

'Have you anything to say for yourself?' Brad asked.

Anger surged up inside her. 'You know what? I have. I know you don't believe me, but Raphael and I wrote "Jewel", not Cam. I didn't do a naked streak round Charlotte Island, somebody stole my clothes. And I don't even like the taste of alcohol, so I don't know what happened that night.' Sapphire fought back tears. 'I know I've disappointed you, but I honestly didn't do it on purpose.' Brad was looking at her, his face unmoved. Sapphire composed herself – there was no way she was going to start blubbing. 'Thank you very much for having me as your guest, you've been more than generous.' And with a sudden feeling of freedom, she turned and walked out.

Madison could literally hug herself. It had all worked out so perfectly. She couldn't believe how *gullible* some people were – *as if* Cam Tyler would have ever been interested in that lame-ass runt! All it had taken was a cunning plan to make out Sapphire was a complete slut and the rest had just fallen into place. She knew how the music industry worked; although Cam was fast on his way to becoming a household name, he wasn't earning big bucks yet. The lifestyle that went with being a pop star – the entourage, the stylists, the chauffeurs – all came out of his own pocket.

Once Madison realised he wasn't mega-loaded, she'd kinda gone off him. Cam had told her in confidence and asked her not to tell anyone, and the only reason Madison hadn't blabbed was because there was no one to blab it to, apart from Simonetta. But it *had* got her thinking. When she'd approached Cam and told him her idea – that she wanted him to seduce Sapphire and make out he was interested in her, Cam hadn't taken much persuading. Madison had promised him that if he helped get Sapphire out of the way, she would give him a chunk of the money if she was chosen as Brad's heir. They'd even drawn up a contract to make it official.

When Raphael had stepped into the picture, Madison's scheming had gone into overdrive. She had told Simonetta about the plan, and even brought her in on the deal. If she won, she'd give Simonetta and Cam a big pay-out. If Simonetta won, she'd do the same. Again, they'd made it official with a contract.

And Brad thinks Simonetta's the one with the business brain.

After that, she'd asked Simonetta to go and see Raphael, to tell him that Sapphire was really into him but was too shy to do anything about it. All that had been left was to tell Cam to turn up and act hurt when he saw Raphael kissing Sapphire, and for her and Simonetta to take Brad on a walk along the beach at the same time. Lo and behold, slutty Sapphire had been exposed. Madison couldn't have wished for it to go better.

The phone had been a nice touch. Cam had asked her to get hold of some of Sapphire's music, so he could listen to it and see if she was any good. As soon as Sapphire had played "Jewel" to them by the pool that day, Madison had known she'd struck gold. All it had taken was for her to take Sapphire's phone and go see Cam. Cam had been blown away. *'This has*

Number One written all over it,' he'd said. *'Madison, I have to have it. Who's gonna believe Sapphire over me?'*

Madison had been impressed; she'd had no idea Cam could be quite so devious. Once he'd recorded it on to his own phone, she'd deleted the version on Sapphire's phone as if it had never been there. Then she'd left the phone in an obvious place in the garden, where Sapphire could have easily dropped it. The only thing that Madison was pissed about was the fact she couldn't tell anyone. She was a frickin' *genius*.

Now that she'd got rid of Sapphire, there was just one more person Madison had to deal with. Simonetta, her partner in crime. Madison had no use for her now, and she'd been holding on to the final, golden nugget of information until exactly the right time. Once Brad found out Simonetta was in masses of debt, there was no way he would let her inherit his fortune. Madison smiled to herself. She could almost *smell* the scent of success. Picking up her mobile, she called Brad's number.

'Brad? It's me, Madison.' She gave a convincing sob. 'I have to come and talk to you. I think Simonetta's in some kind of trouble…'

chapter forty-five

London, one month later

It was starting to rain as Sapphire made her way home from Jerry's shop. The skies above were heavy and grey, while an autumn chill filled the air. It was a million miles away from the paradise of Capri and Florida, but Sapphire didn't care. She'd missed the noise, the smells, the red buses, even the traffic. Now she was home, and it was the best feeling in the world.

It had all happened so quickly that day. Before

she'd known it, her case had been packed and she had been on a flight back to Heathrow. She'd gone first class, the last bit of luxury before returning home to reality. Sapphire didn't care; she'd almost wept with happiness when she'd walked back into the flat again. Beatle had ambled up and stuck his nose in her hand as if she'd just popped out to the shops, while her mother had rushed from the kitchen with a shriek of surprise and thrown her arms round her.

Sapphire had made the decision on the plane: she wasn't going to tell her mum the real reason she'd left. It was too raw, too soon, and she wanted to tell Leonie in her own time. So she told her mum that she'd been homesick and had decided to come home. Leonie had perceptively backed off until her daughter was ready to confide in her. For the first few days, Sapphire had stayed in her bedroom or taken Beatle out on walks to clear her head. Part of her was still seething with the injustice of it all, and she passed her time imagining horrible ways to get back at Madison and Simonetta. But she knew it wouldn't make her feel better; she simply wasn't programmed like that.

When her mum had gently suggested getting herself out and about again, Sapphire knew she was right. Jerry had welcomed her back into the shop with open arms and Sapphire threw herself into the start of the autumn term at college. Before long, the summer seemed like one strange dream. Her only reminder was the expensive watch that had been pushed to the back of her underwear drawer, hidden out of sight.

Yet despite her efforts to move on with her life, one person kept swirling round her mind: Raphael. Sapphire thought about him almost constantly, wondering what he was doing now, and if he ever thought of her. She had so much she wanted to tell him, like how well her studies were going and how impressed Jerry had been with her melodies. *You helped me so much,* she thought, *and I kicked you in the face in return.* She'd even plucked up the courage to phone Casa Eleganza one day, and had spoken to Tito. He'd been delighted to hear from her, but when Sapphire asked if she could speak to Raphael, he had sounded surprised.

'Raphael has gone back to Rome. I think only Brad had his number.'

That had been that, then. There was no way she was calling Brad to ask for Raphael's number, not after everything that had happened. He probably wouldn't have given it to her anyway. Bitterness and regret had churned in Sapphire's stomach. She hated the way it had all turned out.

The flat was quiet when she let herself in, no Beatle waiting for her in the hallway. Her mum had probably taken him for a walk, even though his tired old legs couldn't carry him far these days. Sapphire hung up her coat and went into the kitchen to put the kettle on. She got a packet of biscuits out of the cupboard and then switched the radio on. Suddenly, Cam's voice flooded into the kitchen, singing his hit from the previous summer. Sapphire's stomach did a nasty roll. Even though she had seen his true colours, it was still a shock when she heard him on the radio, or saw him on TV. She hadn't played 'Jewel' since she got back to England and was waiting, any day now, for Cam to release it. The thought made her feel sick, but what could she do? As Brad had pointed out, Cam was a world-famous music star and she was just some nobody from London.

She was dunking her second chocolate chip cookie into her tea when the doorbell rang. Brushing the crumbs off her front, she went to answer it. As she pulled the door open, her mouth fell open. There, standing on the doorstep with an umbrella, an expensive suit and a deep brown tan, was Brad.

He smiled at her. 'Hello, Sapphire.'

'Brad!' she gasped. 'What are you doing here?'

'Can I come in?' he asked. 'I'd forgotten how bad the weather is in England.' Sapphire looked behind him for the chauffeur-driven limo, but there wasn't one. 'I caught the tube,' Brad said with a smile. 'I have to say, it was quite an experience.'

Still slightly speechless, Sapphire led him into the living-room. He sat down in one of the armchairs. He looked out of place amongst the cosy clutter and Leonie's many hand-knitted throws and cushions.

'Can I get you anything?' she asked. 'Tea, coffee?'

Brad shook his head. 'Thank you, but no. I realise it must be quite a shock, me turning up like this.' Nervously, Sapphire sat on the arm of the other chair. Brad looked at her for a long time, making her feel even more anxious. 'Sapphire, I flew in especially from Rome to see you. I wanted to offer you my congratulations personally.'

Sapphire was confused. 'Congratulations for what?'

Finally, Brad's face broke into a big grin. 'I'm making you my heir. You're going to be a multi-millionaire!'

For a moment, his words didn't sink in. 'You're *what*?' she spluttered. 'But how, what? I don't understand!'

Brad's face suddenly grew serious. 'Sapphire, I haven't been entirely straight with you. But I had to do what I did to protect my assets, and to make sure I chose the right person. I hope you'll understand.'

Sapphire was totally confused now. 'Understand what?'

Brad looked at her. 'Sapphire, I knew the whole time what was going on. With you, Madison and Simonetta. I know you wrote "Jewel".'

'What?' she gasped. 'But how?'

Brad looked a bit shamefaced. 'I planned the whole summer, Sapphire. I knew I had to find out what each of you was really like, so I asked Cam to come and stay. Luckily, he needed a place to write.'

Sapphire's head was spinning. 'You asked Cam because of *us*? What do you mean?'

Brad gave a rueful grin. 'In my experience, there's nothing like putting a handsome young man into the mix for young ladies to show their true colours.'

A sick feeling started in Sapphire's stomach.

'I knew about it all from day one, Sapphire,' Brad said. 'Cam came and told me.'

'Cam was *in* on it?'

'I asked him to keep his eyes and ears open, and report back to me.' He paused, his voice suddenly gentle. 'Madison and Simonetta asked him to appear interested in you, to try and make out you were no good.'

Sapphire felt like she'd been kicked in the stomach. 'It was a *set up*? But Cam, he seemed so real…' She trailed off, feeling utterly humiliated.

Brad frowned. 'I must admit, I wasn't sure about that one. I told Cam as long as it didn't go too far…' He stopped and gave her a sympathetic smile. 'From what he told me, Cam didn't have to act very much. He thought you were a really great girl, Sapphire. He said to say sorry that he led you on. Especially as Raphael is in love with you.'

Hold on, this is too much. Sapphire felt her head spinning. Raphael? In *love* with her? 'What the hell are you talking about?' she gasped.

Brad was the one who looked confused now. 'I guess Cam spoke to him. I thought you knew…'

Sapphire couldn't speak. She felt utterly numb. Brad carried on.

'When I heard about their plan, I was surprised but not shocked. When you're in my business, you quickly learn some people will do anything for money. But I wanted to see just how far Madison and Simonetta would go, so I asked Cam to get hold of one of your songs and pretend to pass it off as his own. I knew the girls had heard your version – Cam told me. So when they denied it, they totally put themselves in the frame.' He looked regretful. 'It wasn't nice to find out my daughters could be so deceitful, but I do understand their motives. As I said, money makes people act in a funny, often desperate way.'

Sapphire sat still. 'So you knew all along?' she repeated.

Brad nodded. 'I know it wasn't ideal, Sapphire, but it was the only way I could find out who wanted the money and who really wanted to get to know me.' He smiled across the room at her. 'You're that person, Sapphire. From the start, you always made an effort with me, and it was obvious money wasn't the driving force.' He reached in his pocket and pulled out a CD. He handed it to Sapphire.

'What's this?' she said stupidly.

Brad smiled. 'It's yours and Raphael's demo. Of course, the sound quality isn't very good, so we'll get you in the studio to record it properly.'

Sapphire was lost again. 'I don't understand.'

'As soon as Cam played "Jewel" to me, I knew how good it was. How good *you* are. Sapphire, I'm giving you a recording contract!' His eyes twinkled. 'Pretty cool, huh? An heiress and a pop star in one day! What are you going to do with your money? I know I can trust you to spend it wisely.'

Sapphire was so angry she couldn't speak for a second. She stood up, her face furious. 'I don't want your money! Or your recording contract! You talk about Madison and Simonetta being devious and underhand, but you're just as bad as them!'

Brad looked shocked. 'Sapphire, I know it's a lot to take in, but please believe me when I say I acted with your best interests at heart.'

Sapphire couldn't stand it. The thought of Raphael, and the missed opportunity they'd had, burned through her like physical pain. 'Don't you mean protecting *your* interests? You've totally messed up people's lives, Brad. You talk about what money does to people – well, I can see what it's done to you! And Cam... I can't believe what he did.' *It was almost as bad as stealing my song*, she thought.

'Sapphire—'

'I mean it, Brad! Can't you get it through your head – I don't want your bloody money!'

Sapphire expected Brad to tell her off for swearing at him, but she was so angry she couldn't help it. But there was no tirade. Instead, Brad looked at the floor, silent. All Sapphire could hear was the sound of her own agitated breathing. When he finally looked up, his eyes were full of regret. 'I've made a complete pig's ear of this, haven't I?'

'Just a bit,' Sapphire said hotly.

Brad sighed heavily. 'You're right. I've been playing with people's lives. I had no right to do that.' He paused. 'I just thought that if it wasn't too late, I'd try and be a good dad, make my daughters happy. I guess I've still got a lot to learn.' He smiled ruefully. 'Maggie hit the roof when I told her everything that's happened. She's still not speaking to me.'

'That makes two of us then,' Sapphire retorted. 'What about Madison and Simonetta? Have you told them that you knew?'

'I hinted at it,' Brad said. 'They know I'm not happy.' He grimaced. 'Madison wasn't best pleased when I told her I was making you my heir. I'm hoping she'll have calmed down by now. She comes from a wealthy family anyway, so I know she'll be all right. That girl's one hell of a force to be reckoned with.'

'And Simonetta?' she shot back.

Brad sighed. 'She'd got herself into a bit of bother and I've helped her out. I hope it's set her back on the right path. She's got a great business brain, if she can just see through the superficial. Once she's had time to dwell on what she's done and hopefully learnt from it, I'm thinking of offering her a job at Brad Masters Enterprises.'

Sapphire wondered whether he knew about the bulimia, but as Brad didn't say anything, she didn't bring it up. She was still reeling from all the revelations. Raphael was really in love with her? It couldn't be true! The thought that it had all been messed up for them made her feel physically sick.

'I know you're angry with me,' Brad said.

Sapphire shook her head. *You've got no idea, mate.*

'Please, Sapphire.' Brad's voice was sad, pleading. 'I only did what I thought was right. Try to understand that.'

Understand? The irony that her mother had said almost exactly the same words when Sapphire had found out Brad was her dad didn't escape her. Adults were a nightmare! She was sick of them making decisions without telling her. But her sharp reply fell away when she saw Brad's face. He wasn't faking it. They stood looking at each other, trying to work out what the other was thinking. Suddenly, Brad stood up. 'Have you got a DVD player?'

'What?' Sapphire asked. Surely now wasn't the time to start watching TV!

'I've got something I'd like you to see.' He handed her the DVD. Still in a daze, she went over to the television and put it in. A few moments later, the screen flicked to life. She was shocked to see Madison and Simonetta looking into the camera. Madison looked as sick as a pig.

'Hi there, dear sister!' she gushed. 'We just wanted to say how *pleased* we are that Brad has chosen you to be his heir.' She looked like it physically pained her to say the words. Madison elbowed Simonetta. 'Aren't we?'

'*Si,*' the model drawled. Sapphire noticed she didn't look as pissed off as Madison. In fact, she looked quite happy.

Madison gave a fake smile. 'Anyway, honey, if you need anyone to go on a shopping trip with, you know where to find me! Baby, you are gonna be Amex black card *all* the way from now on.'

The screen faded away.

Brad chuckled. 'I made them send you a message of congratulations. I wouldn't want to think what

Madison said once the camera was switched off.' He looked back at her, his face quizzical. 'So you're really going to throw it all back in my face, Sapphire? I'm offering you the dream here.'

She shot him a look. 'It probably sounds completely stupid to you, but I want to make my *own* dreams. I want to achieve things through my own hard work, not have it handed to me on a plate. So I don't want any recording contract – unless it comes from someone who's heard my music and doesn't know who I am.'

Brad cocked his head, smiling. 'It doesn't sound stupid. Maybe we're more alike than I realised, you and I. After all, I started with nothing as well. But I know just how hard it is, what sacrifices you have to make. Will you at least think about my offer? I think you could do wonderful things with the money.' His voice suddenly sounded thick, like he had a cold or something. 'Most importantly, I've found you. And I don't want to let you go again, *any* of you. You're all such unique, vibrant young women, and despite what Simonetta and Madison have done, I'm proud to be a father to all of you. Sapphire, will you at least give me the chance to try and be a real dad?'

He looked so sincere and sad that Sapphire felt a jolt on her heartstrings. After a moment's pause, she nodded. 'OK. Just don't expect me to start calling you Dad yet. That's going to take a lot of work.'

Brad gave a mock salute. 'Yes ma'am!'

Sapphire managed a small smile. 'I think you'd better go now. Mum's due back any moment and she'll have a heart attack if she finds you here.'

At the mention of her mum, a strange expression came over Brad's face. It almost looked like sorrow. Sapphire took a deep breath. There was something she'd wanted to ask him ever since she'd found out he was her dad. 'Did my mum ever mean anything to you? Why did you leave us?'

Brad looked at her, his face full of emotion. 'I don't know how to say this, so I'll come straight out with it. Sapphire, your mum left *me*.'

'Why did you break it off with him, Mum?' Sapphire said. They were sitting in the kitchen drinking tea, Beatle curled up in his basket in the corner.

Leonie sighed. 'I was so young and free-spirited

then, I didn't want to be tied down. Brad offered me everything: security, wealth, but I didn't want it. He was already working so hard by then, and I wanted my own career. I didn't want to follow him round the world, leave you with a succession of different nannies. That was no way to bring up a child. The only thing that nearly stopped me was Maggie. She adored you, you know, but even she could see I wasn't happy.'

'Maggie was really nice to me,' Sapphire said sadly.

Leonie smiled. 'She's a wonderful lady. I knew she would look after you, that was one of the reasons I let you go.'

Sapphire hesitated. 'Did Brad try and, you know, make you change your mind? He can be very persuasive.'

Leonie smiled regretfully. 'A few times, but he knew it was no use. I was so headstrong back in those days; I thought I knew it all. And by the time I came to the conclusion I may have made the wrong decision, well, it was too late by then. Brad was so famous at that point, I didn't want people thinking I was just after his money.'

She looked at Sapphire, her eyes brimming. 'I'm so sorry, darling. I've deprived you of the father you never knew you had, all because I had some pigheaded notion of us making it on our own.'

Sapphire leant across and hugged her. 'Mum, it's OK. I understand why you did it. Anyway, I had Bill.'

Leonie's eyes filled up again. 'Dear, sweet Bill.' She reached for a piece of kitchen roll and blew her nose. 'Brad named a boat after me once, you know. *Spirito Libero*, it was called, which means "free spirit".'

'I've been on it!' Sapphire said excitedly.

Leonie shook her head thoughtfully. 'After all this time.'

Something else came to Sapphire. 'I think he's got a picture of you in his study as well, a black-and-white one of you, standing by a sunflower.' She hadn't made the connection at the time – now it was so obvious.

Leonie looked astonished. 'Oh my goodness, that's a blast from the past.' She smiled, remembering. 'That was when we first met, Brad and I. We had our whole future in front of us...' She stopped and looked at Sapphire. 'Sapphire, this Raphael...' Over several cups of tea and a whole packet of biscuits, Sapphire had finally told her mum the full story.

'Yes, Mum?'

Leonie leaned across the work surface and grasped her daughter's hand. 'Darling, you must try and make it up with him.'

Sapphire sighed. 'How can I, Mum? He hates my guts and besides, he's back in Rome. He might as well be on a different planet.'

Leonie looked into her daughter's eyes and smiled. 'I know you'll find a way. True love may only come along once in a lifetime, Sapphire. Don't be a fool and throw it away like I did.'

Later that week, Sapphire received a call from the last person in the world she was expecting. The background noise was so loud it was hard to make out who it was at first.

'Simonetta? Is that you?'

'*Si*. I am back in Roma.'

'Oh.' Sapphire didn't know what to say. The last time she had seen Simonetta, she was being driven out of the gates of Homelands, because of something

Simonetta had done to her. There was an awkward silence.

'Sapphire, please do not hang up on me.'

Despite the urge to tell Simonetta where to stick it, Sapphire didn't. In spite of herself she was intrigued to see why Simonetta had called. She wasn't about to apologise, was she?

Simonetta cleared her throat. 'I wanted to call and tell you that I am seeing an eating disorders counsellor.'

Sapphire's eyebrows shot up in surprise.

'Sapphire? Are you still there?'

'Yeah, I am. That's really great.' She meant it too. Even though Simonetta had been such a cow to her, this was a big step forward.

'Yes, well.' The Italian girl sounded thoughtful. 'I know it won't be easy, but I am determined. It was you, you know, who made me think about things. What you said about our past not controlling our future. You finally helped me figure it out.' The hint of a smile entered her voice. 'For that I thank you, strange little English girl.'

Sapphire couldn't help but smile back. She knew it

was hard for Simonetta to tell her this. 'You might not believe it, but I'm really proud of you.'

There was a pause at the other end. 'I am not so proud of myself, Sapphire. I have treated you very badly. I have treated a lot of people badly. You may not believe me, but it wasn't personal. I just wanted to win, to become Brad's heir and then all my problems would stop. I now realise this was not the way to go about things. I truly am sorry.'

Sapphire bit her lip. Part of her still wanted to tell Simonetta exactly what she thought, how she'd helped mess things up with her and Raphael. But there was no point now; it was water under the bridge. She was never going to see Raphael again anyway. Sapphire sighed. 'Apology accepted.'

There was another silence, one that Simonetta didn't seem to be in any rush to fill. 'Er, have you got any modelling jobs coming up?' Sapphire asked, trying to make conversation. Simonetta had said her piece, hadn't she? Why didn't she just ring off?

'Actually, I have decided to give up modelling for a while. It was making me into a person I did not want to be. I am enrolling on a college course, to study business instead.'

Sapphire couldn't help but be impressed. 'Wow, that's great! Sounds like you're making some big life changes.'

'Well, we will see.' Simonetta hesitated. 'So you want to meet up some time? I can come to London.' She paused again. 'Is it true?'

'Is what true?' Sapphire asked, even though she knew exactly what Simonetta was talking about.

'That you are giving me some of your fortune?'

Sapphire didn't answer for a moment. It had been a big dilemma for her. Despite what they'd done to her, Sapphire felt some responsibility to her sisters. They were flesh and blood, no matter what.

'Uh, yeah.' She still felt a bit weird, having all this money.

Simonetta was quiet for a moment. 'I don't deserve it.'

'Forget about it,' Sapphire mumbled. 'You can put yourself through college.'

Simonetta exhaled loudly. 'Thank you.'

'S'all right, I've given Madison something as well.'

'Sapphire, you are a saint!'

'Not really.' Despite the awkwardness, Sapphire grinned. 'There's one condition, though, before Madison can get the money.'

'Oh?' Simonetta sounded intrigued.

'She has to go and work in an animal charity for a month. I suggested dogs – I know how much she loved her puppy swap idea.'

Simonetta let out a shriek of laughter. 'Oh, *mio Dio*! I wish I could have seen her face.'

Sapphire giggled. It was nice to hear Simonetta sounding so happy and free.

'And now I have something for you, to make up for being such a bitch,' Simonetta said.

Sapphire raised an eyebrow. 'What's that then?'

She could almost hear Simonetta smiling down the phone. '*Si*, my contacts have served me well. It is the address and phone number in Rome of a certain Raphael…'

epilogue

'OK, folks, that's a wrap.' Jerry looked at them both and grinned. 'Kids, I've been around a long time and I know when I hear something special.'

Sapphire did a little jog of joy and threw her arms round Raphael's neck. 'I can't believe we've got our own demo tape!'

He squeezed her hard in return and she stayed close to him, lost in the moment. A discreet cough brought them both back.

Jerry was smiling. 'Now get out there and start hounding those record companies!'

Sapphire gave him a hug as well. 'Thanks, Jerry. You're the best.'

Outside the record shop, Raphael bent down and gave her a long kiss. Sapphire's body melted into his, enjoying the moment. 'I am so pleased you came to Roma to find me,' he murmured.

'And I'm so pleased you let me talk you round,' she whispered back. And they really had *talked* – about everything: her and Cam, Brad's secret plan, the fact that she, Simonetta and Madison were all half-sisters. It turned out Raphael had had his suspicions all along. Those green-gold eyes of his had seen a lot that summer. And even after what had happened with Cam, he still wanted her. Sapphire couldn't believe what an amazing bloke he was. It made her realise her feelings for Cam had been nothing in comparison.

As if aware of her thoughts, he stood back and cocked his head. 'What are you thinking?'

She touched his face tenderly. 'All good stuff.'

He tucked a strand of hair behind her ear. 'It's going to be complicated, you know. Me in Italy and you here.'

Sapphire grinned. 'Good, I like complicated.'

Raphael laughed. 'Me too.' His penetrating eyes looked into hers, as if he knew every inch of her soul. Raphael's intense beauty still took her breath away. Slowly, he took her face in his hands, his face filled with emotion.

'I love you, Sapphire.'

Sapphire stared at him, not quite believing it.

Raphael smiled at her quizzically. 'Did you hear what I said?'

A rush of excitement and happiness flooded her body. 'Yes, yes, I did! Raphael, I love you too.'

Their kissing was interrupted by Sapphire's mobile. With some reluctance she pulled away and took it out of her pocket. It was Brad's number. Still holding Raphael, she answered it. 'Hi, Dad. Did you get my message? Mum wants us all to have dinner together at ours next week.' She listened. 'Cool.' Raphael started kissing her again, making her laugh.

'Dad, one more thing,' she managed to say, as Raphael's soft lips found hers. 'I hope you like lentil curry!'